"Vampires don't change, right? I'm never going to get any older, and I'll always look like this. Short. Doughy. If I can't lose weight on an all-blood diet—"

"So is that why you wanted me to go outside with you? You were going to drink my blood?"

Doug dropped his eyes, but then he was just staring at her bare belly, at the hypnotic whorl of her navel that would certainly bewitch him, make him stupid with want.

"Only if you wanted me to," said Doug. "I just would've showed you my fangs and then . . . maybe you'd be, you know . . . into it."

"Okay, time to go," said a really tall guy who came out of nowhere. He grabbed Doug's arm and escorted him, backward, stumbling, toward the door.

"Don't be too mean to him," the girl called after them.

Don't be too mean to him, thought Doug. Not *too* mean. He was fifteen years old, he would always be fifteen years old, and it was possibly the nicest thing any girl would ever say about him.

# FAT
## VAMPIRE

**A NEVER COMING OF AGE STORY**

# FAT VAMPIRE

:

## A NEVER COMING OF AGE STORY

## ADAM REX

BALZER + BRAY

*An Imprint of* HarperCollins*Publishers*

Fat Vampire: A Never Coming of Age Story
Copyright © 2010 by Adam Rex
All rights reserved. Printed in the United States of America.
No part of this book may be used or reproduced in any manner whatsoever without written permission except in the case of brief quotations embodied in critical articles and reviews. For information address HarperCollins Children's Books, a division of HarperCollins Publishers, 10 East 53rd Street, New York, NY 10022.
www.epicreads.com

Library of Congress Cataloging-in-Publication Data
Rex, Adam.
Fat vampire : a never-coming-of-age story / Adam Rex. — 1st ed.
p.    cm.
Summary: After being bitten by a vampire, not only is fifteen-year-old Doug doomed eternally to be fat, but now he must also save himself from the desperate host of a public-access-cable vampire-hunting television show that is on the verge of cancellation.
ISBN 978-0-06-192092-9
[1. Vampires—Fiction.  2. Television programs—Fiction.  3. Foreign study—Fiction. 4. High schools—Fiction.  5. Schools—Fiction.  6. Humorous stories.]  I. Title.
PZ7.R32865Fat   2010                                                2010009616
[Fic]—dc22                                                          CIP
                                                                    AC

Typography by Martha Rago
11  12  13  14  15    CG/BV    10  9  8  7  6  5  4  3  2  1
❖
First paperback edition, 2011

FOR MARIE

# FAT
## VAMPIRE

**A NEVER COMING OF AGE STORY**

# THE

## FALL

**DOUG CAME TO**, lying on his back in what felt and smelled like a field. A gray, milky sky gaped over him. He took it in too quickly and fluttered his eyes.

Why was he on his back in a field? What was wrong with his chest? This last thought came suddenly as he sensed something pressing down on him. He lifted his head, and for a kaleidoscopic moment glimpsed the wooden stake in his heart before his vision swam black and his head hit the dirt again.

"Oh yeah," he whispered. "Forgot."

"You keep passing out," said a voice. "You wake up, look at the stake, pass out again. But shouldn't you be dead? I thought a stake through the heart was supposed to kill you."

"It seems like a good . . ." wheezed Doug, "guess to me."

High above, a crooked line of birds perforated the lightening sky. It was very cold.

"I think . . . I think sometimes you think you're the hero of the story, and sometimes you think you're the victim," said the voice. "But you're not either."

# THE
# PREVIOUS
# SUMMER

# 1:

## MY DORK EMBRACE

**DOUG SAID,** "Hi," and the girl turned. The perfect girl with red hair and a nearly empty cup of yellow beer turned and looked at him. He tried to relax his eyes, take all of her in at once—the blue belly shirt, the bottomless cleavage—without appearing to ogle. He didn't know her or practically anyone else at the party. She didn't know him. She wouldn't have any reason not to talk to him.

She found a reason. Look—it was all there on her face. She'd seen through his disguise—the hair gel, the too-tight shirt from Apparel Conspiracy. He was a completely surprising form of life, something that should not be at a party, shouldn't be addressing her. A gorilla maybe, frantically signing *Koko want kitten. Koko want kitten.*

"What?" she said. Not superinviting.

"Hey. I'm Doug."

She seemed hesitant to give her name, like she might get it back with gunk on it. But then, "Carrie. My friend's coming right back."

"That's . . . cool. So what school do you go to?" he asked. Not that he knew any schools in San Diego.

"Garfield," said the girl, but as she did so she arched her neck to look over his shoulder. Her long, soft, beautiful neck.

Koko want kitten.

"It's . . . kind of crowded in here," said Doug. "Don't you think? You want to go outside? Get some fresh air?"

"I'm waiting for my friend," said the girl. And then her whole posture relaxed, and a sudden brightness in her eyes told Doug that she'd just seen this friend, the friend was close, like the friend had just pressed the button on her key chain that made the headlights flash and the locks pop.

"Just for a second," said Doug. "Really quick. I want to show you something."

"*Ew.*"

"No, it's not like . . . Just trust me . . . Come outside . . . It's totally amazing . . ."

The friend was back. The friend was right there, and Doug heard himself say, "I'm a vampire."

Both girls stared at him for an airless moment, possibly deciding how they were going to take this. Funny or Scary? Funny or Scary?

"A creature of the night," Doug continued. "Cursed like Cain to wander—"

"Aren't you a little fat for a vampire?" asked the friend.

*Funny it is, then.* Doug sighed. "I guess."

"Oh, my god, are you one of those comics convention people?" asked the friend. "Paul said there wouldn't be too many of them."

"Look, sorry," said the girl, the girl whose name Doug had to admit had already escaped his mind. "I'm here with my friend. Maybe someone else will go see your comic book thing." They turned to leave.

"I wasn't trying to show you a comic book!" said Doug as he followed them. "I'm a vampire! I'm a fat vampire, okay? I was trying to lose weight before I got bitten. Now I'm screwed."

The girl faced him. A second or so later her friend realized she was walking all by herself. She clucked her tongue and came back.

"Why are you screwed?" asked the girl.

This was something. Not really the topic Doug wanted to talk about, but at least they were talking.

"I'm . . . cursed," said Doug. He was going to have to come up with another word for cursed. "For all eternity, always alone, never able to quench my dark—"

No, he could see in her face he was losing her. Something else.

"Look," he said, "vampires don't change, right? I'm never going to get any older, and I'll always look like this. Short. Doughy. You know I haven't had anything to eat or drink except blood for the last month? And nothing. No change. If I can't lose weight on an all-blood diet—"

"So is that why you wanted me to go outside with you? You were going to attack me?"

"No! No, I—"

"You were going to drink my blood?"

Doug dropped his eyes, but then he was just staring at her bare belly, at the hypnotic whorl of her navel that would certainly bewitch him, make him stupid with want. He glanced to her right and noticed a few bystanders were listening, their conversations ebbing away. Beautiful people with faces like flowers, turning slowly to bask in someone else's blazing embarrassment.

"Only if you wanted me—"

"What?" said the friend. "We *CAN'T HEAR YOU*."

"Only if you wanted me to," said Doug. "I just would've showed you my fangs and then . . . maybe you'd be, you know"—when he finished the thought it was barely there—"into it."

"Okay, time to go," said a really tall guy who came out of nowhere. He grabbed Doug's arm and escorted him, backward, stumbling, toward the door.

"Don't be too mean to him," the girl called after them. "He didn't do anything."

*Don't be* too *mean to him*, thought Doug. *Not* TOO *mean*. He was fifteen years old, he would always be fifteen years old, and it was possibly the nicest thing any girl would ever say about him.

Doug dug in his heels. "Wait," he said. "I can't leave without my friend. I dragged him here."

His escort appeared speechless that Doug had been able to

**8**

stop their momentum at all. Another tall, good-looking teen-ager had to step up to the plate.

"Fuck, there are more of you?" he said. "Where's your friend?"

"Probably hiding in a bathroom."

This second guy went off to look, leaving the first to stand there and hold Doug's arm and glare.

"Look, you can let me go," said Doug. "I'm not going to turn into a bat or anything."

"Heh. What? Shut up."

"Seriously. I'll leave as soon as my friend gets here."

"I think you can let him go," said someone new.

Doug's escort let him go. "Whatever. Your house, Paul."

"Oh," said Doug to the new kid. "You're Paul. Nice party."

"Thanks. How did you find out about it?"

"I found a flyer at the convention center. At the pre-con party. It was under Stan Lee's foot."

"Someone must've dropped one," said Paul. "Sorry, it was more of an invite-only thing."

"I didn't know."

Just then Jay appeared with a tall guy holding each arm.

"Here he is," one of them said. "People in the bathroom line said he'd been in there a half hour."

Doug glanced at his watch. That sounded about right.

⁝

Outside, Doug and Jay shuffled through wet grass, aware of the gazes of two or three guys standing guard on the front porch to make sure they didn't double back, sneak in through a window, slide down the chimney. Crash the party and get dork all over everything.

"Don't take this the wrong way," said Jay as they reached the car, "but that would have been a great moment for you to turn into a wolf or command rats or something."

"Yeah. And then you could have gone and done recon in the bathroom again. Everything secure in there? Did they have enough guest towels?"

Jay didn't reply.

They drove off into the dark street.

"I have to feed soon!" said Doug. "I feel like I'm starving and going crazy at the same time. I'm curs— damned! I'm damned to forever yearn for the . . . vile . . ."

"Vile crimson ichor?" offered Jay.

"No. For the vile . . . for the sweet, vile . . ." Doug trailed off. Damn it, "vile crimson ichor" had been pretty good.

"Will you die?" asked Jay. "If you don't . . . feed? Will you die again?"

Doug exhaled and watched the houses pass.

"I don't know. It was bad enough the first time."

"You said it was awesome," said Jay. "Before, you said that getting turned into a vampire was better than sex."

"Yeah . . . but—"

"You said it was like your penis went bonernova—"

"Can you not say 'penis'? Please? It's like I get the exact opposite of a bonernova whenever you say it. Say 'dick' or—"

"I don't *swear*," said Jay. "You *know* I don't."

"Look. Okay. *Obviously* . . ." said Doug, "obviously the getting-turned-into-a-vampire part was great, and the vampire chick was hot and everything, but the actual dying part sucked. Obviously."

"Oh. Sorry."

"'S okay."

Doug rolled down his window a few inches and wedged his nose into the gap, inhaling the thick, salty air. Anything to keep from smelling the one hundred and fifty pounds of blood and best friend in the driver's seat next to him.

"You're the one with family here," said Doug. He and Jay were staying with Jay's aunt and uncle during the convention. "Are there any farms close by?"

Jay thought a moment. "I don't think so. Maybe some citrus orchards. Ha! Maybe some *blood oranges*."

"Jay—"

"No. No farms."

"Well . . . there has to be *something*," whined Doug, "someplace with big animals. Big enough so I won't kill them."

Jay was quiet. Then he made a turn toward the freeway.

# 2:

# ENDANGERED SPECIES

**THE SAN DIEGO ZOO** is located within a twelve-hundred-acre expanse of garden and cultural attractions called Balboa Park and encircled by lush palms and meticulously trimmed topiary elephants. Its outer wall is thirty feet high and can be scaled by an out-of-shape vampire carrying a friend if he sits down for a while afterward.

"Just a sec," Doug huffed for the second time. His head was spinning, and the first verse of a song he didn't like was going around and around in it. Jay cast his eyes about with his hands over his nose and mouth. He flinched at every noise. Finally he went to stand behind a cart that sold T-shirts.

"We should meet back here if we get separated," he whispered. "Right at this cart."

"Why would we get separated?"

"I don't know. If guards chase us."

"Jesus, there won't be any guards in here. Why would they be on the inside? No one else could climb that wall. If there are guards, they're probably all out there."

Jay said nothing, but after a minute he stepped out into view.

"Okay, I'm ready," said Doug. "You know, if I was full of blood, I bet I could have hauled ass over that wall. I could have carried two of you. I could have carried a whole cheerleading squad."

"Why a cheerleading squad?"

"I dunno . . . girls like animals."

They chose a path at random past the gift shops and snack stands, and wended their way into the heart of the zoo.

Jay looked at a sign nearby. "'Capybara,'" he read.

"Too small."

"It's the world's largest rodent."

"Good for the capybara. I hope it has a coffee mug that says so. I'm not putting my mouth on it."

They continued down the winding path, peering into the dark, quiet habitats. Doug sang under his breath, "'What the world . . . needs now is love, sweet love. It's the only thing that there's just . . . too little of'— Oh, great. Perfect."

"What?"

"Why can't I have a good song stuck in my head?"

"My uncle doesn't like people messing with the radio. He says he has it just how he likes it."

"It's a terrible song."

Jay shrugged.

"No, seriously," said Doug. "It's stupid. I mean, love is the only thing that there's too little of? What about . . . uh . . . coal? Or trees?"

"'Jaguarundi.'"

"What?"

"'Jaguarundi,'" said Jay, reading a sign. "They're endangered."

"Right, see?" said Doug. He looked at the sign. "I probably shouldn't feed on something endangered, right? Plus it's too small."

"How about the . . . Bornean bearded pig?"

"No."

"It's over three hundred pounds," said Jay. "It'll be okay."

"No. I . . ." Doug searched for the right words. "I don't want you to think I . . . this is going to sound kind of weird, but . . ."

Jay looked up at him.

"I was hoping for something a little more . . . sexy," said Doug.

*"Sexy?"*

"Not actually sexy! Not, like, I'm into animals or anything. Just . . . it's bad enough I have to drink from an animal in the first place, you know? There has to be something more . . . elegant than the whatever bearded pig."

Jay read the next sign.

"What about the 'Southern bush pig'?" he asked. "That's sexier, right?"

"You really don't know the answer to that question, do you?"

Jay blushed the color of raw meat. Doug had to look away. An awkward moment passed between them like a cripple.

"At home you feed on cows," said Jay finally. "Cows are sexy?"

"No, it's all . . . In my head the blood drinking is about either romance or food. It's complicated. The perfect animal . . . would be, like, a real pretty doe."

"Or a unicorn," said Jay.

"Don't be stup—" Doug began. "Okay, yes. Or a unicorn. But this zoo doesn't have any unicorns, and I don't know if a doe weighs enough. I might kill it."

"A tiger?"

"It might kill me."

"Um," said Jay, casting about for an idea. "Ooh! This way."

:

"A panda?"

"Sure," said Jay. "It's at least sexier than those pigs, right? And it's big and gentle. They're like huge babies."

"Huge bear-shaped babies." *Huge*, endangered *bear-shaped babies*, Doug realized with a pang. But what with all the bamboo-eating and never-mating-in-captivity, he thought they might be endangered because they were just kind of stupid.

"Yeah, but they're not really bears, are they? I think they're more closely related to the raccoon or something," said Jay, but he didn't look sure.

The raccoon comment was undoubtedly meant to reassure Doug, but it only made him think of rabies and bandit faces and those sharply determined little hands. He leaned forward, his stomach against the railing, and searched the enclosure.

"I don't see it," he said.

"They probably have someplace in there where she stays at night," Jay said, pointing to a sort of cave opening in the back wall.

Doug stared at the cave. A light breeze tickled his skin and made him shiver—a by-product of being so low on blood, he thought. After a feeding he could barely feel temperature at all. Suddenly his ears pricked at an unexpected sound.

"'What the world . . . needs now,'" sang Jay.

"Wait, *shh*. Someone's coming."

"I can't hear—"

"Dammit," whispered Doug. "Hide."

Jay lurched in one direction, jerked back, lurched in another, tripped for no reason. He finally made it through a gauntlet of invisible obstacles and crouched behind a water fountain shaped like a hippopotamus throwing up.

Doug scrambled over the railing and found a ten-foot drop into the panda yard. He hung by locked and aching fingertips from the top of the wall as a night watchman ambled into view.

*Nothing to see*, Doug thought at the watchman. *Just walk on by . . .*

The night watchman sat down on a bench with his back to the panda pen.

*Son of a*—thought Doug, as his grip failed and he tumbled noiselessly onto the lush grass below. He paused and listened. Jay was okay. The man above was unwrapping food and singing something in a mumbly hum, something about life being a highway. He sounded like he might be a while.

The yard behind Doug was still pandaless and quiet. He hurried, hunched, through the grass, past a thicket of bamboo, a pond, and stopped at the mouth of the cave Jay had pointed out before. It had a gate, but the gate was unlocked, designed only to keep pandas in, he supposed, not vampires out. It opened with a high squeal that Doug was pretty sure only he could hear. He, and any dogs nearby. And maybe pandas. He really wished now that he knew more about pandas.

Once inside, Doug got a good look at the panda and had to admit he'd been worrying too much. It appeared to be asleep. It appeared, actually, to be just a huge stuffed toy, the kind stepdads buy for their stepkids when they're overcompensating. The illusion was supported by a rubber pig, which probably squeaked, nestled beside it on the straw bed. And a plastic xylophone hanging from the bars of a narrow window. And a big pink ball that had settled where the bare concrete floor sloped downward to a drain. It was like the toy department of a prison.

The floor curved up into the walls, one of which was nearly hidden behind a wide fan of bamboo stalks. The floor was painted bright white. All in all, the whole space wasn't any larger than a two-car garage. It smelled the way a garage would smell if you left a bear inside it too long.

Doug breathed through his mouth and tiptoed over to the

**17**

panda, its body slowly inflating and deflating like a fur balloon.

He realized, suddenly, that there was a significant difference between this panda and the cows back home. With the cows, it was easy to sniff out a vein, break the skin, take care of business. Here, he could imagine biting down and getting only a mouthful of hair.

He leaned over the animal, fangs bared, his hesitant hands hovering clawlike in the air, lacking only a black cape and high collar to finish the picture. Then a faint whirr from above caught his attention. Light glinted off a single lens, a glassy eye in the corner that motored slowly upward to look from panda to Doug.

*Is that a camera?* thought Doug.

The camera angled down again, past the panda, square on the rubber pig toy, and Doug wondered, *Is that really a rubber pig toy?*

He stepped around the panda and crouched on his hands and knees in front of the thing. It wasn't a toy. It was some kind of animal. It looked like a naked rat.

*What the hell IS that?*

# 3

## THE MAGIC KINGDOM

**"OW. OW. OW,"** said Doug from under his white plastic poncho.

"It's only a little farther," said Jay.

"Ow. Why would anyone want to live in a place this sunny? Is it leaving marks?"

Doug imagined what a pretty picture he made—zinc oxide on his nose, his cheeks greased with SPF 80. A small crack in the left lens of his spare glasses. Jay bent over to look under Doug's hood.

"No. You're just kind of red."

"Ow."

"Does it hurt?" asked Jay.

"What have I been saying for the past eight blocks?"

"It's only a little farther," said Jay.

"Actually, that's what *you've* been saying for the past eight blocks."

It was the first day of Comic-Con International, a four-day event in San Diego and the largest comic book and pop-culture convention in America. A building like a shopping mall with fins housed acres of elaborate booths with Jumbo-Tron displays and life-size sculptures of superheroes and signings with actual comics artists and creators. All right next to game-playing stations where you could try out *next year's* video games and talk to the programmers and then mosey over to the seller's area with its hundreds upon hundreds of long boxes packed with hard-to-find-issues and action figures—but who has time for action figures when you have to rush to make the eleven o'clock panel discussion with the creator and stars of *Nebula-Bravo* followed by a nap-inducing lunch in the food courts where you were forced to eat soft pretzels and pizza because they didn't sell anything else.

Doug was really going to miss the soft pretzels and pizza.

"Ow. I'm going to have to drink someone soon," he told Jay, and realized he was slurring his speech. Was this what it felt like to be drunk? "I've got the shakes. And I was totally getting somewhere with that girl last night, too."

"Sorry," said Jay, for maybe the thirtieth time. Doug's gut twisted. He hadn't meant to squeeze another apology out of Jay. He hadn't meant to give the impression that they'd only been thrown out of the party because of Jay's monopoly of the hall bathroom, either, but somehow he had.

"What happened after the panda hit you?" asked Jay. "Can you remember now?"

"No. I can remember everything up to— Well, I noticed the camera, and it's looking at me, and then it looks down at this little pink thing next to the panda, so I look, too, and it's this tiny animal."

"Baby Shuan Shuan," said Jay. "You're so lucky."

"I feel lucky. So I'm looking down at this tiny hairless panda when I hear footsteps, and a door bursts in, and these uniformed guys with metal poles start tasering me. And you know what doesn't work when people are tasering you? It's shouting 'Stop tasering me.' If they're tasering you already, they won't stop because you ask them to."

"No," said Jay.

"The Tasers aren't working so well on me, maybe because I'm a vampire, but they really, really hurt, so I back up, trying to get away from the guards, and I guess I get too close to Baby Ching Chong because that's when the panda punches me in the head."

"Yeah."

"Then there's a scene missing, because the next thing I know I'm back out in the zoo, in the bushes, without any clothes on. So you gotta figure that's one hell of a missing scene."

"Uh-huh."

"And then I go to find you, but you're *not where I left you*—"

"I said we should meet by—"

"—but you *are* by the exit, and the exit is by the T-shirt stand, so I don't have to drive home naked. So that's fine. Ow."

Jay looked glum.

"We should have left money on the stand," he said. "What we did . . . it was bad enough without stealing a T-shirt."

Doug sighed. "Yeah."

They crossed the train tracks to the convention center.

"But it was a stupid shirt," Doug added. "They can't expect anybody to actually pay for a shirt that says, 'I (picture of an elephant) the San Diego Zoo.' What does that even mean?"

"Oh, man," said Jay. "Look at that line."

Doug looked up, but his glasses went foggy from the smoke suddenly rising off his cheeks.

"AAH! Dammit!"

"Sorry."

It was still ten minutes until the doors opened, but they walked to the front of a grumbling line of fanboys, cosplayers, furries, goths, and a smattering of girlfriends that were there out of curiosity, or there to be supportive of their boyfriends, or maybe there because they had assumed they'd be a singularity—the only queen in the anthill, with all the power that implied. This last type was easy to spot, dressed in clothes so brazenly revealing they could pass for Halloween costumes. Doug knew there would be a lot of girls here who genuinely liked comics, too, though they never seemed to like the same kind he did. Still, it gave him hope that he'd eventually get lucky. He'd be at his local comic shop or maybe (why not?) even at this very convention. He and some beautiful girl would reach for the same back issue of *Young X-Men* at the same time. They'd have a laugh about it. They'd get to talking and discover they shared a great love of anime and customized action figures. Then they'd have sex on the fucking Batmobile or something.

"No cutting!" shouted Doctor Doom, or someone dressed just like him.

"That's a really good Doctor Doom costume," said Jay. "Look at those rivets."

"Movie or comics version?" asked Doug.

"Comics."

"Hold on," said a large bald man whose costume was a simple black T-shirt that said his job (or name or personal motto) was Security. "Are you an exhibitor?"

"No—"

"Do you have an exhibitor's badge?"

They didn't.

"Back of the line, then."

"My friend can't stand out in the sun like that," said Jay. "He has really sensitive skin. See?"

Jay lifted the hood of Doug's poncho just slightly.

"Christ," whispered the man. He lifted a walkie-talkie to his mouth. "This is Craig at D stop. I got a situation."

The walkie-talkie squawked something only Craig could understand. He said, "Copy" and returned it to its holster, all the while staring fixedly at Jay.

"It'll just be a minute."

"Okay," said Jay. "Thanks."

Craig nodded. "So . . . he likes comics?"

"Yeah."

"He speaks English, too," said Doug.

Craig was joined by another big man in identical clothing, apart from a black baseball cap that said HEAD. Doug thought it seemed awfully literal.

The man said, "I'm head of security, boys."

*Oh.*

"What's the problem?"

"These two want in early," said Craig, "on account of this kid can't be out in the sun."

"Oh, yeah," said the head of security, looking under Doug's poncho. "He's got some kind of skin thing, right? They can wait in the lobby."

"You're not surprised?" said Craig.

"Surprised? Hell, no. This is the big comic book weekend. If the freakin' boy in the bubble rolled up here, I wouldn't be surprised. Hey, watch this."

He called out to the queue. "Anyone lose an inhaler?"

About one in ten checked his pockets.

"See?" said Head, loud enough for anyone to hear. "Look at that lineup. It's like all the kids picked last for every kickball game in America."

"Hey, screw you!" shouted a boy in a Gorillaz T-shirt. "I'm on my high school swim team!"

"Ooh." Head laughed. "Swim team."

"We went to state last year! What'd you ever do, fat ass?!"

"Hey!" said Head. "Watch your mouth or I'll watch it for ya!"

**24**

"He wants to watch your mouth," said another boy.

"Yeah," said a third attendee, one in his twenties, "because that *is* all he does, right? That's his job. Watching things. Whereas this line is full of geniuses and software engineers."

"Maybe I'll hire you to watch my mansion someday, dickpipe!" someone shouted.

"That's it! Back of the line!" said Head.

"Maybe I'll hire you to clean my pool!" said someone else.

"Back of the line! All of you!"

"Can we go in?" Jay asked Craig.

"Knock yourselves out," said Craig.

**:**

In minutes they were in a zigzagging line of low curtains, and they slalomed through it, alone; right, left, right, toward a row of tables manned by seated, serious women. Each woman looked like she was someone's least-favorite aunt. Each woman had something to bestow on Doug and Jay, and the two boys walked in procession and received each of their tokens in turn.

Marjorie gives the Guide to Programming, your companion to the kingdom that awaits.

Wendy grants to each an Official Badge, which Mustn't Be Lost.

From Ellen comes the Bag of Holding, filled with buttons, key chains, and all manner of promos.

And from Madge, the Book of Coupons. A thirty-dollar value.

Then, part the thin gray curtains and step, if you're ready, into the Great Hall and taste of all its—

"Jesus," said Doug. "*Look.*"

Almost immediately a girl sauntered by dressed as Femininja—which is to say, in a black bikini with a sword.

"Huh," said Jay.

"My spidey sense is tingling," Doug whispered, and looked over at Jay, who possibly hadn't heard him. He'd spent an afternoon several weeks ago thinking of funny comic book things to say when girls passed. He had a notebook full of them.

The exhibit space on the ground floor was like three football fields of stands, booths, and tables, behind each of which was something to want, or some*one* to want, or someone to want to talk to. Directly in front of them now was the original captain's chair from the set of *Gastronauts*, a book-brick bunker of manga and imported action figures in packages dashed with Japanese, and Lou Ferrigno.

"Why does everything look cooler with Japanese on it?" asked Doug.

"Huh?" Jay said absently.

They strode forward, slowly, deliberately, taking it all in—this goblin market at the nexus of all realities where a circa 1980s Iron Man and an original 1963 Iron Man and Naruto and Sherlock Holmes could all be waiting for the same bathroom. Would it convey the scale of the thing to know that there was a person who elected to dress as the Kool-Aid Man? Would it convey it better to know there were two?

"Look," said Doug. "Those two Kool-Aid Men are fighting."

"I don't know what to do," said Jay. "I don't know what to do."

"About what? The Kool-Aid Men?"

Jay shook his head. Then he motioned at the whole thing, at *everything*: the comics and the culture and the people pulling the first Kool-Aid Man off the second Kool-Aid Man.

"We're going to walk around and look at things," said Doug.

"But what things? Which ones? What if we don't see all of them? What if we look at the wrong things?"

"Look. Calm down. We're just going to get the lay of the land. We're going to skim through the program and circle things. If someone tries to hand us something, we let them. If we pass a trivia quiz, we're going to shout '*Crisis on Infinite Earths!*' because that's usually the answer. Are you going to be okay?"

Jay swallowed and nodded. The convention hall was filling with people. Someone in Spider-Man tights crouched near them and pointed with two web-slinging fingers.

"Hey, true believers!" he said. "The Marvel Entertainment Group is in booth six thirty!"

Doug gave a hesitant thumbs-up. "Thanks."

"Thank you, Spider-Man," said Jay.

Spider-Man leaped away and delivered his line again to a group of Japanese girls.

The two boys tunneled through the feedlot of warm bodies to visit every table and booth in turn. They got writers and artists to sign comics and a model dressed as Punching Judy to sign Doug's arm. It would have been a good opportunity to say one of the funny comic-book lines he'd thought up ("You're making me horny. You wouldn't like me when I'm horny."), but he couldn't quite manage it. Punching Judy was getting dirty looks from the writer/illustrator of *SuperBitch*, who was talking to a local news crew from her adjoining booth.

"Superhero secret identities are like virginity," she told the camera. "All these sweaty boys want to see the day when she gives it up, the day everyone *knows* her, but then after it's gone, they're disappointed. They want her to have a secret identity again."

Doug supposed that was true. It was always this big euphoric event in a comic when the hero's girlfriend or whoever learned his secret. Everybody wanted to read that story, but a year later the writers would probably give the girlfriend amnesia. You always wanted to put the cat back in the bag.

He'd blown his cover last night at that party, but Doug was going to be more careful from now on. He sort of wished he hadn't even told Jay.

They watched the world premiere of a new movie trailer and then attended a ten thirty panel discussion with DC comics editors, where there was a prize: a light-up resin Green Lantern ring, one of only five thousand produced.

"Cool," said Jay.

"Green Lantern's gay," said Doug.

The panel moderator flashed it off and on a couple of times. "Is that not awesome?" he said. "And the ring goes . . . to the audience member who has traveled the farthest to be here!"

"Philadelphia!" shouted Doug. A dozen other attendees

shouted their hometowns, too. The ring went to a man from Belgium wearing a Tintin shirt.

"We don't live in Philadelphia," whispered Jay.

"We live in a suburb of Philadelphia. You think they know where Ardwynne is?"

"I know you thought that was it," the moderator continued, "but it just so happens . . . yes, I think I may have another ring . . . for whomever's traveled the farthest from within the United States?"

"Philadelphia!" Doug shouted again.

"Bangor!" shouted some kid from Bangor.

"Bangor is farthest!" said the moderator.

"No, it isn't!" Doug protested. He got to his feet. "No, it isn't. Not if you take into account the curvature of the Earth, which—"

"Bangor's farther, kid," said the moderator.

Doug sunk into his chair. "Let's go," he said to Jay. "Panels suck."

"You don't want to sit awhile? You look tired."

Doug answered by rising and walking out the side door while a fan asked the panel about an obscure Superman versus Muhammad Ali comic from the seventies.

"Sorry you didn't win," said Jay when he'd caught up. "I think Bangor is farther, though."

"I don't care, I just wanted the ring to sell it. I didn't really expect to win. Nobody ever wins anything."

Twenty minutes later Jay won a new shirt for shouting, "Crisis on Infinite Earths!" a fraction of a second faster than seven other boys. It read, MY MOM AND DAD WENT TO THE

**29**

NEGATIVE ZONE AND ALL I GOT WAS THIS LOUSY T-SHIRT. By twelve o'clock it was covered by thirty-one free buttons.

"I'm having a really good time," he said. "Aren't you?"

Doug didn't answer. Jay looked him in the face for maybe the first time in an hour, and turned pale.

"We should . . ." he said, "we should find you somewhere to sit down. And get something to eat."

Doug nodded.

**:**

"What about a milkshake?" Jay asked when they found an empty table near the snack bar. "Or, like, a smoothie?"

"That sounds . . . like the worst thing in the world," said Doug. "Seriously, if I . . . if I'd had an appetite for anything these past weeks, I'd have eaten it. I'd eat my own hand if it sounded good. I don't want anything anymore."

"You look a little better."

"It helps to sit down. Away from everyone else."

Jay flinched as someone at a far table shouted "'UP *QAGH!*'" and thumped his chest.

Doug and Jay turned to watch the largest of four Klingons pound the tabletop with his world-shattering fist, bouncing half-eaten French bread pizzas off paper plates made translucent by grease.

"Sooo," said Doug, "why so many Klingons, do you think? I mean, there have been *Star Trek* comics and all, but they're not popular or anything."

"I think they just have the outfits all ready from the last Trekkie con," said Jay. "So they're coming here and they think, why not show colors?"

"My party wants your ketchup," said a very short Klingon who was suddenly at Jay's flinching shoulder.

"Oh," said Jay. "Sure, you . . . We're not using it."

The short Klingon held the ketchup bottle aloft and turned to address his table.

"*Qettlhup!*"

"*QETTLHUP!*" the others answered in chorus.

The Klingon departed.

"I gotta go," said Doug. "Can we go? I just want to lie down for a while. I thought here at the con I could take my mind off it, but—"

Jay's face fell, and Doug's gut twisted again. He understood how Jay felt—he didn't want to have to leave either. This was where they belonged. These were their people. The San Diego Comic-Con was a mystical city that only appeared for a few days each year, like Brigadoon.

"There's still three more days," said Jay, brightening a little. "I've heard it's best to buy old comics on Sunday. Maybe we can figure something out for you tonight. Find you some blood."

"Gah!" moaned Doug. "That's the frustrating part! It's everywhere! It's all I can smell! People full of it! And do you know how many characters I've seen today with blood in their names? There's Bloodstorm, Bloodaxe, Bloodlust, Bloodhawk, Baron Blood, Baro*ness* Blood, Bloodhound, the Blood Brothers . . . Even the superhero on that kid's bag over there looks like a big drop of blood with a cape."

Jay looked. Doug looked again. It *was* a big drop of blood with a cape. It said "Type O Hero!" on the side above the Red

**31**

Cross logo. Jay jumped out of his seat.

"Excuse me," he said to the kid. "What's that bag about?"

"It's full of free comics. If you give blood outside."

"Outside?"

"At the bloodmobile."

*Bloodmobile*, thought Doug. He could drive that around all day.

# 4

## QUICK, ROBIN. . .TO THE BLOODMOBILE!

**I**T **WAS IMPOSSIBLE** to miss—a long white-and-red school bus parked on the broad sidewalk where the line had been that morning. It must have pulled up after the convention started.

"What are we going to do?" said Jay.

"We're both going to—ow—we're going to say we want to donate," said Doug from under his poncho. "You'll go first, and I'll scope out the bus, try to figure out where they keep the blood. Then you create a diversion, and I make off with a jar or two."

"They put it in jars?"

Doug adjusted his hood. "I don't know. A jar or a tube or— It doesn't matter."

They stopped next to the bus, near the open donor entrance. There was no line here. In the shade, Doug could manage to lift his chin a little and see Jay's troubled face.

"What kind of diversion?" said Jay. "What should I do?"

"I thought of the creating-a-diversion part," Doug said. "Can't you at least come up with your own diversion?"

Jay thought about it a moment with a Charlie Brown look on his face.

"I could . . . freak out," he said. "I could pretend I don't like needles."

"There you go. Perfect. And can you still throw up at will like you could in sixth grade? That would be good."

They stepped up and into the bus. A woman in Muppet-print scrubs came to meet them.

"Will you be donating today?" she said, then frowned. "Are you both eighteen?"

"Oh, sure."

"Uh-huh."

"Can I see some ID?"

"WE DON'T HAVE ID," said Jay, loudly. "'CAUSE WE'RE CANADIAN. WE DON'T USE ID . . . THERE. AND THAT'S WHY WE LOOK SO YOUNG. 'CAUSE WE'RE CANADIAN."

Doug stiffened. Jay sounded crazy. Doug tried to look extra sane to even things out. The woman raised an eyebrow.

"And you're not maybe just trying to donate to get the free bag of comics?"

"Oh, no, of course not," said Doug. "Free comics? No, you

**34**

don't even have to give us those. We just want to help out."

The woman's face softened. "Well, all right, I guess. Who's first?"

"He is," said Doug.

"You can have a seat by the donor beds while I ask your friend some questions and check his vitals," she said to Doug, then led Jay toward a private room the size of a closet.

"What part of Canada you from, honey?"

"THE LEFT PART," said Jay.

Doug sat down in a plastic chair. There were two thin beds in the bloodmobile, and one of them was occupied. The boy had a needle and blood-filled tube snaking out of his arm and into a plastic bag attached to the bed. He was attended by another woman in scrubs and gloves.

"Whoop, you done already," she told him. "You fast."

"I've been drinking a lot of water," the boy said.

Inside the private room, Doug could hear Jay having his blood pressure checked and his temperature taken. Then the woman in Muppet scrubs launched into a questionnaire. "How do you feel today?"

". . . Okay."

"Have you had a tattoo in the last twelve months?"

"No."

"Have you spent a total of three months or more in the United Kingdom since 1985?"

"No."

"Have you ever had sexual contact with another man, even once?"

"W-what? No."

"Have you ever paid for sex or accepted money or drugs for sex, even once?"

"No. What is that?"

"Just a little rubbing alcohol, honey. I have to prick your finger to test your blood. Do you now use or have you ever used intravenous drugs?"

The other woman by the beds pinched off the boy's tube, removed the needle, then pressed cotton to the wound and told him to hold it there with his arm straight up.

A voice called out from the private room where Jay had gone.

"Kendra? Can you . . . Kendra, can you come here?"

"Just a sec," said Kendra as she removed the full blood bag from the bed and placed it on a nearby counter, *right next to another bag.*

"Kendra!"

*Here we go*, thought Doug.

"All right, all right," Kendra answered, and turned to the boy. "You just lie there a minute till I get back."

She passed Doug and joined Jay and Muppet scrubs in the little room. "He's a fainter, help me lift him," said Muppet scrubs, and Doug had to admire Jay's dedication to the role. If he'd only thrown himself into last spring's *My Fair Lady* auditions like that, he could have played Henry Higgins for sure.

The door closed and Doug was alone with the blood and the boy with his arm in the air. He leaped from the chair to the counter, paused for a reverent moment over the plump red bags, considered biting into one right then and there. Instead, he tucked a bag under each arm and turned.

The boy on the bed studied him. "Hey . . . that's my blood," he said.

Doug hadn't intended to hiss just then, couldn't remember thinking it was a good idea, but then suddenly he was hissing, with an itch in his gum line that told him his fangs were bared.

"*Shit*," said the boy.

Doug bolted for the door of the bloodmobile but found his way blocked by the two women and a drowsy-looking Jay. Again he showed his teeth.

"Don't you hiss at me," said Kendra. "What you doin' with blood that don't belong to you?"

Doug froze, then closed his mouth. He wondered briefly if anyone in the history of the world had ever been asked that question before. There didn't seem to be a right answer. He hissed again, but his heart wasn't in it.

"I aks you a question. You better put that blood down and stop your hissin'. And take those Dracula teeth out your mouth."

Jay began inching toward the door. The other woman leaned into Kendra.

"He's trying to steal the blood."

"I know he is," said Kendra.

"He thinks he's a vampire maybe."

"I've taken blood from a stormtrooper and a Superman and at least three cartoon characters today," said Kendra. "He can think he's whatever he want, long as he *TURNS HIS ASS-FERATU AROUND AND PUTS BACK THAT BLOOD.*"

Jay made a run for it. He threw himself down the steps at the school bus door, and Doug thought, *School bus.*

"Okay," he said, returning to the counter. "I'm just putting it back."

Kendra nodded. Doug hesitated. The boy on the bed gaped at him.

Then Doug ran for the back of the bus, and his heart lifted when he saw it—the emergency exit. He didn't know a student who hadn't thought of using it at least once on the way to school, at a stoplight . . . maybe the stoplight right by the miniature golf place on Route 30.

"Oh no you don't," said Kendra, behind him.

Doug fumbled with the latch on the door, trying not to lose his armpit grip on the fat red tubers that were getting slick with sweat. He could feel heavy footsteps through the floor behind him, but then the door swung free—and he fell, like a turd out of the ass of the bus, to freedom.

# 5

## :

# AMERICAN INDIAN

**FOR THE THIRD TIME** since the plane landed Sejal fished the curling photograph out of her backpack and studied it. She walked as she looked at her host family, posed and smiling before a softly blotchy blue backdrop. Everyone wore a different kind of sweater. The father was tall with large-framed glasses and a tawny sweater vest the color of chinaberries. The mother's wide frame was seated below him, pink skinned and in a pink-on-pink cardigan and sweater ensemble—so round and bright that Sejal's father had taken to calling her "gum ball woman" when Sejal's mother needed cheering. The photo family's oldest daughter, who was now away at college, wore a lavender sweater. Sejal panicked briefly as she realized she could not remember the girl's name. She went to a college out of state, and wasn't expected to be around much during Sejal's stay, so her name hadn't been important enough to stick. At least she remembered Catherine's—the other daughter, the daughter who was Sejal's own age, wore a black-and-white striped sweater two sizes too large for her. The tips of her fingers looked like tiny pink tongues, barely emerging from the gaping mouth of her sleeve to taste the cotton candy fuzz of her mother's shoulder. Her face was pale, no makeup. Her dark blond hair was long in front and shaved on the sides in a style Sejal had never seen before.

"She does not want to be there," Sejal's father had said, with what would prove to be his characteristic insight. "Look at her hand. I don't think she even touches her mother's shoulder."

"Felu, stop," her mother said then. "You want to turn Sejal against them before they even have a chance."

"Did I arrange this photo?" he protested. "The evidence is all there. I'm not the one who killed this poor girl and stuffed her and posed her in this clearly unrepresentative manner. Look at her."

Mother laughed. Sejal looked. Catherine's tight smile seemed suddenly like rigor mortis compared to her family's sunny grins.

Now, in the airport, Sejal walked out past security and looked up from the same photo, expecting at least three of its four subjects to be standing there smiling and half smiling, perhaps with the softly blotchy blue backdrop somehow behind them, and Catherine posed awkwardly like she'd been placed in the wrong exhibit. A crow among canaries.

There were families here, but none of them the right family. There was a strangely madeup teenage girl who appeared to have already found the passenger she was meeting, and a group of blond girls in matching sorority sweatshirts holding a handmade sign that read WELCOME BACK, CASSIE!

Sejal stood still as fellow passengers streamed past her, pressed too close, their swinging arms and hot breath fanning a guttering panic in her chest. She had been traveling for eighteen hours and she felt worn and thin. *What now? Would they be waiting in the baggage claim instead?* But her host father, Mr. Brown, had been so insistent. Weirdly, overcautiously insistent. In his email, and in all caps, he'd assured her that they would BE WAITING JUST OUTSIDE SECURITY, IN A-WEST TERMINAL, RIGHT NEXT TO THE CASH MACHINE NEXT TO THE VIDEO SCREENS THAT SAY "ARRIVALS," and that they would LOOK LIKE THE PEOPLE IN THE PHOTO. There were two people standing by the cash machine, but they were only the teenager and a female passenger from Sejal's flight. Sejal approached.

Both girls turned. One was a fellow Indian, the other a girl with dangerous-looking bottle-black hair and thick eyeliner. Blue lips. Pale skin. Black everything else.

"Oh, thank goodness," said the Indian girl in Hindi. "Do you speak English? This very odd Amrikan girl will not leave me alone—do you know how to tell her that I don't want any pamphlets or whatever it is she's selling?"

Sejal turned to the American girl. "Are you . . . Catherine?" she asked.

Catherine glanced at the other passenger in confusion, then back to Sejal.

"Oh, shit," she said.

:

"Please don't tell my parents I did that," said Catherine as they walked to baggage claim. "It took so long to get them to let me pick you up myself. I had to promise to rake leaves."

Sejal smiled, pleased to be worth bargaining for.

"I did not know you at first either," she said, looking down at the photo in her hands. "You look different than your picture."

"Oh Jesus. Don't look at that." She snatched it from Sejal and ripped it in half. "I thought I'd gotten all of these."

Catherine threw the pieces of family to the floor, then stopped.

"Sorry," she said.

She took two steps back, picked up the pieces, and presented them to Sejal.

"Sorry, that was yours."

Sejal took the two halves and reconnected them in her hand.

"It is fine."

"No, I'm acting stupid. You're going to think I'm stupid."

"I am not. I think you are . . . interesting. I think you have interesting clothes."

*Way to go*, thought Sejal. *Well said. She's going to think I'm insulting her.* But Sejal did find her clothes interesting. They looked like she felt. She thought with some embarrassment about the skirt and sweater outfit she was wearing now, as though she'd meant to audition for a spot in the Brown family portrait.

Catherine watched her face as they mounted the escalator. Sejal tried to look as earnest as possible, and after a moment Catherine smiled.

"Well, I like your . . . sweater," she said. "Really yellow."

They held each other's gaze for another moment, then laughed.

"Thank you, Catherine."

"Ooh. Call me Cat. My parents won't, but . . . I was hoping you would."

"Of course."

They found the baggage carousel that corresponded with Sejal's flight and staked their claim to a small gap between other passengers. For reasons she didn't entirely understand, Sejal did not look forward to seeing her luggage. She had already claimed and rechecked it twice, the last time being in New York's JFK airport only a few hours ago, and each time she had seen her big pink bag it had seemed less like a thing that belonged to her, more like something that should have stayed in Kolkata with the mess she'd left behind. She considered grabbing another bag, one of the nondescript black ones that just now thumped onto the conveyor, and taking her chances with someone else's affairs.

"India seems so cool," said Cat.

"Truly?"

"Sure. I guess, right? At least it's not here. I don't know why you wanted to come here."

Sejal had not often thought of her home, or of India as

**43**

a whole, as cool. She was dimly aware, however, of a white Westerner habit of wearing other cultures like T-shirts—the sticker bindis on club kids, sindoor in the hair of an unmarried pop star, Hindi characters inked carelessly on tight tank tops and pale flesh. She knew Americans liked to flash a little Indian or Japanese or African. They were always looking for a little pepper to put in their dish.

"India and I had a talk," Sejal said finally, "and we decided it would be best to see other people for a while."

Cat stared for a moment, not laughing. Sejal had to smile to let her know that she could, too.

"You were joking," said Cat.

"Yes."

"It didn't sound like you were joking."

"Perhaps it is my accent."

⋮

This was the second time that day that Sejal had used what she'd considered to be a discreet and charming line about India and her needing some time apart, and in neither instance had it gone well. On the flight from JFK she'd been asked the same question by a University of Pennsylvania undergrad, and had given the same answer.

"What do you mean?" the coed had asked. "Are you in trouble with your government or something?"

"No," Sejal answered. "I am sorry. I only mean that I had a . . . personal situation back home. It was a good time to try some studies abroad."

"What was the problem?"

Sejal had pulled her arms closer to her sides and folded her hands.

"Nothing so terrible. Just a situation."

"Yeah," said the girl, "but what was it?"

Sejal lowered her eyes to the seat pocket in front of her.

"C'mon," the girl prodded, leaning close. "You can tell me."

Sejal sighed. "I have the Google."

"Oh. *Oh*," said the girl, and she pulled back against her seat.

⁝

Sejal had been one of the first clinical cases. India was a bit of a hot spot, Kolkata in particular. So many software companies, so many new jobs making web protocol work better, faster. The old system had been pieced together by all kinds of different people in cubicles and basements all over the world, and it worked about as well as a steam-powered igloo. The last couple years had seen significant upgrades. There were suddenly so many sites and stats and blogs and vlogs that you could search your own name and find out what you had for breakfast that morning. You could download a widget that graphed your last five haircuts. Webcams were everywhere.

Some people couldn't deal with all the new information. They couldn't pull themselves away from their computers. But that had always been a problem. That was nothing new. The people who contracted a clinical case of the Google couldn't pull themselves away from themselves. With everyone online, there was always somebody mentioning you in a blog post, and you were always in the background of someone's video. The new search engines could show these things to you. They could show *you* to you. The internet knew what you looked like. The internet had your scent. And if these rumors and blurry visitations weren't enough (and they weren't), you could move out of your body and onto the web's muddy crossroads for good, forever.

It was like a great democratic future where everyone had his own television show—the perfect realization of Andy Warhol's fifteen minutes of fame, one streaming minute at a time. Shows and shows about shows and shows showing people watching shows.

It got so she was on all the time. She had old friends and new friends and real friends and web friends with blogs and video blogs, and she checked them every day. Then it was a few times a day, just in case. Then she started a vlog of her own. Her parents were working long hours and had no idea how much time she was spending on it. They had no idea how much time she spent just watching her old posts, admiring the better things she'd said, obsessing over the little mistakes.

Gradually, it all became more real to Sejal than the real world. Gradually, online Sejal became actual Sejal.

She once saw a banner ad that read, "If a tree falls in the internet and no one's there to stream it, does it make a sound?" On some level Sejal understood that it was meant to be funny, but she didn't sleep for three days.

Then one night, her mother came home from work and poked her head through the curtained door of Sejal's room.

"Hello, princess," she said.

Seconds passed before Sejal answered. Ten, twelve seconds. She sort of half turned to her mother and said "Hey" before her head jerked back to the screen again.

"What are you looking at?" said Amma, entering the room. "Sejal? What are—"

"*Shh,*" said Sejal.

Amma looked over her shoulder. It was Sejal's own video blog, and it was live. Sejal stared back from the screen, and just now her mother's mouth and chin entered the picture.

"You're home from work," Sejal said to the screen with a smile.

". . . Yes. Darling, do you think maybe you've been spending—"

"*Shh-shh.*"

"Sejal, I really think—"

"Amma, *shh,*" she hissed. "Something might happen and I don't want to miss it."

:

"It is not contagious," Sejal told the girl on the plane.

"I know. Sorry. So you guys . . . have the internet in India?"

Sejal laughed. "We have the internet. Both my parents are computer programmers. Our connection speed was *supernatural,*" she said, aware that her voice had become draped with a flowery longing.

Her American foster family had assured her parents in writing that they had only dial-up.

:

The baggage carousel was filled with luggage now, and it was beginning to thin out as passengers took up their lives again and wheeled them out the sliding doors. Sejal saw her bright pink bag, as radiant as a wound, and when it came within reach she didn't move to claim it.

"What does yours look like?" asked Cat.

Sejal followed it with her eyes.

"I do not see it yet."

:

"I can't believe they lost your bag," said Cat from the driver's seat of her black Jetta. "Those meathead asswipes."

Sejal smiled faintly in the passenger seat, shifting her feet to avoid the seasick tide of bottles and empty drink cups on the car floor. *Sorry about my car*, Cat had said when they'd found it in the airport parking garage, but it had turned out she was apologizing not for the mess but for the simple fact that it was a Jetta.

"We should have waited at that counter longer. Or gone to find somebody," Cat added.

"We can maybe call tomorrow?" said Sejal. "I'm anxious to see my new home. And my new bed."

"Oh, right. You're probably tired."

"Very tired."

"Only I think my mom has a special dinner planned," said Cat, wincing.

"Oh!" said Sejal, brightening even as her heart sank. "Of course, that is wonderful, no? My first American home-cooked meal."

"Actually," said Cat, "I think we're going out for Indian."

**48**

The Brown house was larger than Sejal expected. She glanced around it cautiously while Cat and Mr. Brown shouted at each other.

"What were you *thinking*?" Mr. Brown shouted. "Were you thinking at all? What is Sejal going to wear?"

"It isn't my fault they sent her bag to the wrong city!" Cat answered. "Why don't you call up those asswipe . . ."

"Catherine!" Mrs. Brown gasped.

". . . airport . . . bag . . . people and yell at them?" finished Cat.

"I will call them, but you should have stayed and talked to someone! If you don't get them looking for a lost bag right away, they'll never find it!"

"*I didn't know!*" Cat moaned. "Call them then, and stop yelling at me!" She tore out of the room and up the stairs. Mr. Brown stomped into the kitchen. There came from above a whuffing noise, the sound of a door that was too light to slam.

Mrs. Brown was wearing two different kinds of orange. Her small, quiet smile seemed at odds with her outfit, which announced CAUTION: ROADWORK AHEAD. "How was your flight?" she asked.

"It was my fault about the luggage," said Sejal. "I told Cat I wanted to go."

"You couldn't know," said Mrs. Brown, patting at her curly hair. "But in America we get our bags. They're not supposed to get lost."

When she'd first arrived, Sejal had deliberated over

whether to bend down and touch the Brown parents' feet. She considered how it might look in a nation of firm handshakes and high fives, and let the moment pass. Now Sejal could only smile reflexively and glance around the room again. She was finding it difficult to look directly at Mrs. Brown, a condition for which she blamed her father. The woman looked, at the moment, not so much like a gum ball as a goldfish. One of those very round goldfish with the cauliflower heads.

Mr. Brown emerged suddenly with a cordless phone. "I don't know how to spell your name," he told Sejal. "Could you speak to this person a moment?"

Sejal got on the phone. "Namaste."

"Yes, Ms. Namastay," said a dull voice. "Can you spell that?"

"No, I was merely saying hello. My name is Ganguly."

"Please spell it, Ms. Namastay."

Sejal thickened her accent to molasses as she tried to spell as swiftly and unhelpfully as possible. She hoped each odd stress and pause would string out an uncrackable code between her and the bag she did not want. Then, pleased with herself, she said her good-byes and returned the phone to Mr. Brown.

"Are you feeling hungry?" asked Mrs. Brown. "We should leave soon to beat the dinner rush."

"I'll go tell Cat," Sejal answered.

:

"You see what I have to put up with?" Cat said immediately upon opening her door. Behind her, on walls the color of eggplant, were black posters and clippings from magazines. Many

**50**

photos of girls looking morose in cemeteries. People in complicated outfits; black and red and white material laced up backs; arms and legs waffled by fishnet. A chunky laptop and a cherub-shaped lamp with a counterproductively black lampshade stood on a desk so haphazardly piled with CD cases it appeared to be molting. "Sorry your room isn't cool like mine. I'll show you."

Sejal's room was through the next door down the hall. It was stupefyingly beige. It had a beige computer in it and an off-white bed.

Neither this computer nor Cat's antique laptop had stirred more than the slightest pang in Sejal. If she were an alcoholic, these machines would have been weak lemonade shandy. She felt intellectually safe but oddly claustrophobic.

"Your mom wants to leave soon," said Sejal.

"To 'beat the rush,' right?" said Cat in an impersonation of her mother, if her mother had been a dim-witted cartoon bear. "It's like, there's a reason they have a dinner rush—that's when all normal people eat."

"Do you think we can wait a bit? I promised my mother I would have a puja in my new room."

Cat wrinkled her nose. "That can't possibly mean what it sounds like."

"It's only a . . . small ceremony about new beginnings. You bathe and burn incense, and offer flowers and sweets to Ganesha—"

Sejal gave a small cry and tented her hands over her face.

"What?" said Cat. "What's wrong?"

"Ganesha is in the bag I . . . lost," Sejal said.

"Ganesha . . . Is that the god with the elephant head?"

Sejal thought of her little pink Ganesha figurine in her big pink bag, turning slowly on the dull airport merry-go-round. She nodded.

"The airport lost your elephant god," said Cat.

Both girls slumped onto the bed.

"Asswipes."

# 6

## PLASMA TV

**TV'S ALAN FRIENDLY** strode down the corridor of Belfry Studios, a DVD in his hand. Occasionally he pumped this hand in the air, watching the light glint dazzlingly off the disk's iridescent grooves. *This would look good on tape,* Alan thought. He wished someone were taping him. Someone usually was.

He hosted a hit basic cable television show called *Vampire Hunters* on which, over the course of two and a half seasons, they had not only failed to ever successfully hunt a vampire but also failed to collect adequate proof that such a thing even existed. And yet people watched. Every week, their numbers were as good as the weaker network shows, even in reruns. It was all a lot of stumbling around in the dark, filming everything with those green night-vision cameras, hanging around New Orleans nightclubs when there were no leads to take them elsewhere. So many false alarms with wealthy homosexuals and goth kids, never any legitimate bloodsucking anything, and still the nation watched. It had made Alan feel invincible, like he could put anything on television and make money. *Miniature Bigfoot Hunters. Sixteen-Foot-Tall Invisible Robot Hunters.*

Then came the *Saturday Night Live* skit thing. Last Saturday's host, Cody Southern, had once starred in an 80's teen vampire picture (*Love Bites*, 1987, starring Cody Southern and Cody Meyer) that had become the sort of movie that was on TV every Saturday afternoon your whole life. So the SNL writers and cast cooked up a *Vampire Hunters* parody in which a fake Alan and his team followed the real-life Cody everywhere—to the dry cleaners, to his kid's piano recital, always impotently waving crosses and garlic in his face and trying to stake him.

It shouldn't have been important. There was a school of thought (and a school of thought that Alan had been hearing a lot lately, especially from the people who worked for him) that said getting spoofed on SNL was a good thing—it proved that they'd arrived, that the country was talking about them. And the following week they had their best viewer share ever. But the week after that they had their second worst. And that was the same week that Alan lost a sponsor. That was the week an anchor on *TV Now!* said his name like it had quotes around it. That was the week his coproducers started looking like they'd awoken abruptly from a confusing dream in which they had, for some reason, financed a man with a vampire-hunting show based on little more than the fact that he had an English accent and his own stake.

But that was old news. The DVD made it old news.

"Ha-*ha!*" Alan trumpeted as he entered Props. "I have it! The news affiliate sent it over this morning."

Mike didn't look up from his workbench. "I've already seen it on YouTube," he said.

"Not like this. Not like this. The quality is much better. Look."

Mike flinched as if Alan had slipped a wet finger into his ear, rather than a DVD into his laptop. "That better be clean," he said. "Nobody but me ever scans for viruses around here."

The video started itself. It looked down onto a concrete zoo enclosure and a sleeping panda. And a kid or a short man hunched over the panda. Seconds later there was the bang of a door and two more men appeared, and there was a struggle, and then a moment that was difficult to explain.

"There!" shouted Alan, thumping out the punctuation against the workbench, then cradling his bruised hand. "There."

Amid the tangle of bodies a shape had seemed to collapse in on itself and rise, flittering, into the air. Where there had once been three people, now there were only two zoo guards and what looked, conceivably, to be a bat. Especially if you wanted it to be a bat.

"There," Alan said again, gesturing at the monitor. "This is a big break. Before now we weren't even sure a vampire would show up on tape."

"What do you mean? Why?"

"Because of the whole no-reflection thing. And some people claim they can't be photographed."

"That's the stupidest thing I've ever heard. Light either reflects off something or it doesn't. If it doesn't, you wouldn't be able to see the vampire with the naked eye, either."

"Well . . ." said Alan. He wasn't used to having this sort of conversation about what he did. Most of his staff were fairly uncritical believers, or pretended to be. And until recently his coproducers hadn't cared either way.

"And this is supposed to be the same person who stole some blood at a comics convention."

"He fits the description."

"Comics fan donors," Mike snorted. "That's gotta be some watery blood." He pushed back his chair. "By the way, your Stake-O-Matic is done."

Alan squealed and leaned over Mike's shoulder.

"It eats up a lot of compressed air," said Mike. "You'll have to wear some kind of whippit bandolier."

It was a gun, there was no pussyfooting around that. It was a homemade air pistol with a wide, open barrel.

"It takes a standard three-quarter-inch dowel rod," said Mike. "Can stake a vampire-shaped thing at ten yards."

"Do you have any stakes already sharpened? I want to try it."

"I'm an applied sciences genius. I don't whittle sticks. You want a stick whittled, find an intern."

"But it kills vampires?" asked Alan.

Mike sighed. "If vampires, like most people, don't like

**56**

getting things stuck in their hearts, then, yeah, okay. But if I really thought you were going to be aiming this thing at any vampires, I wouldn't have made it in the first place. I'm envisioning a lot of footage of target practice at dummies with the word 'vampire' written in Sharpie."

"That footage says this kid is a vampire."

"That footage could have been faked. Are you kidding? I could have made that at home on my Mac. But if there are such things as vampires, it's because they're people with a disease or a disorder. Light sensitivity plus anemia, or something. Even if this kid is out there hurting people you're not allowed to just go shooting things into his chest."

"If he's . . ." said Alan, "if he's a murderer, it'll be justifiable."

"Sure. And *Vampire Hunters* will join the great tradition of television shows predicated on vigilante homicide. On-camera, vigilante homicide. Oh, wait—there aren't any shows like that? I wonder why that is."

"Look," said Alan, "it's not called *Vampire Killers*. It's *Vampire Hunters*. We should be able to string out the hunt for this kid for at least five episodes. We'll figure out what to do with him when we find him. But focus groups say they like our gear. Our tools. So we need more swag like the Stake-O-Matic. There are licensing possibilities."

"Whatever."

"Four more Stake-O-Matics just like this, plus another four for backups, plus we're not calling them Stake-O-Matics anymore. They're now called Redeemers."

"I don't care."

"Also, I'm encouraging each crew member to name his personal Redeemer—maybe after an old girlfriend or something. But! The point is, the hunt is on! There's a vampire in San Diego!"

"Sunny San Diego," said Mike.

# 7:

## THIS WEEK,
## ON *VAMPIRE HUNTERS* . . .

**ON THE EVE** of the first day of the new school year
Sejal sat on the floor of Cat's bedroom, looking at CD liner
notes.

"I like them," she told Cat. "They're almost Bollywood
but slower, no? How do you say their name again?"

"Like 'Suzy,'" said Cat into her cavernous, dark closet.
"Siouxsie and the Banshees. They're totally old school, right?"
She parted and reparted the dark curtains of her wardrobe,
tossing this and that onto the bed.

"Thank you again for lending me clothes," said Sejal, who
at that moment was wearing a pair of Cat's jeans and a cast-
and-crew T-shirt from her high school production of *My Fair
Lady.*

"It's perfect. I used to be more Elizabethan, but now I'm strictly Batcave, so I was probably going to sell these clothes anyway." Cat had taken to the task of dressing Sejal with great enthusiasm, as though she'd been sent a huge doll with MADE IN INDIA stamped on the foot. "Are you okay? You seem a little fidgety."

"I am like that only. And I'm anxious about school. I—I feel I should tell you I've sometimes had panic attacks. Not for a long time now, but . . . I do not want to freak you out."

"'Cause of . . . the Google?"

Sejal nodded at her feet. Panic attacks when reminded that she could not just close her eyes and vanish from the real world with its fleshy claustrophobia. Panic at the thought that she'd failed to log on and check her status for two hours, a day, four months. She pictured the complicated yoga of it—hands at her temples like blinders, bent at the waist to gaze at her own navel. Downward spiral pose.

Panic, especially, with the memory of what had happened. Of what she'd done.

"Huh," said Cat. "You want some Prozac? Or a Xanax? I don't need it, but my parents got me all kinds of that shit after I started dressing this way. I don't think it's expired or anything."

Sejal shrugged. *Her* parents had been very strongly against drugs, but she was an American girl in training. "Maybe a half a pill."

Cat produced an amber bottle from a drawer in her nightstand and tossed it onto Sejal's lap. "It says Niravam but it's totally Xanax," she said, as though Xanax might be a name she would know and trust, like Coca-Cola.

Sejal didn't open it. She felt a little better just knowing it was there. "I like the cover of this Cinema Strange album," she said. "Can we listen to it next?"

"Yeah, but we'll have to stop it when— Aw, crap!" said Cat, looking at the clock on her nightstand. "It's already started!"

"What has?" asked Sejal, drawing her legs up quickly as Cat thundered past.

"*Vampire Hunters*. It's this rad show on the Crypt. Last week they totally almost caught this one vampire, but it turned out he was just German."

She clicked the TV on her dresser through a dozen channels, finally stopping at a commercial for paper towels.

"These are European vampires then, isn't it?" asked Sejal. "Like Count Dracula? We have stories about vampires in India, but they are not the same."

"It's American vampires, mostly. And they're not really like Dracula. They're more like the sort of people you'd meet at a gallery opening, you know?"

"Not really."

"Shh! It's on!"

INTRO MUSIC
INT. *VAMPIRE HUNTERS* STUDIO

ALAN FRIENDLY
What really happened in San Diego,
California, just a few short weeks

ago? What dark predator stalked
these idyllic shores?

EXT. LOCATION SHOTS OF SAN DIEGO—STOCK
FOOTAGE OF A WOMAN IN A BIKINI ON
ROLLER SKATES

          ALAN FRIENDLY (V.O.)
On August third, not every visitor
to this harbor city came in search
of fun in the sun. On such a
summer's day, one young man was
California dreamin' . . . of blood.

EXT. HOME OF PAUL KLEIN AND FAMILY

          ALAN FRIENDLY (V.O.)
Our hunt begins at the home of
Paul Klein, straight-A student and
artist. On this first Wednesday in
August Paul hosted a few close
friends for a quiet get-together.
How could Paul and his friends
know that their party would soon be
crashed by darkness?
Friends like Carrie Lawson.

INT. KLEIN HOME—MEDIUM SHOT OF CARRIE
LAWSON AND PAUL KLEIN

CARRIE LAWSON

He came right up to me, out of all
the people there . . . and he starts
talking in this real player voice,
like this hypnotic voice—

ALAN FRIENDLY (off camera)

What did he look like?

CARRIE LAWSON

He was tall? Like, average height?

PAUL KLEIN

He was short.

CARRIE LAWSON

Like kind of a tall kind of short.
With dark hair and eyes. You could
tell he was really rich, like he had
a really big house.

ALAN FRIENDLY

Did he mention where to find this
house?

CARRIE LAWSON

No. But right away he tries to get
me to go outside with him. He says
he wants to show me his fangs, to

share his eternal curse, right? My
friend Trish was there, too, but he
wasn't into her at all.

                PAUL KLEIN
That's when a couple of the guys
decide he has to leave. They say
he was really strong, for a little
guy. He wouldn't leave without his
friend.

                ALAN FRIENDLY
There were two vampires?

                PAUL KLEIN
What? I don't know. He was there
with a friend. The friend had locked
himself in the half bath. We found
him and they left together.

FOOTAGE OF HALF BATH SHOT IN GRAINY
HANDHELD VIDEO

                ALAN FRIENDLY
Folklore experts tell us that a
vampire cannot enter a home without
first being invited. Did you invite
this dark stalker inside?

PAUL KLEIN
No. Well . . . he had a flyer.


CLOSE-UP OF PARTY FLYER, TURNING
SLOWLY COUNTERCLOCKWISE OVER CEMETERY
STOCK IMAGE FROM EPISODE 1.7. MUSICAL
STING #9 (FOREBODING HORN SECTION),
TRANSITION TO DRIPPING BLOOD EFFECT #2
(BLOODY CURTAINS)

ALAN FRIENDLY (V.O.)
Did a canary-yellow flyer promising
two-dollar beer cups and vodka-
soaked watermelon slices make an
altogether more sinister promise to
two thirsty children of the night?
Is this all the invitation a vampire
requires? Phoenix Community College
Professor Charles Hargraves says
yes.


INT. PCC TEACHERS' LOUNGE

PROF. HARGRAVES
There is an account from nineteenth-
century New Hampshire in which the
citizens of a certain village were
invited, via a broadside posted

**65**

on a certain tree, to come view
the wealthy ironmonger's new water
closet. This was the only invitation
the infamous Manchester Vampire
needed to enter the home, kill the
ironmonger and his family, and steal
twelve dollars.

INT. *VAMPIRE HUNTERS* STUDIO

ALAN FRIENDLY
When we come back—what dark business
did these evil forces have at the
San Diego Convention Center? And
does the blood of baby pandas have
the power to turn ordinary vampires
into supervampires? Plus, we'll give
you a first look at the new weapons
in the *Vampire Hunters* arsenal.
Watch your backs, Army of Darkness—
here come the Redeemers!

OUTRO MUSIC, SCREAM SFX #6, FADE TO
COMMERCIAL

Doug had the phone up to his ear before the first ring
finished.
"Hello?"

Jay's voice came through in a panic. "Are you watching—"

"Yeah."

"They're talking about us! They're hunting us!"

"They're hunting *me*."

"Well," said Jay, "they made it sound like I'm a vampire, too. Maybe if they find me they'll just . . . stake first and ask questions later, right?"

"Did you hear that girl from the party talking?" asked Doug. "She sounded totally hot for me."

"And what was that about new weapons?" wondered Jay. "Redeemers? Sounds holy. Maybe it's something with holy water."

"Maybe I could visit San Diego again . . . over a three-day weekend. Or over Thanksgiving break. 'Course, my parents would kind of notice I was gone . . ."

"Does holy water even really work on you? Do you have to be religious for it to work? We should know these things. I can't believe we haven't run . . . tests or something."

"I can't believe these commercials last so long. Hey! Back to *Vampire Hunters*, all right? No one cares about term life insurance!"

"I'm going to do some more research online," said Jay. "We should test out everything everybody says about vampires, shouldn't we? I mean, if those vampire hunters track you down, we need to know what's real and what isn't . . ."

"Shut up, it's back on."

"Like, that getting-invited-into-houses thing they

mentioned. Is that true? Like what if they were chasing you and you tried to hide in a building or house, but you couldn't because you couldn't get in—"

"Will you shut up already? TV!"

>            ALAN FRIENDLY
>      —was when we knew it was time to
>      head back to our roving headquarters
>      for a new tool against these two
>      foot soldiers in the army of the
>      undead.

>      CLOSE-UP OF REDEEMER, ROTATING SLOWLY
>      WITH VITAL STATS RUNNING COMPUTER-STYLE
>      DOWN THE RIGHT SIDE OF THE SCREEN LIKE
>      IN THOSE CRIME SCENE INVESTIGATION
>      SHOWS. MUSICAL STING #24 (REDEEMER
>      THEME)

>            ALAN FRIENDLY (V.O.)
>      Vampires, say hello to the Redeemer.
>      Ancient wisdom meets twenty-first-
>      century know-how in a repeating
>      stake launcher that can neutralize
>      fifteen vampires per minute at thirty
>      yards.

>      EXT. BALBOA PARK, SAN DIEGO

>                    ALAN FRIENDLY (V.O.)
> I prepared my personal Redeemer, Ann
> Marie, and assembled the *Vampire
> Hunters* team outside the gates of
> the San Diego Zoo, where the trail
> suddenly went cold . . . cold as
> death.

INT. OFFICE OF BILL WINCHELL, CHIEF OF
ZOO SECURITY

>                    BILL WINCHELL
> We don't know how he got in . . .
> whoever got in that night. The
> gates, all the service entrances
> were secure. We might have missed
> it, if not for the call from a panda
> lover, watching our webcam.

STILL IMAGE OF BLOODRED TELEPHONE AS
RECORDING OF EMERGENCY CALL PLAYS

>                    ZOO SECURITY
> Hello, Zoo Security.

>                    CALLER
> Hi, I was just watching the
> PandaCam?

> ZOO SECURITY
> This is not the information line,
> ma'am. Zoo hours are—

> CALLER
> I know, but I was just watching, and
> in the panda room? There's a guy.

(SILENCE)

> ZOO SECURITY
> What?

> ALAN FRIENDLY (V.O.)
> Security officers rushed to the
> enclosure where panda Lee Ling and
> her baby, little Shuan Shuan, slept
> peacefully, unaware that a predator
> had invaded their happy den. We can
> now show you enhanced webcam footage
> of the next few chilling moments.
> Don't take your eyes away for an
> instant.

Doug didn't. Jay didn't. The video played out silently on their television screens.

"I . . . turned into a bat," said Doug.

"Oh, wow."

"That's what happened. I turned into a bat," Doug

whispered as they aired the webcam footage a second time but slower. "Look, I left my clothes behind. There was a skylight in the ceiling. I must've flown up out of the skylight."

"Oh wow."

                    ALAN FRIENDLY (V.O.)
               We present now an artist's rendering
               of a possible panda-empowered
               supervampire.

ARTIST'S RENDERING OF PANDA-EMPOWERED
SUPERVAMPIRE. MUSICAL STING #11
(DISQUIETING FLUTES)

"Meet me at the farm," said Doug, and then hung up.

# 8

## BATTING PRACTICE

**THE PROBLEM,** it seemed to Doug, was that he wasn't even sure how it worked. Did he just *think* about being a bat? Picture a bat in his mind? Contract his muscles? Shout, "Up, up, and away?"

"Up, up, and away," Doug said under his breath.

"What?"

"I said, 'This is stupid.'"

Doug had arrived before Jay and had used the time to take blood from one of the docile cows near the greenhouses. He'd done it so many times before, but now it left him feeling empty. He'd tasted real blood, *human* blood in San Diego. He'd felt strong. Invincible. He barely even noticed the sun, for a while. But those two small bags had only lasted a couple of weeks.

"That webcam video was pretty grainy," said Doug. "Maybe it just looked like—"

"But we know vampires really can do it, right?" said Jay. "How else could you have gotten out of the panda den? And you said the vampiress did it. You said she made it look easy."

"Yeah, well, she's probably been doing it for five hundred years. Her mom probably made her practice when she was a kid."

"That doesn't make any sense—"

"Just shut up and let me think about bats, okay?"

A long minute passed, with only lowing and the distant sounds of traffic reaching Doug's ears. *Bats. Small, furry, screeching, winged bats. Bats, bats, batty—*

"Screw this," Doug said finally.

"No," said Jay, "c'mon. We can figure this out. There's just something we haven't thought of."

They thought.

"Hit me," said Doug.

"What?"

"I think you're gonna have to hit me."

"Why? I can't do that."

Doug sighed. "If I've ever done this before, it's because I was just hit in the head by a bear. Plus tasered a bunch of times."

"We don't have any Tasers," said Jay.

"Thank you for laying that out for me. In lieu of Tasers, you'll have to hit me. Hard as you can. Then maybe some kind of fight-or-flight response will kick in and I'll turn into a bat to get away from you."

"Fight or flight."

"Yes."

"Only half of that is flight."

Doug almost said, "Duh," but then he got Jay's point.

"I promise I won't attack you," he said.

"But what if you do?" asked Jay.

"I won't."

"But what if you do?"

"Then . . . make the sign of the cross or something."

"You're Jewish."

"I really, really don't think I would attack you—"

"I can sort of make a Star of David with my fingers," said Jay. "Look."

"I'm starting to consider it, though," said Doug. "You know. Attacking you. I'm going to keep my options open."

"All right," said Jay, with his fists curled in front of his face like an old-timey pugilist. "I'm going to hit you."

Doug closed his eyes. "Do it."

"Are you ready?"

"Don't wait until I'm ready. Just—"

Jay rushed toward Doug and threw a wild haymaker into his shoulder. Doug staggered and Jay fell into a spinach plant.

"Ow."

"Ow."

"Okay, don't do the running start," said Doug. "Did you close your eyes? Don't close your eyes. Stand right in front of me. Yeah. Okay, now—"

Punch.

"Ow! Jeez!"

Punch, punch.

"Okay, no, this isn't—"

Punch-punch-punch-punch.

Jay's blows were growing harder. It was entirely possible he was getting into it. Doug backed away, but Jay followed, punch-punch-punch-punch-punch.

"Ahh! Fuck! Stop it! Stop—"

Something happened. He felt something new, and heard Jay's sharp gasp. He held his breath and tried to slide into it, but it was like trying to stay underwater while his fat body and airless lungs drove him to the surface.

"AHHHHHHHH!" Jay screamed.

*"What?"* Doug said, or tried to. His shrill voice squealed through sharp teeth like he was whistling for a cab.

"AHHHHHHHHHHHHH!"

Doug looked down at himself. His body was covered in coarse, curly hair. He'd shrunk a bit—his clothes sagged—but his fingers were twig thin and distended, the webbing between them stretched tight as a drum. He'd changed, all right, but only halfway.

"AHHH—guh," said Jay, then he doubled over and vomited into a row of parsley.

*"Stop screaming,"* said Doug, as low as he could, but his voice still cracked into the ultrasonic. Dogs barked in the distance.

Jay sputtered and sat down in the dirt. "Change back. Please."

Doug tried. He hobbled around on stubby legs, cradling his head inside his gigantic fan-hands. But how did he change back? *Not* get punched? He was already not getting punched.

"*I can't believe this,*" he squealed. "*The night before school starts. It's like all the puberty I've been missing till now just hit me all at once. Like I've been saving it up.*"

"Except you're shorter now."

"*Except that. It's like I've been whacked with the puberty bat.*"

"It's like you sort of *are* the puberty bat."

"*Can you maybe help me?*" squeaked Doug. "*Instead of making fun?*"

"What can I do?"

"*I don't know. Don't punch me. What's the opposite of punching someone? Shaking his hand? Buying him dinner?*"

"We should get out of the open," said Jay. They were standing far from the road but were still pretty exposed.

"*And go where?*" asked Doug. "*I can't go home. My mom noticed that time I trimmed my eyebrows. She's gonna notice this.*"

"I can . . . hide you in our shed," said Jay.

Doug sighed like a tin whistle. "*Okay . . . but I need a lift. I don't think I can ride a bike like this.*"

They walked to Jay's car—a long walk, now that Doug was roughly the size and build of E.T. He imagined himself riding home in the front basket of his own bike.

Jay loaded Doug's bike into the trunk and helped him into the backseat, where he could lie down. And as they drove he felt unexpectedly childlike, lying in the back of the car at night, listening to the road hum through the seat, someone there to take care of him.

He'd known Jay forever. They hadn't gone to the same elementary school (Jay had been homeschooled) but had met through Jay's mother, a noted doctor of the hair and scalp. Dr. Rouse had chosen her specialization mostly out of frustration from dealing with her own son's uncombable hair syndrome. To this day if you google "uncombable hair syndrome" you can easily find a photo of Jay from a scientific article written by his mother, his eyes masked by a scandalous black rectangle.

As a toddler he'd had pale, shimmery dandelion hair that could not be combed down nor back nor parted or tamed in any way. Like a spray of fiber optics. Like something that should be plugged in at Christmas. This and a naturally inquisitive temperament had given him the appearance of always being startled.

At the age of six Doug had taken part in a study conducted by Dr. Rouse to investigate a new head lice treatment. He had even been persuaded to have his picture taken for a series of informational posters (caption: Sleep tight. Don't let the head bugs bite) that hung in hospitals and clinics. These posters now fetched upward of fifty dollars on eBay. A hundred if they were signed. Doug didn't really understand it, but that didn't stop him from selling signed posters.

Jay and Doug had met in Dr. Rouse's office, and once Doug's lice had cleared up, the boys fell into an easy routine of play in the common areas and empty clinical spaces. They hid in cupboards and wore rubber gloves everywhere. They made spaceships and Podracers out of stethoscopes and vaginal specula.

Doug's eyes welled up just thinking about it.

"Jay . . ." he said, "I . . . *really appreciate all you . . . I'd have been screwed these last few weeks without you. You're a good friend. I know I'm not, sometimes.*"

"What did you say?" Jay called over his shoulder. "I can barely understand you."

"*Nothing.*"

# 9:

## SOUND BITES

**"HELLO?"**

"Mr. Lee? This is Jay."

"Oh, hi, Jay. Is Doug with you? He hasn't come home yet."

"He's here. We wanted to know if he could spend the night at my house."

"Tomorrow's the first day of school, isn't it?"

"Yeah, it's okay, though. He can ride in with me. He has his book bag."

"Why didn't he call me himself?"

"He said you'd say no. We want to play D&D."

"One last hurrah, then it's back to the coal mines, is that right?"

"Um . . . right."

"Well, I suppose. Don't stay up too late slaying elves!"

". . . Okay. Thanks. Good-bye."

"Bye, now."

# 10
# :

## CONFLUENCE

**THE NEXT MORNING,** Sejal followed Cat to the high school office. She'd taken half a Niravam with her orange juice and her surprisingly bacon-oriented American breakfast and was feeling okay.

"Hope we have some classes together," Cat told Sejal. "Probably not, though. You're way smarter than me."

"That is not true."

"It is. Plus you speak three languages and you're Indian and you don't use as many contractions as I do. That alone'll get you into AP everything."

"Hmm."

"Don't worry about it," said Cat. "I can always rely on my

breathtaking hotness, right? See you at lunch."

"By the tree, *na*?"

"By the tree."

Sejal entered the office and stepped up to a wide counter. Beyond this were a pair of desks, one of which was occupied by a middle-aged woman as blond and toothy as an ear of corn. Sejal waited to be acknowledged. After a while this didn't seem to be working, so she cleared her throat.

"Hello," said Sejal. "This is my first day."

The woman didn't look up from her computer. "This is a lot of people's first day, hon. Take a seat."

Sejal blinked and looked around her at the otherwise empty office. She sat down in an unfriendly chair next to a fake plant.

There were no sounds, save the faint clicks of a mouse and the constant sigh of an unseen air conditioner. Each click sent a little tickle up her spine. She willed herself to be at peace. She tried to quiet her mind. In moments like these she once would have been texting or talking or checking her email. Now, more often than not, she found herself filling the void by twiddling her thumbs. Honest-to-gods thumb twiddling, but it helped.

Her heart and soul were off someplace, hopping from one computer to the next. They were riding the rails like hoboes.

On a wall behind the counter a framed poster said POSITIVITY, beneath a photo of a blizzard-battered penguin cradling an egg on its feet. Below the frame was a cartoon cat who hated Mondays. Sejal rather thought the two posters canceled each other out and searched for a third to break the tie.

The office door opened and a boy entered. He was

gathering up a rain poncho as if he'd just been holding it over his head, though a glimpse of the sky outside confirmed that it was just as sunny and cloudless as it had been a few minutes ago. The boy stood at the counter and waited.

The blond woman rose and said to the boy, "Now then. It's your first day?"

"What? No, I'm just late. I need a late pass."

"It is my first day," said Sejal, standing.

"Oh my dear!" the woman said to her. "You're our foreign exchange student, aren't you? Why didn't you tell me?"

"I'm sorry, I didn't think it made a difference," Sejal explained, though clearly it had already caused this woman to double the volume of her voice.

"Say-jall . . . Gangooly?" the woman ventured, reading Sejal's name from a file. "From India?"

"Yes. Kolkata."

"It says here 'Calcutta.'"

"It is the same thing."

"And this is an Indian dress you're wearing? It's very exotic."

The boy was frowning at it. "It's from Dark Matter," he said. "In the mall."

The corn woman's entire demeanor went stale as she turned to the boy.

"Name?"

"Um, Doug. Douglas Lee."

"Reason for being tardy?"

"It . . . took me longer to get ready this morning than usual."

The woman sniffed. "That's no excuse. I'm afraid I'm going to *have* to give you a Tardy."

"Right. Hey," said Doug, pointing at Sejal's file, "that says she's in the same Pre-Cal class as me first period. I can show her the way."

:

Pre-Calculus was held in one of the temporary buildings ringing the parking lot, and Doug felt the sun crackling on his skin as he escorted Sejal. It could have felt worse, though—he had recently fed—and there was no way he was going to duck and cover around the one girl in school who hadn't already decided he was a loser.

"I hate that word," said Doug. "'Tardy.' Don't you?"

"I had never heard it before a minute ago," said Sejal.

"Oh. Well, school's the only place you'll ever hear it. It just means 'late.' And they invented it because they really needed a special word for kids that means 'late' but also sounds like 'retard.'"

Sejal laughed. The sound of it rang Doug like a bell.

"So . . ." he said, "when did you get here? To America?"

"A week ago."

"You like it?"

"I like it. Everyone has been . . . very nice."

"Yeah, well . . . high school's just starting. Give it a few days."

A brittle silence passed.

"So," said Sejal. "You are interested in fashion?"

"What?"

"You knew from where my dress had come. The boys back

**84**

home would never—"

"Well . . . you know, I think guys can be interested in that kind of thing without being . . . you know," Doug said in what he hoped would be taken for a confidently masculine voice. He only recognized the dress because he'd spent several summer afternoons at Dark Matter attempting to meet a nice girl with a vampire fetish.

They stopped outside the classroom door. The walk had been too short. And now Sejal was already frowning at him.

"What's wrong?"

"I'm sorry," said Sejal. "Your face . . . you look like you've had a lot of sun, no?"

"Oh. Yeah. I spent a lot of the summer at the beach. You know."

"I didn't notice it in the office."

"Also . . ." said Doug, "also I caught some sort of sun allergy. My skin's really sensitive."

*Sensitive*, thought Doug. *May as well ask her to braid my hair.*

"Oh. I was going to ask you where you eat lunch," said Sejal, "but you wouldn't want to eat outside, then, by the tree."

She was inside the classroom door before he could answer.

# 11

## FIRST ISSUE

**"I DON'T WANT TO** eat lunch by the tree," said Jay to Doug as they walked from math class to Spanish. "All the drama kids eat there. The popular ones."

"Well, so what?" said Doug. "You were in the musical, right? You played that waiter character— What was his name?"

"Waiter."

"See?"

Specifically, the kids who ate by the tree were the ones who got good parts in the plays. Lead actors, plus maybe an assistant director or two. Less popular were the kids who got small parts and nonspeaking roles, but at least they were still members of the cast. Doug was crew. Crew were like the friends you called only when you needed help moving furniture.

Doug always tried out for a part in each production, and so far he'd always failed to get one. He often thought about how his life would change if he landed a lead role, but on some level he understood what everyone in Masque & Dagger understood: you weren't popular because you'd played a lead role, you got lead roles because you were popular. Or, rather, your popularity and your distinguished high school drama career both stemmed from some effortless charisma that shone from your face and spilled from your lips—a shower of quarters when you opened your mouth, a trail of flowers and corpses in your wake.

Doug was just as nervous about lunch as Jay. More so, perhaps, as he assumed he was more highly regarded and therefore had more to lose. At least the rest of his classes were indoors, so he expected his skin to clear up by lunch.

"I should have brought a baseball cap from home," he said. "I was in such a rush."

"You were hard to wake up," said Jay.

"I only got like an hour of sleep! My body won't let me sleep at night anymore. I maybe nodded off around six thirty."

Jay had woken him at 7:30, and then again at 8:00. At some point, while he dozed, Doug had changed back to normal. Then he had had only thirty minutes to bike home, watch Mom and Dad pull out of the driveway, sneak into the empty house, shower, and change. In the foggy bathroom mirror he glanced quickly at himself to be sure. Pale. Hairless chest. The impression of being clammy even when he wasn't clammy. Normal, or what passed for normal now.

The kids in Spanish class were broken up into groups of two and three, and Doug and Jay took up their usual spot near a poster from the Spanish board of tourism. Mr. Gonzales wandered around the room.

"She seems really nice," said Doug. *And short enough. And kind of pretty.* "I just need a chance to talk to her more. Maybe she could be, you know, the one."

"Would you turn her into a vampire?" asked Jay.

"I don't know. If she wanted. I don't even really know how to do that."

"The vampiress drained all your blood, right?"

Doug nodded slowly at the tourism poster, an unfinished cathedral in Barcelona with facades like two rows of sharp teeth.

"I think so," he said.

:

*July in the Poconos, near Hickory Run. Alternating sun and clouds, rain every few days. Biting insects, mosquitoes that swarm your ankles and arms like you're passing out little supermarket samples of blood. New Product! A hundred discrete marks on your skin.*

*You were out late again, alone, watching the spiders ticktack across that field of boulders between the trees. You had to feel your way back to the family cabin through the fireflies and the moonless night.*

*The vampire came at you then, milk white. Naked. Howling through the trees. Wounded, open chested, it oozed its red center. The spill collected in tangled crotch hair and traced ligatures down pale legs.*

*The vampire pressed down on you. There was no beguile-ment, no charm or enchantment. You were held fast by the hair as the vampire tore you open and siphoned off your life. Your blood mingled. It wasn't romantic.*

*The vampire made a wrenching noise and folded in on itself. Now small, it flapped thin wings and disappeared into the trees.*

*You were left too weak to stand. Your lungs fluttered in your chest and you were desperately thirsty. Your death was like a slow fall into a deep well.*

*When you stirred again, it startled two coyotes that were sniffing at your carcass. The vampire's blood laced your empty veins; tensed their red, spindly fingers; and closed you up like a fist over the closest animal. It thrashed, but you drank it dry and rose unsteadily, needing more. Still night. A hundred yards distant you could tell (without any trouble at all) that the second coyote had paused to look back. You chased it for an hour and fell upon it in a copse of trees.*

*When your mind found its place again, you collapsed and dry heaved into a creek and washed the stains from your skin. There were no wounds on your body, save a long, dry welt on your neck. But your clothes were covered in blood. You buried them.*

:

"*Bienvenido al supermercado,*" Jay was saying. Doug just stared at him for a dim moment, dumbfounded by this talking animal and his Spanish classroom exercise.

Oh, it was Jay.

"This would . . . this would all be a lot easier if I was just an asshole," Doug said. "I could just find someone and hold them still and feed. I wouldn't even have to kill them. I could just take a pint or two, like I do with the cows. I wish I could be sure that wouldn't turn them into vampires, too."

Jay pushed aside his textbook. "There's gotta be a way," he said. "Look."

He produced his calculator from his backpack.

"Say you drink from someone once a week. Is that about right?"

"Yeah," said Doug.

"So if your first victim becomes a vampire, then in a week there are two vampires who need to feed. You and him."

"Me and *her*," Doug stressed.

"And then in two weeks there's four vampires, and in three weeks eight, and on and on. So guess how many weeks it takes before everyone on Earth is a vampire."

"I dunno." Doug sighed. "Ten."

Jay frowned. "You don't think that. You just guessed low so my answer won't sound amazing."

"So what is it already?"

"It's, like, thirty-four. Thirty-three and a half."

"That's really amazing."

"Anyway," said Jay, sounding deflated, "it means there must be a way to just feed, like we thought. Maybe even a way to feed so the victim forgets, like some kind of vampire hypnosis, or else there'd be news reports of vampire attacks all the time."

"I don't like that idea," said Doug. "Hypnosis. It'd be like slipping something in her drink."

"Well, what if the person . . . gave you permission?"

Doug covered his face. "We've been through this. I appreciate the offer, but it just seems . . . *gay*. I'd rather drink a little cow here and there and try to meet some girl who's into it. Like this new girl. She's pretty goth for an Indian."

"I'm not saying I want you to do it," said Jay. "It's just . . . hard to see you hurting so much. You could just drink a little of my blood, just to see—"

"Uh-uh," said Mr. Gonzales as he loomed suddenly over their desks. "*No inglés. En español, por favor.*"

Jay glanced in the teacher's direction, then stared at his hands. "Um . . . *Podría usted . . . beber un poco de mi . . . sangre? Es correcto? Sangre?*"

"*Sangre es* 'blood,'"

"*Sí*," said Jay. Doug pretended to read his book. Mr. Gonzales coughed.

"You're supposed to be pretending to buy pineapples," he said.

# 12

## PACK LUNCH

**S**EJAL CARRIED her lunch through the center aisle of the crowded cafeteria like a bride, aware of the careless stares of other students, the brush of their eyes on her skin— the designs that they left there, some pretty, some not. For the second time that day a boy asked in a loud stage whisper as she passed if Sejal had ever read the *Kama Sutra*. Maybe the same boy.

"Dude, I think she heard you!" said another. Laughter all around.

*That's what I get*, she thought. It hadn't been necessary to walk among them all like that. She could have skirted around the side, but she'd made the effort to be visible, to be an actual actor in the actual world. As if, as the new girl, she really needed to give them an excuse to stare.

She dipped her head, let her hair fall in front of her face.

She had to remind herself of one of the points her psycho-analyst was always trying to drive home: that the internet was *less* inviting, that it was even *more* critical. Her conspicuous stroll through the cafeteria of the internet would have started a flame war. Each nasty comment would burn like a match against her skin. How could she miss the warmth of all those matches?

She exited the cafeteria and walked toward a large tree in the center of the quad, drawn to a shining, friendly face like a smiley. A face that seemed just now to be lit with the divine light of the universe.

"There she is!" said Cat. Cat stood and invited Sejal to sit in the grass with a tight cluster of other kids.

"Hi," said a girl with long, slender arms. "I'm Ophelia. Cat's probably told you about me."

Cat had, in fact. She'd given Sejal a rundown of a dozen different names, most of which were promptly forgotten. Sejal shook Ophelia's hand, let her eyes linger over the soft brown feathers and long pink bangs of her hair. Sejal wanted this haircut.

"This is Troy and Abby and Sophie and Adam and Phil," Ophelia said, christening each with a flick of her wrist. They became more animated, as if made real by the gesture of Ophelia's invisible wand.

"Where are you from again?" asked Sophie.

"Kolkata. In India."

"Ohh," said the girl with a sad tilt of her head.

It was a response Sejal would hear a lot in the following weeks and which she would eventually come to understand meant, "Ohh, *India*, that must be so hard for you, and I know because I read this book over the summer called *The Fig Tree* (which is actually set in Pakistan but I don't realize there's a difference) about a girl whose parents sell her to a sandal maker because everyone's poor and they don't care about girls there, and I bet that's why you're in our country even, and now everyone's probably being mean to you just because of 9/11, but not me although I'll still be watching you a little too closely on the bus later because what if you're just here to kill Americans?" There was a lot of information encoded in that one vowel sound, so Sejal missed most of it at first.

"Christ, Sophie, my gyno is Indian," said Ophelia. "Just because she's from the Third World doesn't mean she eats bugs. No offense if you do, Sejal."

"*'Felia*, you can't call them Third World anymore," said Troy. "It's hurtful."

"Says who?"

"Mr. Franovich."

Ophelia farted through her teeth. "Franovich."

"What are we called, then?" asked Sejal.

"A Developing Nation."

"Ha!" said Ophelia. "Developing! Like they're getting their boobies."

"Isn't that one of your old dresses, Cat?" asked Abby, who was similarly attired.

"The airport lost my bag," said Sejal, "but Cat and I wear the same size."

"Really?"

"That's sad," said Sophie. "About your bag. You probably had all kinds of beautiful kimonos or robes or whatever."

"Just one sari," said Sejal, "and a salwar kameez my mom made me pack. Mostly it was jeans and shirts."

"And your elephant god," Cat reminded her.

*And that*, Sejal thought with a guilty pang. The faces of the other kids had soured suddenly, as if they could taste her shame. But then someone new spoke up behind her.

"Wow, you smuggled Ganesha in your suitcase? Isn't he pretty big?"

Sejal turned to see Doug and another boy from math class. She smiled.

"Not always. Sometimes he rides a mouse."

Doug sat, followed by the other boy, who pulled a book from his backpack and began to read.

"Hey, Meatball," said Cat. Doug returned the greeting and extended it to everyone else. The other kids responded with nods or leaden "heys" of their own.

"Meatball?" asked Sejal. It sounded like an insult, but nobody laughed, and Doug had taken it in stride.

"God, it's like you know everything," Sophie half sneered at Doug. "Why do you know G'daysha?"

"Ganesha. I don't know, from books. He's . . . heh . . . he's in this comic book called 'The God Squad.' You ever read that one, Adam?"

Adam started. His face contorted with hammy confusion as he muttered that he had no idea what Doug was talking about.

"You sure? They have a huge God Squad poster on the wall at Planet Comix."

Adam shrugged. "Whatever, Meatball. I don't remember. I haven't been there since junior high."

"Meatball?" Sejal said again.

"Yeah," Doug explained now. "People just—I've always been called Meatball. Since, like, the fourth grade. I can't even remember how it started, anymore."

No one offered to remind him.

"And you don't . . . mind it?" asked Sejal.

"It's just a nickname," Ophelia reassured her, "it doesn't mean anything. Like Dutch or Lefty or whatever. It's not mean." Her smile was peaceful and blameless. Most of the group nodded faintly, as if they'd needed reassuring, too. Even Doug.

"Ah! He's blushing!" said Troy, pointing at Doug. "You're *so* pink right now."

"Oh, he's not blushing," Sejal said, and turned to Doug. "Right? You told me this morning."

"Yeah. Yeah, over the summer I developed this sun allergy. It comes and goes."

"I have that!" shouted Abby. "I totally know what you're talking about. It's, like, sometimes, when I'm out in the sun awhile my skin gets this very fine layer of ash."

"Really?" said Sejal.

"Really?" said Doug. Behind him, the other boy glanced up from his book.

"And now you have an aversion to crosses, too, right?" Ophelia asked Abby. "And it all started—lemme guess—it all

**96**

started when that emo boy gave you a hickey at Stacy's pool party?"

Now Abby blushed. "Maybe."

Ophelia pulled a compact mirror out of her purse. "Ooh, let's see if you have a reflection. Whoop, you're still in there. Not a vampire."

"Did this emo boy break the skin?" asked Troy. "Maybe she's just turning into a vampire really slowly."

"That reflection thing doesn't work anyway," Doug's friend said suddenly. All eyes turned to him, and time stopped. There was a great black hole where his head should have been, sucking all light and heat and conversation. He hid behind his book again.

Doug rose, then, and strode off without warning, as if he'd seen someone or something he wanted. The other boy glanced over the edge of his paperback in surprise. Then his eyes returned to the group, his possum face flashing "flee or play dead?"

"Your name's . . . Jay," said Cat. "Right?"

"What?" said Jay.

:

Doug crossed the quad to the boys' locker room and pulled his poncho back over his angry skin. The day was actually looking up. This new Indian girl continued to be nice to him. And he thought he might start working on Abby now, too. She was obviously dying to be made a vampire. So to speak. He wouldn't have wished to leave the drama tree just then but for two things: one, the almost subconscious knowledge that the longer he stayed, the more likely he was to screw everything up. And two: he'd just spied Victor Bradley, walking alone. Not surrounded by sycophants or anxious girls, but alone.

And now Doug was, of his own free will, walking into the locker room. He hadn't been required to take phys. ed. after freshman year, and since then this entire section of campus had been an ecological dead zone as far as he was concerned. This felt reckless and stupid. Not-ready-to-face-Lord-Vader stupid.

He was a vampire, sure, but the jocks were werewolves. They always had been, he understood that now. They had been bitten by something as kids and had changed in ways he hadn't, and you needed a farmer's almanac and a tent full of gypsies to foresee their sudden, savage benders.

He knew what happened when a vampire bit a person, and turned him. How much worse when a vampire turned a were-wolf?

"Victor?" Doug said. His voice echoed through the stink. Was the locker room always this bad? No, of course not—it was his new heightened sense of smell. It always buzzed at human odors. Others, not so much. But this was even worse than he would have expected—it was sewage, rotten eggs, sulfur.

"Victor?"

Victor appeared then, from behind a locker bay. Half undressed. The star of the football team. The Boy Most Likely. He wrinkled his nose.

"Is that you?" Victor said.

"Yeah, if you mean . . . What do you mean?"

"Is it you that smells like that. It smells . . ."

"Dead," said Doug. "It's us, isn't it? We smell each other."

The locker room was cool and windowless, like a crypt. They stood silently, neither really looking at the other.

"I was out of my mind that night," said Victor.

"I know. I mean, I figured."

"I didn't even know it was you. Not at first. I could barely remember what happened, so if you want to blame someone—"

They heard the locker room door open again. More boys approached, three more werewolves. Their barking voices went silent when they saw Doug.

"What's this little faggot doing here?" said Reid, an enormous senior built like a stack of hamburgers. There wasn't any laughter. The issue of the little faggot in the locker room was a very serious one that demanded answers.

"I think he came to get a look at Victor," said another guy just like Reid but larger. "I think he's got a big faggot crush. Right, Victor?"

Victor rushed Doug then, half naked, white skinned, like that night in the forest. He pressed Doug back over a bench and against the lockers.

"I don't have a crush on you, Victor, I swear—"

"Shut the fuck up. Jesus."

"I just need to talk to you about—"

Victor punched Doug right below the ribs. And so Doug would not be finishing that sentence or starting any new ones for two or three minutes.

Victor's face was close.

"Four o'clock," he hissed quietly through his teeth before throwing Doug out. "The drainpipe behind the soccer fields. *Alone.*"

# 13

## NOCTURNAL ADMISSIONS

**DOUG COULDN'T** concentrate for the rest of the day and did little more than watch the clock until three thirty. He didn't know if he was going to a secret meeting or a fight. Maybe more than a fight. Maybe Victor was going to kill him. Maybe he enjoyed it so much the first time he wanted to do it again.

"Why . . . exactly . . . are you meeting Victor Bradley by the drainpipe?" asked Jay after last bell.

"We just have some business to talk about. Or he wants to beat me up. I'll find out when I get there."

Jay was thinking hard. You could tell because he looked like he was cleaning his teeth with his tongue. "I'm going with you. Even though I'm still mad at you for ditching me. Although I think I really scored some points with the drama kids—"

"I'm supposed to go alone," said Doug.

"Yeah, right—so then Victor can show up with the whole football team?"

"Are you really suggesting he's gonna need *help* kicking my ass?"

Jay shrugged. "You have vampire strength now."

"Not during the day I don't. Look, thank you, but I'm going to go alone. If I don't call you by five, then you can panic," Doug said. He was annoyed with Jay, annoyed with himself for even telling Jay about it. Plus people were making fun of his poncho.

He walked out past the bus bays and the throngs of people, across the parking lot and the soccer field, through a hole in the chain-link fence, and down an embankment. Victor was already there, alone. Victor who, if possible, was even better looking now that he was a vampire. It made his eyes smolder or something. It made Doug look like a blind cave fish.

The day was humid and close. The area around the pipe was rocky and lush green. Flies punctuated the air over something furry and dead. It smelled worse than Victor. Victor he was starting to get used to.

"I checked up on you," Victor said. "I did. After I figured out it was you that I attacked. I came by your family's cabin and made sure you were okay."

"Thanks," Doug said, and wanted to slap himself. He

was thanking him for *this*?

"And then when I saw you *were* okay," said Victor, "I knew I must have made you. I guess because I took too much?"

"I wonder if it's because you were bleeding, and I got some of your blood in me. You haven't made any other vampires?"

"I don't think so."

"So you were made right before you made me. I was your first feed."

"Yeah. I didn't know what I was doing. You could have been anyone. Anything."

Doug nodded. He was sweating under his poncho. "You looked pretty fucked up that night," he said.

"She was really rough," Victor admitted.

"She?"

"My vampire. She was a total piece of ass. French. Looked maybe nineteen, but who knows, right? She could have blown Napoleon for all I know."

So there *were* hot vampire chicks, at least. That was comforting.

The fact that Victor wasn't being a complete dick was coming as something of a surprise to Doug. That Victor was aware that Napoleon was both French and lived a long time ago wasn't entirely expected, either. He supposed he was going to have to give Victor more credit. He hated giving people more credit.

They had known each other since they were little kids. Never were great friends, maybe, but they'd played together during the summers at their families' cabins. They'd always gotten along when there were no other kids around to complicate things. Then the two boys got older, and Doug simply assumed in Victor a growing cruelty and stupidity to balance out his more appealing qualities. Sure, after high school he might become a better person, find God or something, but for now, didn't he almost have to be evil? Wasn't that part of the deal?

"You haven't told anyone, have you?" asked Victor. "About any of it?"

"Oh . . . no. No. And if I was going to tell anyone, I wouldn't tell them about you. I'd probably claim my vampire was a hot girl, too."

Victor gave a satisfied nod. Maybe he'd just gotten what he was looking for. Doug still had some unanswered questions.

"What the hell am I doing wrong, Victor?" he said. "I mean, look at you—you don't hide under a poncho all day. And that bat thing—"

"Yeah, well I figure I'm some kind of special vampire," said Victor. "One that doesn't burn up in the sun. You're not 'cause you were an accident."

"Oh," said Doug. "I thought maybe being able to stand the sun was normal, like in *Dracula*."

"Dracula burns up in the sun, dumbass."

"Not in the book, remember?"

Victor frowned, and then looked down the drainpipe. "I haven't read it."

Doug's eyes popped. "You haven't read *Dracula*? Are you kidding? I read it, like, first thing. Well, *re*read it first thing."

"Yeah, big fuckin' surprise," said Victor. "Meatball gives himself extra homework to do."

"But it's like . . . our instruction manual, right? And in Stoker's book, Dracula can walk around in daylight all he wants. He's just powerless then."

Victor picked up a chunk of concrete and pitched it down the drainpipe. Both boys paused to admire the firecracker sounds it made as it fractured and ricocheted in the darkness.

"Well . . ." said Victor, "so much for your instruction manual. I haven't read it and I'm doing a hell of a lot better'n you."

Doug had to admit that was true.

"What've you been drinking?" asked Victor.

"Nothing," said Doug reflexively. "I don't drink."

Victor gave him a look.

"Oh . . ." said Doug. "Right. Well, there are these cows at the university farms—"

"You've been drinking cow? Jesus! Aren't there at least some, like, dork girls you could feed on?"

"I'm working on it. I don't want to just attack anyone."

"Hey, who's attacking people? The girls I feed on *want* it. It's better than sex," said Victor, then he looked thoughtful. "In fact, afterward, they seem to think all we did was have sex. They go into a kind of daze when I'm doing it, you know?"

*No.*

"I'm getting really good. I barely leave a mark, and I only take a little. Like as much as a Coke. But I do it enough so's I'm always full as a tick."

Doug had stopped listening. He was listening, rather, to a rustling echo of footsteps coming from down the pipe. He held up a hand. "Shh, hold on."

The boys squinted down the dark tunnel of the drainpipe. A man was walking slowly down its center, slightly hunched, carrying a silver tray. He wore a knee-length jacket, a vest, a tiny tie. His long face and tired eyes were a perfect mask of boredom.

"The hell?" Victor whispered.

They had all the time in the world to study his approach, though to Doug he gave the impression of the kind of unhurried cartoon tormentor who would always be calmly on your heels, no matter how hard you tried to get away.

He slowed to a stop at the lip of the pipe and glanced with distaste at the decaying animal in the rocks.

"An auspicious place to find you, young masters," he creaked. "My compliments."

"Who the hell are you?" asked Victor. "Why are you here?"

"Remarkable. The incisive quality of your questions staggers me. Allow me a moment of quiet awe."

The man took his moment. The boys looked at each other.

"Now then. I am but an unworthy messenger," the man rasped. "Please accept these gracious invitations from my mistress."

On the silver tray were two small scrolls, tied with red ribbon. Doug hesitated, but then Victor took one, so he did, too.

*You Are Invited*

*to attend*

*a Light Supper*

*and*

*Willing Congregation of Like-minded Individuals*

∽

*at the Home of*

*Signora Cassiopeia Polidori*

*Midnight*

*The Hawthorne*

*Chestnut Hill*

⊱⊰

*Watch Your Fingers*

No sooner had Doug read the last line than he noticed his invitation was on fire. So was Victor's. The messenger flipped closed a Zippo lighter as the boys dropped their scrolls and stamped them out.

When the ashes were scattered and dead, the boys turned to watch the man retrace his steps down the pipe.

"Fucking crazy old fuck," said Victor.

"He smelled like you," said Doug. *Except not as bad*, he thought.

"He smelled like *you*, you mean. 'Cept not as bad."

"Finally," said Doug. "Cool vampire shit. A secret society."

"I dunno. I'm probably not gonna go. Could be dangerous. You shouldn't go either."

Doug thought about the *Vampire Hunters*. He supposed it could be a trap.

"Go drink some blood and stay home," said Victor as he walked away. "You look terrible."

# 14

# DARK STALKER

**DOUG DIDN'T** drink any blood, and he didn't go home. Instead, he rode his bike to the street on which he thought Cat lived, and traced and retraced a long figure eight in the road. He thought he knew which house it was, which house Sejal was in. He'd been to Cat's once freshman year, when she'd hosted the cast party on the closing night of *Guys and Dolls*. But he wasn't certain. He wore his uncertainty like a veil. If he wasn't positive, he could be excused for not riding up the driveway and knocking on the door.

:

"Is he still out there?" asked Cat. Sejal spied through the black curtains of Cat's upstairs bedroom while Cat and Ophelia rifled through clothes. After learning of Sejal's baggage mishap Ophelia had also accepted with brio the responsibility of dressing her. She'd arrived minutes before Doug with a Macy's bag full of outfits.

"He is," said Sejal.

"He probably followed me here," said Ophelia from behind a sheer green blouse. "It's weird how many guys are already into me this year."

"Nah, he's here for Sejal. Did you see how he looked at her at lunch?"

"Should I go say hello?" asked Sejal.

"No way," said Ophelia. "If he can't come ring the doorbell himself, then screw him. Besides, it's only Meatball. I mean, no offense—maybe in your country the weird-looking guys are the hot ones, I don't know."

"I'm not certain he knows which is the correct house."

"He knows," said Cat. "Go talk to him if you want. He's smart. Pretty funny, too."

Sejal smiled. "I'm not interested in him as a . . . suitor."

"Suitor?" said Ophelia.

"Whatever." Cat grinned at Sejal. "It's fine."

"Truly, I am not."

"Truly? Suitor?" Ophelia smiled at Sejal, too, a movie-star smile. "Are you the cutest thing ever?"

⁝

Doug was on the verge of giving up and leaving, as he had been for ten minutes, when the front door of the house-he-was-pretty-sure-was-the-house opened, and Sejal walked out. She was barefoot, in black jeans and a black T-shirt.

"Hello," she said.

"Hey. Hey, I . . . *thought* this was your house, but . . ."

"Your skin looks better."

"It's cloudy out."

"You could carry an umbrella, no? For when it is not?"

"No, too faggy," said Doug. Did Sejal's smile falter, then? "Sorry, I mean . . . too *homosexual*."

Sejal folded her arms and looked at her feet. Her startling toes clutched at the grass.

They were like hazelnuts. Her toes, her feet were a golden brown—the same color as the rest of her, really; Doug couldn't imagine why it surprised him. He couldn't fathom why it made her feet look more naked than other feet.

:

*Doug is staring at my feet*, Sejal noted. She supposed she'd just been looking at them herself, so she couldn't really . . . No, now he was watching that bird in the yard. Now a glance at her chest, now a pause at her shoulder. And again the bird. He was like a cat. He was like a cat at a mirror, looking anywhere and everywhere but at the pair of eyes in front of him.

She considered suddenly that he might be *her* reflection. There was something familiar about his eyes, his look of distraction. He was lost, maybe missing something, like she was. Perhaps he'd left his heart someplace, too.

Then he cocked his head and looked up at her face at last.

:

"Hey, you have a nose earring. I mean, a nose ring," Doug said, though it wasn't actually a ring. "A nose . . ."

Sejal brightened and touched the small silver stud with her finger. "My mother convinced me that in America I should

**111**

leave the piercing empty, isn't it? Then I meet Ophelia, and she has one, too! It feels different, like it's a different kind of hole in you, here."

"Uh-huhey, do you want to go see a movie sometime?" said Doug before he had a chance to think, or inhale.

Sejal reacted as if she'd just been pinched unexpectedly in the ass. "I don't know, Doug . . ."

"Oh, that's cool."

"I arrived so recently, I still feel very . . . unsettled."

"I totally understand. I just thought you might be interested in seeing an American movie, because you're probably just used to those kinds of dancey movies they show on Desi TV. That's this late-night channel here, I don't know if you've seen it."

Sejal smirked. "Okay. I do not think I've seen any of the current American movies. Why not."

"Hey, all right! Great. Um, well, I have this big dinner party to go to tonight, but Friday?"

"Yes."

"Okay," said Doug. "Well, I'll see you at school!" He stood hard on the pedals, then biked quickly away, before he was overcome by it. Before her yes could catch up to him and set him ablaze.

# 15

# TESTING

**THE PHONE WAS** ringing as Doug entered the back door of his home. He let it ring, went upstairs, rubbed lotion into his dry cheeks. Then he sat at his computer and called for messages as he searched for "The Hawthorne Chestnut Hill." It sounded familiar.

"You have . . . four . . . new messages. New message."

"Hi, Doug . . . it's Jay. You were supposed to call by five, so . . . just calling to—"

"Message has been deleted. New message."

"Hi, Doug . . . it's Jay. I hope everything's okay. "I don't—"

"Message has been deleted. New message."

"Jay again. Call me as soon as you get this, I'm really wor—"

"Message has been deleted. New message."

"It's Jay. I'm really, really—"

"Message has been deleted. End of messages."

Doug laid the phone down on his desk. The Hawthorne turned out to be an eighteenth-century mansion in Chestnut Hill, another suburb of Philadelphia. It was going to be kind of far to bike, though. He'd probably have to take a train, change at Thirtieth Street, take another up there. If he went, that is.

Outside there was a squeal of brakes, the slam of a car door, and then, a few seconds later, the doorbell.

Doug answered the doorbell. Jay was on the step, bobbing like a balloon.

"Oh, hey," said Doug. "I just tried to call you. Had you tried to call? I didn't get the messages yet."

Jay just narrowed his eyes and frowned like a bulldog and shook his head. Then he turned and started back to the curb.

"Hey! Seriously! I just got home! Some crazy shit happened at the drainpipe! Secret meetings and this-message-will-self-destruct kind of shit. I need to tell you about it. I need help deciding what to do."

Jay paused at the car door.

In what felt like the marathon of run-on sentences, Doug caught Jay up on the events of the day. Sort of. In this version Victor just wanted to talk to Doug about some private math tutoring, and the dead butler didn't arrive until after Victor left. When Doug finished, the sun was behind the trees and his mom and dad were returning home.

"Hi, kids," said Dad.

"Hello, Mr. and Mrs. Lee."

"Mom, can Jay stay for dinner?"

Mom paused in the driveway, her arms hugging her briefcase and two bags of groceries. Her expression conveyed to Doug, via a bit of family-only telepathy, that he *knows he's not supposed to ask in front of Jay like that because now how can she say no even though they're only having Manwiches?* "If it's okay with Jay's mom" was all she said out loud.

"You can help me figure out the best route to ride my bike to the party," Doug told Jay when his parents were out of sight. He hoped that hook wasn't too flagrantly baited, but what he really wanted was for Jay to offer him a ride.

"You're definitely going?"

"I don't think it's the *Vampire Hunters*. Do you? It doesn't seem like their style."

"No," Jay admitted. "Do you want a ride? You don't want to show up all sweaty."

"That would be awesome."

:

The boys ate and finished their homework. Then they drove early to the Hawthorne to be sure they could find it.

"This has to be it," said Doug. "It's perfect. You can't even see the house from the road."

Past a NO OUTLET sign the dark and quiet street stretched into a sharp, thin curve. The front gate of the Polidori residence was garnished with thick ivy. You didn't borrow a cup of sugar from this sort of neighbor. This neighbor had no sugar for you.

Jay backed out to the NO OUTLET sign again and turned around.

"We'll go down to the creek somewhere," said Jay.

"Good," said Doug. "We should have done this before. I want to go into that house with as few questions as possible."

They walked through the shimmering trees toward the smell of water. Jay carried a grocery bag in addition to his schoolbag, and it was from the former that he produced a set of high galoshes. He sat on a rock and slipped them over his shoes.

"We're going to the other side of the creek," he said. "There'll be less chance of running into anyone else over there."

"Uh-huh. Where are my galoshes?"

"I didn't think you'd care. You don't really feel cold when you're full of blood, right?"

"But I still feel this acute sense of embarrassment when I show up for a vampire party later with wet feet."

Jay avoided his eyes. "Oh. Well, you'll be dry by then, with this wind," he said, and started across the rushing water.

There was nothing else to do but follow. Doug didn't feel the cold, but he felt the damp, and there was no mistaking the transcendental goose of a suddenly wet crotch. He stumbled over the slick rocks and leaned into the incline on the other side.

"Sorry about that," said Jay after a few minutes of walking, "but that was actually the first test. Some sources say that vampires can't cross running water. It didn't hurt or anything?"

"Of course not. That was a test? I've crossed running water all kinds of times since getting made. In planes. In cars. I'm even the only guy I know who washes his hands after he pees. Not that I pee much anymore . . ."

"Can cross running water," said Jay as he made notes in a big red binder. "Doesn't pee much. Okay"—he brandished a big silver crucifix from his backpack—"take that!"

"Take that?"

"Yeah. Anything?"

"No, but like you said before, I'm Jewish. Where'd you get that thing?"

"Dark Matter. Here."

Jay threw Doug the cross. Doug fumbled it, picked it up off the wet leaves. "What am I supposed to do with it?" he said.

"It's real silver. Plated. It doesn't hurt?"

"Silver is for werewolves."

"Some sources say vampires, too. Try sucking on it a little."

Doug sucked on the cross. It tasted like fork. "Nothing."

Jay crossed the cross off his list, then they repeated the whole process again with a Star of David.

"Nope," said Doug.

Jay tossed a pile of rice at Doug's feet. Doug looked at the rice, then back at Jay. "What? Do I eat it?"

"How many grains are there?" Jay asked.

"I don't know—I'm not autistic, I'm a vampire."

"But you don't care? Some sources say if you toss grain on the ground in front of a vampire, he has to stop whatever he's doing and count it."

"These 'sources' wouldn't all be Wikipedia, would they?"

"Mmmmm," Jay hummed, "mostly no. In fact—you know something? Remember when *Vampire Hunters* mentioned that thing about vampires having to be invited in? I remembered today where I'd heard it before. It's in that Cody Southern vampire movie that's always on cable. *Love Bites*."

"I don't remember that."

"No, it's true. I wasn't sure either, but you can watch the whole thing online. And you know what else? Practically all the good vampires turn normal at the end because they kill the head vampire."

Doug nodded slowly. "Yeah. Yeah, I've read a comic like that, too. If you kill the vampire that made you a vampire you're not a vampire anymore."

"Well," Jay interjected, "in *Love Bites* it had to be the head vampire. Like, he's the top of the family tree. Killing the gang leader vampire wasn't good enough—Cody had to kill the antique store owner who made the whole gang."

"That's just a movie, though."

"Yeah. It doesn't really make sense, anyway. Like, how do you know who's the head vampire? Wouldn't the vampire that made the head vampire be the real head? Or the one who made him? How far back do you go?"

Doug thought about this.

"Anyway," said Jay. "The list. So. I know you usually cut

through that Presbyterian parking lot on the way to school."

"Yeah."

"Do you still? Because then we'd know you can walk on hallowed ground."

"Well, I can definitely *bike* on hallowed ground. If the hallowed ground really extends to the parking lot," said Doug. "Is this really an issue? Cemeteries are hallowed ground. Old-school vampires *lived* in cemeteries."

"Hmm, yeah. Never mind." Jay consulted the binder again. "We know already that you have no trouble with mirrors, of course. Right?"

"Right," said Doug. What he didn't say was that in the weeks since the change he had avoided seeing his reflection whenever he could. It was superficially the same, but he felt no connection to the boy in the mirror. Victor had taken that, too. There was only an empty stranger; a funeral mask; a pair of weird, dead eyes. He didn't see himself reflected at all.

He'd taken to keeping his bedroom mirror covered with a sheet, as if someone had died. Someone *had*, actually.

"Right," said Doug again.

"And you've probably had garlic."

"Oh, yeah. My mom puts it in everything. There was extra garlic in those Manwiches. Do you remember," said Doug, "in fifth or sixth grade, when she read that it was good for your heart or something? She used to have my dad and me take garlic pills, eat garlic at every meal . . ."

Jay was looking more and more uncomfortable. He nodded gravely as if recollecting some great tragedy, until Doug finally said, "What?"

"That's why . . ." said Jay, "people call you Meatball."

"What? No, it's not."

Jay stared at the ground.

Doug was incredulous. "They call me Meatball because I'm short and . . . husky."

"And smell like Italian food."

"Shut up!"

"You don't anymore!" Jay rushed to add. "But you did back then. Especially during PE. It was like you sweated garlic."

"Why didn't you tell me? Shit!"

A fresh breeze ruffled the trees. A dead leaf caught in the hair of Jay's heavy head.

"I don't think anybody means anything by it anymore," he said. "It's just something to call you. Cat isn't being mean. She's nice. Stuart calls you Meatball, but you guys are still friends, right? And Adam? He wasn't even in sixth grade with us. He's a senior."

"*Adam*," Doug snarled. "That guy is completely full of shit. I saw him in Planet Comix over the summer. Twice. You were with me one of the times, for the McFadden signing."

"Yeah. I guess he doesn't like admitting he reads comics."

"I guess he doesn't like admitting a lot of things. You ever notice how he's nicer to us when we're away from school? But even then he's still looking over his shoulder like the girls' volleyball team is gonna jump out from behind a tree."

Jay shrugged.

"Look, never mind," said Doug. "Just . . . what's next."

Jay looked at his list. "Holy water. But I couldn't get any."

"And after that?"

"Um . . . here. Eat this mustard."

# 16

## SECRET VAMPIRE SHIT

**At FIVE TO MIDNIGHT** the boys approached the gate of the Hawthorne for the second time.

"I'm going to get in trouble for staying out this late," said Jay.

"I know."

"I'm sorry about the garlic thing."

"I know."

They unloaded Doug's bike from the trunk and tucked it behind a hedge.

"I have my phone. I'll call you if . . . something happens." Doug thought this sounded stupid as soon as he said it. Of course "something" was going to happen—he was going to walk into a house full of vampires. The thought that this alone was not necessarily going to be the lead story of the evening made him suddenly cold. He marched quickly from the car before Jay could offer any words of encouragement. His feet were damp.

The gravel driveway looped like a racetrack around spare ornamental shrubbery and an expanse of lawn so large and plain that it seemed designed to testify to how much land this woman could waste. Doug had rarely seen so much grass in one place without a soccer net at each end.

The home of Signora Polidori was huge, redbrick, and brightly shuttered, more blandly Colonial than Doug would have expected. No gargoyles. No severe, Gothic arches. No bat-shaped door knocker. He supposed that last one would have been a little on the nose, actually.

He rang a perfectly ordinary doorbell, and a few moments later the door opened onto the crepe paper face of the man from the drainpipe.

"You honor this house with your presence, dark master," he said, stepping aside to admit Doug. "Truly it has stood patiently these lonely centuries only that it could one day receive such an exalted visitant into its homely blah, blah, etcetera."

Doug blinked as he walked into the hall. He had no idea how to talk to this person.

The interior of the house was more like it. The foyer was aglow with candlelight and clad in marble and bronze. There was a grand curving staircase of the sort that promised majestic introductions. In the movies a staircase like this could only exist to provide a beautiful woman with a decent way to enter a room. This was no movie, however, and the banister was rubbed dull and dry. The center of each velvet step was bald like an old dog. But the beautiful woman was a beautiful woman.

She looked like a college girl but carried herself down the stairs with the air of a woman three times her age. For all he knew, Doug realized, she *was* a woman three times her age. Thirty, even. It didn't hurt that she was dressed like she'd stepped out of a school movie about the cotton gin.

Was this the vampire who had made Victor? She wasn't French, not with *that* name, but what did Victor know? He'd probably think Sejal was French.

"I am Signora Polidori. You may call me Cassiopeia," she added, with a faintly raised eyebrow like a footnote, a little legal disclaimer to explain that she wouldn't normally permit someone like him to call her anything at all. Her voice was the sound of crisp new bills—a little British, not really Italian like Doug expected. More than anything, it had that sound of the East Coast rich that you heard so much in old movies.

She lowered a shoulder. She pointed a toe. She made the gentle tilt of her collarbone into the sort of thing that moved mothers to cover their children's eyes. Doug decided then that, yes, she was very old. She had learned to inflame men in an era when a glimpse of leg could start swordfights.

"You are already acquainted with my thrall, Asa."

"Yeah. Hey," said Doug to the thrall.

Asa somehow managed, without twitching a muscle, to favor Doug with one last, breathtaking display of contempt before leaving the room.

"You are the first to arrive," said Cassiopeia. "How embarrassing for you."

Doug followed her through dark, wide doors into a sort of study. More candles here, and floor-to-ceiling bookshelves and one of those wheeled ladders on tracks that Doug had never seen in real life before. Curved steps at one end of the room rose to a platform that accommodated a small piano and three high-backed chairs.

"You may repose here and await the others. The chairs upon the dais are reserved. Each object in the drawing room is worth a small automobile. Reflect on this before you touch anything." With that, she left.

Doug stood stiffly. The air felt old, somehow, more brittle, and it smelled like books. He tried not to breathe it too deeply. He felt so terribly aware of himself here—heavier, fleshier . . . itchy.

Two guys who looked very much like Victor soon arrived, guys who looked like they were not so much born into this world as hiked, by quarterback, into an American flag. They took up places in the room and stared at Doug like he'd sat down at the cool kids' table. He was certain they were vampires, too, from the smell. With so many in such close proximity the room was growing sour with an old-milk stink that filled your throat. Could regular people not smell this? He realized now that he couldn't trust Jay to tell him he stank, though he was confident Jay's sister would have mentioned it.

Victor himself came next, and stood at the far end of the room, and appeared to pointedly *not* stare at Doug; it was only for this that you might have guessed that the two boys knew each other at all. Doug fumed. They were all junior varsity vampires here, weren't they? They'd all made the team one way or another. In a hot rush he realized that Victor had always planned to attend the gathering. He just didn't want Doug there.

The great door opened and shut again. Finally, another girl. She was the last to arrive and the first who seemed to know how to dress for this sort of thing. She had straight green hair that just brushed her bare shoulders, and Doug imagined riding a tiny toboggan down their powder-white slopes into the foothills of her bust. She wore a black leather halter and skirt that showed a lot of everything. She looked to Doug like a video game character.

Signora Polidori returned now with another man. He was strikingly handsome in a way that looked very foreign next to all the homecoming kings in the room. Victor and his kind were big dogs, but here was a wolf, his face lean and sharp. He and Cassiopeia alighted on two of the three chairs.

"There! now," said Cassiopeia. "All are here who will be here."

*All?* thought Doug. The third chair was still bare as a headstone. He could feel the others beside him glancing at it, too.

"I am, as ever, Cassiopeia Polidori. At my left is Alexander

Borisov. The third place is set out of respect for Mr. David, who enjoys his solitude. Until recently, we three were the only so ennobled for a hundred miles."

"What about Asa?" asked the green-haired girl.

"Asa is not of our kind."

"What is he, then?"

"He is my butler. Now. A gathering of the ton such as this will by no means be commonplace. For reasons you may have already deduced, our breed tend not to mingle." Her nostrils flared slightly, and the point was made. "It is customary, however, for our kind to mentor those they grace—to guide, and to teach discretion. Discretion is paramount. You tell no one what you are. You speak to no one of our concerns."

*First rule of bite club: you do not talk about bite club,* thought Doug. *Got it.*

"But that is not enough. Even in your private affairs must you be utterly clandestine. An elder shows her protégé how this is done. That you have all come so hastily and stridently to my attention suggests that you have not had the benefit—"

The green-haired girl tensed, her whole pointed demeanor aimed squarely at the seated man. "Well, if Count Dickula ever called *like he said he would*—"

"I got very busy," Alexander protested in a thick stew of an accent. He pronounced every word like he was pushing it uphill. "Work has been a nightmare, I can't tell you . . . I was going to call this week—"

"Whatever."

"But when I heard of this party—"

"What*ever*."

A thick silence filled the room. The green-haired girl crossed her arms under her chest, which Doug appreciatively noted had a sort of push-up bra effect.

Cassiopeia sighed. "Perhaps we should try to conclude with the introductions. Short boy, tell them your name."

Doug's face boiled, but he did as he was told. The other kids took their turns.

"Danny."

"Evan."

"Victor."

"Absinthe."

"Absinthe?" slurred Alexander. "At the rave you were called Beth."

"Oh, so you remember *what* to call me, just not *how* to call me—"

"I believe it has been made rather plain how our dear Absinthe became one of us," said Cassiopeia. "I am more interested in the provenance of our other guests."

*Don't call on me*, thought Doug. *Don't call on me.*

"Douglas. Is the kinsman who granted your immortality present here tonight?"

"Uh, no," Doug replied, and did some quick thinking. "No . . . not unless it was Absinthe, I guess."

"Oh, right," said Absinthe. "Sure. It was *totally me*."

"Did she resemble Absinthe?" asked Cassiopeia with a note of surprise in her voice.

"It was dark," said Doug.

"Maybe his was the same one who got me," said Victor. "Doug and I talked about this already . . . we were both attacked in the Poconos."

"Attacked?" asked the signora. Her distaste for the word was palpable.

"Well, not 'attacked,' maybe. It was . . . it was fine."

Doug felt a surge of love and gratitude. He could have cried. He could have bumped Victor's fist, or done one of those complicated handshakes everyone else seemed to know how to pull off but him.

Victor described his vampire then as "college aged" and "hot." Average height. Foreign. Hair that was either black or brown. Danny and Evan, in turn, described their vampires in much the same way. Danny ventured that her hair was really dark brown, not black, and Evan offered that she definitely had an accent but that it wasn't the same as Signora Polidori's.

"You cannot fathom my relief," she said. "Well," she added, sharing a meaningful look with Alexander, "it seems we have an enchanted stranger in our midst. Such intrigue."

"Such a delightful turn of events," muttered Alexander.

"Alas! our mysterious friend has been remiss," she continued. "Each of you should have your tutelage. I will take our Miss Absinthe under my wing; she may do well to have a fairer hand at the tiller than Mr. Borisov's."

"I will take on Victor, then," said Alexander.

"And I will take Daniel, as well."

"Then I will take Evan."

There was a fat pause, during which Alexander cleaned

his fingernails. *Oh, give me a break,* thought Doug.

"It occurs to me . . ." said Cassiopeia airily, "I hesitate only because it occurs to me that, absent though he is from our gathering, Mr. David should know the joys of mentorship as well."

"Oh yes?" said Alexander. "Oh. Yes. Yes, definitely."

"So we are agreed."

"Definitely agreed."

"Douglas"—Cassiopeia smiled sweetly—"you shall have the surpassing benefits of Stephin David's many wise years. I will arrange it personally. It is, I daresay, a perfect match."

She rose to her feet.

"Now! who will have some supper?"

:

It was like eating somebody's stamp collection, this supper. Everything was small and difficult to acquire and had a story behind it that was meant to be interesting, but wasn't. Parakeet's eggs and truffles, roe from an endangered salmon served in a ring of lightly battered kraken. Edible flowers. A supper planned by someone whose relationship with food had drifted over the years. Doug was relieved to see that he was not the only one picking at his plate.

The party broke up at a little after two in the morning. Asa saw all but Alexander to the front door—Doug hadn't noticed if he'd stayed behind or simply left by another route to avoid Absinthe. They walked toward the front gate, the three Victor clones a little ahead, Doug lagging behind and trying to appear to be lost in thought, Absinthe a couple steps behind him.

"Hey," she said. "Douglas, right?"

"Yeah. Absinthe is a cool name."

"Why aren't you up there with the rest of the big bats?"

Doug shrugged. The answer, in fact, was that back here he was maybe Victor's friend. Back here he didn't force Victor to choose whether to accept him in front of the others.

It was nice of her to pretend that there was nothing separating Doug from the other guys. Or it was a *kind* of nice, at any rate. One that allowed her to spotlight Doug's standing in life, his outward flaws, meanwhile casting herself as the sort of guileless ingenue who believes it's what's inside that counts. Or maybe Doug was overthinking things, as usual. He told her he had a lot on his mind.

"I hear that. God, isn't she rad? La Signora? I'm so stoked to see her again next week. Fuck Alex."

Doug didn't know what to say to that. He tried to nod sagely.

"So . . ." Absinthe said, "have you . . . told anyone about becoming . . . ennobled? You can tell me if you have."

"I haven't, though," said Doug. "I . . . almost let it slip to a friend, but I didn't."

"Yeah. Yeah, I didn't either. Signora sounded so serious about that. Like it might be dangerous for anyone you told."

The night was quiet, apart from the crunch of gravel beneath their shoes. Up ahead the other boys erupted into bawdy woofing. The phrase "killer rack" drifted backward on the breeze.

"Hey," Absinthe said suddenly, "if I fly home, would you get my clothes for me?"

"What?"

She answered by changing into a small green-and-brown bat, in a wink, and her clothes dropped to the ground beneath her. She flittered around Doug's head until he bent down and retrieved her garments. He was inches away from what was technically a naked, beautiful girl but he couldn't appreciate it. He folded her clothes neatly in his hands and the bat gave a lyrical chirrup and flew away.

When next Doug looked ahead he saw Victor, alone, by the gate.

"Did she just turn into a bat?" he asked.

"Yeah. She asked me to take her clothes," said Doug, trying to make it sound like this sort of thing was always happening, girls rapidly undressing in front of him and so forth.

"You ever do that?" asked Victor. "Turn into a bat I mean?"

"Once."

"Yeah. I don't like it much. It's like . . . you know when you're driving somewhere and you space out, and when you get where you're going you can barely remember how you got there? Like you just went on autopilot?"

"Not really," Doug admitted. "I don't get my license until next month."

"Oh. How you getting home?"

"Bike."

Lights blinked off in the house behind them.

"You want a ride?"

# 17

## HIGH STAKES

**"THERE!"** Alan Friendly belted. "The San Diego vampires are before us! Present Redeemers!"

Each crew member raised and leveled his stake-firing weapon and squinted down its barrel. Alan stood facing outward for the cameras, his arm extended like the commander of a firing squad. He *was* the commander of a firing squad, he realized with a confusing sort of delight.

"Send those mothersuckers back to hell, boys! Fire at will!"

The crew let loose a volley of stakes, a few of which hit but most of which sailed past the row of dummies on the other side of the field.

"Cut! All right, that's good!" said Alan. "Doesn't matter, doesn't matter. You know we weren't filming the targets anyway. We'll get them later at close range."

The targets were dressmaker's dummies. The art department had scoured flea markets for old ones but eventually just bought a crate full of new models and spent an afternoon staining them with tea and roughing up the edges. Then they sewed a red velvet heart in the center of each. They'd tried paper targets on hay bales but it just looked too much like something you'd seen before.

Alan met his assistant Cheryl by the only dummy that had a stake lodged firmly in its stuffing.

"How was that?" he asked. "Did we get that?"

"It looked hot."

"I said 'mothersucker.' Too much?"

"We'll have to run it by Standards and Practices."

"It just popped out."

They looked in silence at the dummy, and the stake.

"Well, *that's* not the heart," said Alan. "What would that be?"

"The appendix," Cheryl answered. "I have a scar there. Oh—Mike called from San Diego, wants you to call him back."

"Ooh!" Alan rushed for the phone. "He has something? Never mind, he'll tell me." He dialed and rocked on his heels while the line rang.

"Alan," Mike answered.

"Mike! Mikey Michael! Michael P. Pfefferneuse! I don't know your last name, Mike."

"It's Storch."

"Mike Storch! Big Mike Storch! Tell me you have a lead. God, we need a lead."

In lieu of hiring a private detective agency Alan had left Mike and a few other staffers to keep canvasing San Diego after the hunt lost its momentum. They had a police sketch of the main vampire based on a description the girl Carrie Lawson had given, and at least one intern was wandering the Gaslamp Quarter, showing it around. Another was calling hospitals and begging for information about anyone complaining of bite marks. It was vitally important for Alan to show his producers that they could do things on the cheap at the moment, so everyone was doing jobs they hadn't signed on for.

"I do have something," said Mike, "a very little something."

"Tell me. Tell me."

"All right. I talked to this convention center security guard today who had a run-in with a kid, a teenage kid, who had very severe polymorphous light eruption."

"Uh-huh, uh-huh," said Alan. "What?"

"A really bad skin reaction to sunlight. Kid had to hide under a poncho. It was so bad they let him and his friend in early, so he wouldn't have to wait in line. Which is good for us, because they were the only two to pass under the CCTV cameras in the lobby at that particular time."

"And you got a look at the security tapes?" Alan was grinning and drumming on the snack table with his free hand.

"I got a look at the security tapes. And I gotta admit, the

shorter of the two kids could definitely be our guy from Panda TV."

"Yes!"

"But here's the thing: If it is him, then the sketch we have from party girl is bullshit. I think she was very generous with her description. He probably gets better looking every time she tells the story."

"Bloody hell."

"I'm having the sketch artist do a new portrait based on the security tapes, and I'll start sending it around. But, Alan, we're running out of money here."

"Wait," said Alan. "Why don't we just put the security footage on next week's show? Or online? But then, of course, someone else would find him before we do . . ."

"Also? It would be slander. We don't know for certain the kid on the security tape has done anything wrong—the panda room was too dark for a positive match and the Red Cross people won't return our calls."

"Stupid, bloody, pompous Red Cross."

"But, Alan, did you hear me? We need more money."

"You're breaking up, Mike. I'm passing through a tunnel."

"I know you're not driving, Alan."

# 18

## THE SWEET CLOUD
## OF TOGETHERNESS

**DOUG'S DATE** with Sejal had, somehow, become a group thing.

"How did this happen?" Doug asked Jay after lunch. "This is unacceptable."

"You asked Sejal what movie she wanted to see," said Jay, "really loud. You know you did—you wanted everyone to hear."

"I did not say it '*really* loud.' I said it loud 'cause it's loud out there."

"Actually"—Jay sniffed—"I remember it being quiet and uncomfortable because you'd just told everyone about that time I threw up horseback riding."

"What, are you mad about that? It was funny."

They were nearly to the door of English class when Victor and another guy rumbled by.

"Hey, Victor," Doug said, quietly. Victor didn't respond.

"Dude," said Victor's friend as they walked away. "Did Poncho Villa just talk to you?"

"C'mon," Doug said to Jay. They went inside.

"Are you and Victor friends now?" asked Jay.

"I don't know. I don't care if we are or not, he could at least say hi when someone says hi to him."

They took their seats, wrote an in-class essay on *The Metamorphosis,* then broke into groups to plan their oral reports.

"It's understandable that maybe Cat would come along," Doug said to Jay. "They live together. And maybe Sejal wants a chaperone on our first date—I don't know how Indians do things."

"I'm Indian," said Kyle, their third partner. "I don't need a chaperone on a date."

Doug rounded on him. "Sejal's *Indian* Indian, Kyle. You were born in Scranton."

"We're supposed to be talking about 'The Love Song of J. Alfred Prufrock.'"

"Just . . . *fft* . . . go make an outline or something and give us two minutes, okay?"

"Asshole," Kyle said, and moved to an empty desk.

"What really pisses me off," Doug told Jay, "is that Adam's inviting himself along. How did that happen?"

"I think he maybe likes Sophie," said Jay. "I think he's going because she's going."

"That figures. She's his type—not as smart as him and at least two years younger. I don't even remember how *she* got invited."

"Sejal invited her. After she invited Ophelia and Ophelia said no. Look, maybe I can distract them all and get you some time alone. Or we can figure out some plan to get you sitting together."

"How are you going to do that if you're not there?"

Jay's forehead tightened. "Cat invited me."

"Cat can't invite you on my date! My date! And I thought you didn't even like hanging out with this crowd."

Jay shrugged. "I don't mind so much."

"Also, I don't think this is your kind of movie."

"If you don't want me there, fine. Just say so."

"No, no, you can go if you want. What difference does it make now that half the Masque & Dagger club is going."

"I won't go."

"No, go."

They sat in silence for a moment.

"Maybe," said Doug, "maybe you *could* even help distract everyone else a little. Keep them busy. Create a diversion."

"Yeah, that went superwell last time," said Jay.

They both smiled, lips drawn tight to restrain laughter that chuffed out through their noses.

"No needles this time," said Doug, and they laughed some more.

"I hear laughing," said Mr. Majors, "so I know you're not talking about T. S. Eliot."

⦂

*The Rocky Horror Picture Show* was a cult and cultural institution. It was a decades-old campy sci-fi horror rock-and-roll comedy musical that was almost certain to be playing at midnight, somewhere in the world, on every day of the year. Even Christmas. Especially Christmas.

"I think it's gonna be really weird," Doug told Jay in the car. "I've heard things. I should have researched it more online."

"Which house is Cat's again?" asked Jay.

"On the left, with the basketball hoop."

Jay pulled into the driveway.

"Should I honk? Or are you going to go up?"

"I should go up, right? I'll go up."

Doug went up, his guts slithering. It was exciting having something real to do on a Friday night, and it gave him a feeling of almost limitless expectations. He rang the doorbell. It was like anything could happen. It was like this door could open onto the whole rest of his life. And a moment later the door did open on a round, curly-haired woman in a fuzzy yellow sweater set, like a big baby chick. Like a really obese baby chick.

"You must be Doug," she said with a reluctant, simpering look, like she was trying to smile her way through a bad cookie. Doug would have taken it personally, but he'd seen Cat's mother before and was pretty sure she always looked like this.

"Yes," he said. "Hello."

"Here for our little Sejal, then."

"Yes," Doug answered, then nodded slowly and deliberately as if his head might come off otherwise. This wasn't really his area, and he wondered if there was something he was supposed to say or do to produce Sejal faster. He was suddenly anxious he might have to solve a puzzle.

"Mom!" a voice shouted from behind the yellow, and Cat appeared, squeezing herself and Sejal through a gap in the doorframe. "I told you not to answer the door!"

"I don't remember you saying that—"

"It's a blanket rule. Bye, now. Going to a movie. Won't drink or smoke or shoot heroin. Promise not to kill Sejal. Good-bye."

"Hello, Doug," said Sejal as Cat pulled her past and down the path to the driveway. Doug gave chase. When he reached the car, they were already climbing into the backseat.

"Oh, hey, you can have shotgun, Cat," said Doug.

"Naw, you go ahead. Back here me and Sejal can talk in our secret girl language."

"It's mostly hand signals, no?" said Sejal.

"Hand signals and telepathy," said Cat. "Hey, Jay."

"Hi."

They pulled out into the road and a clammy silence fell over the car.

"Has anyone seen this movie before?" asked Jay.

"No," said Sejal, "but I have heard about it. And I like Tim Curry."

"Is that, like . . . a spicy dish?"

Sejal laughed. "It is a spicy man. An actor."

Now Doug was jealous of Tim Curry. He didn't even know who that was.

"Ophelia's told me about it," said Cat. "And I think Abby has been. People shout stuff at the screen, throw food . . . I put the music on my player—can we listen to it in the car?"

"Yeah," said Jay. "Pass it up here."

"Can that program you wrote really clean up my music files?"

"Only if you're running Linux. You're not running Linux, are you?"

"No," said Cat, "but I totally want to. Open-source everything. You wouldn't be willing to set it up for me, would you? I'll buy pizza, it'll be like a really lame party."

Jay laughed. "Sure."

The music played, and Doug twisted around to look at Sejal, gave her an eye-rolling smile. "Finally, someone will use one of Jay's little programs."

"Lots of people use my programs," Jay said faintly. "My vlog widget's been downloaded twelve hundred times."

"Vlog widget," said Cat.

"Vlogwidget," Sejal answered.

"If I ever start a band," Cat said, "I'm naming it Vlogwidget."

:

They pulled into the theater parking lot, where Abby met them dressed like a syphilitic French maid.

"Oh my god," said Cat as they spilled out of the car. "Look at you."

"Yep," said Abby. "Look at me! Get a good long look, children. You have my permission."

"Yeah, well . . . I don't think it would matter if we didn't," said Doug. "You don't dress like that to blend in."

Abby smirked. "You guys are such virgins."

All the supposed virgins shared confused looks as Abby led them up to the ticket line, which contained a second and third French maid, a bald-capped hunchback, a man in fishnets and a pleather bustier, another wearing a nude body stocking with muscles drawn in puff paint, and two long-legged girls in glitter-gold Rockettes outfits. Lots of hennaed hair. Also about a dozen other teens and twentysomethings who looked as unremarkable as anyone.

"Abby!" said the boy in the body stocking. They hugged like it had been ages, like the wall had finally come down between France and Nudistan.

"He's fake naked," whispered Jay.

"Fayked," said Doug. Sejal tittered.

"Are these virgins with you?" the fayked boy asked Abby.

"Why do people keep saying that?" whispered Jay.

"What makes you think we're virgins?" asked Cat.

"Oh, you just have that look about you. Don't worry about it. I'll personally see to it that you all lose your virginity tonight."

A rip-cord laugh buzzed Abby's lips, while the fayked boy air-fucked their personal space. With each pelvic thrust he chanted, "Group sex, group sex," until everyone but Abby felt the need to take a step backward. Abby feather-dusted his crotch.

It turned out the only virginity the *Rocky Horror* regulars were concerned with was the kind you lost simply by watching the film in a theater, preferably with a live cast. And there was a live cast here, dressed in the same peculiar ways as the line waiters outside.

"They act out the movie while it plays on-screen," said Abby as Doug and the rest took their seats. "They're good. I'm second understudy for Magenta, which pretty much means I never get to do a show."

"And you are understudy for the boy there in his underwear?" Sejal asked Fayked.

"No. Why?"

Their row went Fayked, Abby, Jay, Cat, Sejal, Doug. Jay was supposed to sit on the other side of Sejal to cut her off from the others, but when the time came, he failed to stake his claim. Then Adam and Sophie arrived and sat in the next row. Adam turned around.

"Pretty crazy, huh?" he said to no one but Sejal.

"It's about what I expected," she said.

"Really?"

A toilet paper roll sailed over their heads.

"Hey! Hey!" one of the cast scolded. "No premature ejaculations!"

Doug leaned into Sejal's armrest. "So . . . do they do this in India?"

"I don't know," she answered. "There are a billion people there, so I think the safe answer is yes."

"Maybe after this is over, you and I can—"

"Oh!" said Sejal. "Ophelia made it!"

Ophelia was swishing down the aisle like it was a red carpet, with another wisp of a girl closely following.

"I'm here!" Ophelia sang with a flourish. "Start the show!"

"I thought you had a date with a waiter," said Abby, looking suspiciously at Ophelia's companion.

"Make room next to the birthday girl!" said Ophelia, in what was clearly some kind of coded reference to Sejal. Doug scowled but moved two seats down, and was reassured when Sejal moved down as well. Now she had Ophelia on her right, and the new girl between Ophelia and Cat. Cat tried to introduce herself but was met with stony silence.

"All right, you lucky bastards!" shouted a cast member. She looked out of place next to the decadently costumed actors around her. If anything, she was dressed for tennis. "You're about to see *The Rocky Horror Picture Show*! Do you feel lucky?"

The audience shouted, "YOU'RE LUCKY, HE'S LUCKY, I'M LUCKY, THE BANNISTER'S LUCKY!"

"Jesus," muttered Doug. "What the hell was that?"

"I can see from the frightened and bewildered faces out there that we have some *virgins* here tonight!" said the girl. "Virgins stand up!"

Doug hadn't planned to volunteer any information, but Ophelia took to loudly outing all the first timers in their group, so when Sejal stood, Doug did, too. Two cast members stalked the center aisle and examined the

**145**

crowd like they were selecting a lobster.

"Ooh, you're cute," said a top-hatted girl to Adam as she took his hand. "You're coming with me."

A boy wearing nothing but gold hot pants motioned to Sejal. "I like the looks of you, honey. Come down here."

"You don't have to," said Doug to Sejal, but she was already leaving.

Adam and Sejal were made to stand side by side and face the audience. They were loudly married by a tall boy who wore a nun's habit over his garter belt and corset. The recitation was much like a regular wedding service but with a greater emphasis on ass play than Doug thought was customary.

"Now then," the nun boy purred, "do you promise to love, bone her, and fellate—whoops! I mean love, honor, and obey, as long as you both shall live?"

Sejal and Adam each muttered their I dos.

"You may lick the bride!"

Most of the audience showered the theater with rice, which they'd apparently brought from home. Adam and Sejal looked at each other with brittle grins, until Sejal presented her forehead and Adam gave it a kiss.

The rest of the virgins were marked with lipstick V's and had to give the cast pantomime blow jobs.

When everyone was seated again, the movie started. A faceless red mouth appeared, and the theatergoers shouted, "LET THERE BE LIPS!" The lips sang, the credits played, then the first scene opened on a little church. On the screen, and among the live actors down below, there was another wedding scene. More rice was thrown. The hero of the story, Brad, proposed to the heroine, Janet. Every few seconds the crowd shouted something funny, offensive, or offensively funny. Doug couldn't make it all out, but the word "asshole" cropped up a lot.

Doug turned to Sejal, tried to smile at her in a *wow, what a show, who could doubt that we two are the only sane actors on this crazy stage called life* sort of way. But her eyes were fixed on the screen.

There was a lot of singing. Even now Brad and Janet approached a castle in the rain, singing hopefully about their prospects there. The theatergoers waved flashlights, covered their heads with newspapers, and fired squirt guns into the air. Ophelia shrieked, though she arguably should have seen this coming. Her friend hid under her jacket. Sejal giggled, but Doug turned to glare at some kids he didn't know a couple rows behind him. He was certain they were shooting their pistols directly at the back of his neck. His turned head earned him a squirt right in the glasses.

He whispered, "Asshole." Exactly at the same time the rest of the theater shouted it, as it turned out.

Sejal turned her head and smiled at him. Had she heard? He tried to look like he was having a good time. In truth, the evening was giving him the same feeling of anxious dread he got whenever he passed a couple of guys tossing a football around, or a Frisbee. You never knew if it would suddenly come your way, and you'd have to show that you couldn't catch or, should you somehow manage to catch it, throw. This theater was swarming with existential Frisbees.

But then everyone was made to stand and do a dance called the time warp, a dance that was thoughtfully described on-screen, and Doug began to wonder if he might be enjoying himself after all. There was a sweet cloud of togetherness that is perhaps inevitable when a hundred people are pelvic thrusting at the same time.

"They should do this at the United Nations," Doug shouted to Sejal. "World peace!" And she laughed and nodded, because in that moment she knew exactly what he was talking about.

The drag queen mad scientist Dr. Frank-N-Furter joined the scene, a sweet transvestite from transsexual Transylvania.

"Is that Tim Curry?" Sejal whispered to Ophelia. Then, to Doug, "That's Tim Curry!"

Tim Curry looked uncomfortably like Doug's rabbi, but in heels and lingerie. Like Rabbi Bartash was the new Black Queen of the Hellfire Club. Doug wanted to say this out loud, but it was a comic book joke, so Jay would probably be the only one to get it. Maybe Adam. Doug's blood rose when he thought of Adam. Now that he was fake married to Sejal he better not get any ideas.

By the time Doug took notice of the movie again the location had changed. Brad and Janet were in white bathrobes. Tim Curry was wearing a green smock and pearls.

"I think my mom has that dress," said Doug. Sejal stifled a laugh. "I think my mom and Marge Simpson and Tim Curry all shop at the same store."

Now Sejal really laughed, and Ophelia and Cat, too. A boy behind them shushed.

"God, look at that tux with all the turquoise," Doug said, a little louder. "I'm totally wearing that to prom."

This last comment was somewhat drowned out by the snapping of a dozen rubber gloves all around them, but Sejal heard it. Ophelia leaned in and asked Sejal to repeat it, and after she did Ophelia passed it down the row.

On the screen Dr. Frank-N-Furter revealed his creation, an artificial man in a tank. He ordered switches to be thrown and cranks to be turned, and called down a red metal apparatus from the ceiling, hung with multicolored nozzles. The doctor tapped each, and they ran with a rainbow of liquids.

"It's like he's milking a gay cow," said Doug.

Everyone laughed. A boy behind them, maybe the same one, shushed him again. Another said, "If you're not going to say the real lines, shut up."

Abby turned and whispered, "There's no right or wrong thing to say. *You* shut up."

A tense silence followed, or what passed for a tense silence in an auditorium full of people shouting, "*SLUT.*"

In the movie, the artificial man was revealed to be a muscular golden boy under his bandages. Dr. Frank-N-Furter swooned. The boys behind Doug weren't shouting lines with the theater crowd anymore. They were reading from an entirely different script.

"If he doesn't know the talk back, he should be quiet and learn," said one of them.

"He should stick to chess club," said another. "He should stay home and play on his computer."

"He should stay home and play with himself."

Sejal turned to face the boys. Doug stole a glance. She didn't look angry. She just looked naive to him, even disappointed. Innocent.

"You are not being polite," she said.

"Why should I be?" a boy answered. "I don't know you."

"That is the point."

"Turn around and watch the movie, goth girl."

"Yeah, goth girl. Aren't you a little brown for a goth, *Kama Sutra*?"

Here it was. The Frisbee had been thrown, and Doug knew he was supposed to do something with it. He'd read about people for whom time slowed under stressful conditions. People like snipers, or race car drivers, or ninjas. In slow time, the situation presented itself with intricate clarity.

It was always exactly the opposite for Doug. When the Frisbee was in play, time only seemed to speed up. His vision went blurry around the edges. It was like his body was trying to kill him. He could think of only one circumstance in his life when this hadn't been the case, and he wasn't hunting coyotes now. But that wet, visceral memory reminded him that it was night, and he was stronger than these guys. Maybe not stronger than both of them together, but . . . Little by little he turned to face them.

Ophelia did him one better by reeling to her feet. A torrent of screaming fiery hatred scorched the boys' faces. That they weren't allowed to talk about Sejal that way was the basic gist of it. That their dicks were small and embarrassing formed a sort of secondary thesis, but the whole message was illuminated with such a floral rococo of virtuoso cursing that it hardly mattered.

". . . and if you *ass clowns* say *another word* about her, I'll whittle your fuck sticks with my *car keys!*" she finished, and even the film actors' voices seemed for a moment to be reverently hushed.

"Well . . ." said one of the boys, "well . . . she should control her boyfriend more, that's all."

"Why?" said Cat. "Because he's making his *own* jokes? Because you asswipes need a script to be funny?"

A few moments passed. From the front of the auditorium an actor said, "Settle it or take it outside, guys."

In another story, in a Western perhaps, the audience would have erupted into a theaterwide brawl. But these were mostly drama kids, so the girls were more prone to histrionics, and the boys were more likely to throw parties than punches.

"C'mon," one of the boys said. "*Rocky*'s been getting lame for a long time. Let's go to the band party."

"Yeah, go to your band party," Ophelia began, but with a touch on the arm from Sejal she fell silent. Then, surprisingly, Ophelia's friend rose and left without a word. "Chrissy!" Ophelia hissed, and followed.

"Hey, the show's down here," the live-actor Janet called to the crowd. "Leave the drama to the professionals."

The show resumed, and Doug burned happily in his seat.

This was shaping up to be the best night of his teenage life. He tried to share a glance with Sejal, but Sejal's eyes were fixed on the screen, her face reflecting its blue glow. Her moon face shone in the dark theater, unknowable and suddenly very far away.

# 19

## :

## PAJAMA PARTY

**DOUG PEDALED** through the bustling, trolley-tracked streets of West Philadelphia while the events of Friday played over and over in his head. He knew he should stop thinking about it and concentrate—he was biking to the home of his vampire mentor, Stephin David. This was arguably more important than a date. Why didn't it feel more important?

Cat had defended him. Called him funny. And in the parking lot after the show everyone seemed to be on his side—Abby, Sophie, even Adam. Abby said it was proper for *Rocky* watchers to invent new lines to shout. The routine was always changing. She was certain someone would use Doug's "gay cow" line at the next show.

There was an "Us" and a "Them," and Doug was on the right side for a change.

"How about that Ophelia?" said Doug as he, Jay, Cat, and Sejal piled back into the car. "I've never seen her like that."

"I have." Cat laughed. "She was drunk is all. Did you smell her breath?"

"What's up with that girl she was with? Her hair, and her clothes . . . she was like a really pretty boy."

"Her jacket was rad," said Cat.

Doug had no opinion about the girl's jacket. "Ophelia said before that she had a date tonight. Is she . . . ?"

"Gay?" asked Cat. "I've sort of thought so for a while. Gay or bi. She doesn't date anyone at our school anymore."

Doug realized he should have something to say about this, something worldly, but nothing came. He was at sea. He was drifting in unfamiliar waters, and he felt the passing seconds break against him.

"Are you okay, Sejal?" Jay asked. "You're really quiet."

"I'm only tired, thank you," she said. She looked stiff, her small fingers interlaced and tense and pinned to her breastbone. She lacked only a white lily to hold and a plush box to lie down in.

Doug realized now, on his bike, that she'd probably been offended by all the gay talk. India was different. He would have to let her know everything was cool, that he was on her side, whatever side that was. He had to stay on top of this.

After they'd dropped off Sejal and Cat, Doug had explained the situation to Jay. "Adam's after Sejal," he said. "I don't think he cares about Sophie."

**154**

"Really?"

"It's obvious. Did you see how long he hugged her good night? And all his *we're married now, when's the honeymoon jokes . . .*"

"You said he only dates girls who're at least two years younger," Jay reminded him. "And not smart. Sejal's our age and smart."

"Yeah, but she's foreign."

"I don't understand your math," Jay had answered.

"I don't understand *your* math," Doug shouted, now, as he hurtled through the stale bus-and-curry-scented streets. He swerved to avoid a mother with stroller who'd just stepped into the bike lane to watch for larger traffic. Then, with quick reflexes (vampire reflexes!), he hopped the bike onto the sidewalk, his poncho blowing heroically behind him.

Stephin David owned an old row house near a park in West Philadelphia. Doug scanned the porches and steps for house numbers and nearly missed the pink and blue balloons and poster-board sign that said VAMPIRE attached to Stephin's mailbox. Doug hastily tore down the sign and stuffed it in his backpack. In a disoriented rush he also popped the balloons and threw them inside the mailbox. Then he locked his bike to it and started up the path past a small, dry lawn. The door opened as he stepped onto the porch.

"Douglas?" said a man.

"Doug. Yes. Hi."

"Hello, Doug. I'm Stephin. Come in."

He was short, too, only a touch taller than Doug, but with a sonorous voice that seemed to creak up through the floor.

And he was not what you would call classically good-looking. Maybe this was the rationale behind that "perfect match" Cassiopeia had mentioned.

Doug glanced around as Stephin led him through the foyer. If there had been a fourth Little Pig who'd elected to build his house out of cigarette butts it might have looked and smelled something like this place. The walls were as brown as a dead plant, the corners bruised with mold. Here and there the ghostly rectangles of missing picture frames haunted the hall. Books were stacked everywhere, clogging the already narrow artery into the house.

"Are you moving out?" asked Doug.

"It's possible I am. Sometimes it feels like I've been moving out my whole life."

*Okay*, thought Doug. They passed a frame that hadn't yet been removed but was covered with a languid drape of cloth. It was a Jewish tradition to cover mirrors after someone died. Was Stephin Jewish? But, no, when Doug was sure he wouldn't be seen, he lifted a corner of the drape. It was only an old portrait of a Civil War soldier.

Stephin led Doug into a sort of study or den, and invited him to sit in a worn leather chair. He fell into it, suddenly tired. He had been pushing himself a bit out there, actually. All that biking in the daytime. His back was sticking to his shirt, and now his shirt was sticking to the chair. He tried to steady his breathing as he looked around.

Small book stacks ringed his chair like a cul-de-sac. Suburbs. The chair Stephin chose was more like downtown Bookville—literary high-rises, thirty stories tall. In the amber

156

glow of two small lamps the whole room took on the sepia blur of an old photograph. It was steeped in the musty but unaccountably pleasant smell of old paper.

They stared at each other a moment. There was something gnomish and subterranean about Stephin, Doug decided. Maybe he had been an accident, too.

"So," said Stephin. "I haven't done this in a very long time. You'll forgive me if I've misplaced all my old lesson plans."

"Well, should I— Should I just ask questions?"

"That would be fantastic."

Now Doug was being asked to dive in headfirst, and Doug had never learned to dive. He thought perhaps he should start with Stephin himself.

"Are you . . . American?"

"I was born in Scotland. But we came here when I was three."

"Have you lived here long? In Philadelphia I mean. Do you have to move around a lot?"

"About twenty years," said Stephin. "This is not my only residence."

"So how long have you been . . . ennobled?"

Stephin's expression did not change, but when he answered, there was a sour note to his voice. "I'm not as fond as you might imagine of Miss Polidori's delicate little euphemisms. Can we perhaps call the thing what it is?"

"You mean I should just say 'vampire'?"

"If it walks like a bat and quacks like a bat . . ."

"All right, so how long have—"

"One hundred and forty-six years."

"Oh. Well, that's pretty good," said Doug. He hoped he didn't sound disappointed. He kind of wanted Stephin to be hundreds of years old. Even thousands. He didn't think Signora Polidori was more than two or three hundred. He didn't know anything about Alexander Borisov. All the other vampires he knew were recent hires like himself.

"Who's the oldest?" asked Doug. "Like, who's the oldest vampire you know."

Stephin mulled this over a moment. "I suppose the oldest . . . the oldest I'm certain is still in this world is Cassiopeia herself. Born the year of Victoria's coronation, as she likes to tell anyone who will listen. Alexander is only seventy or eighty."

Doug nodded and looked at his feet. There was another pale rectangle here, this one in the center of the floor like the chalk outline of a dead coffee table.

"Are there many vampires?" he asked. "My friend Jay likes to work these things out and—and there were only three vampires here in the Philadelphia area up until a month ago. That's three vampires for six million people. So maybe a hundred and fifty vampires in the whole country. Three thousand in the whole world. And we're guessing there wouldn't be as many in rural areas."

"I suspect it's something like that. I don't have better numbers than you do. I would definitely agree about less populated areas, the countryside . . . It's far riskier to hunt in such places."

"So why aren't there more vampires? Why don't you know any really old ones? It's not like they're dying out or anything—"

With a jolt Doug realized that Stephin was in his pajamas. They were a loose pair of pants and a shirt with large buttons. The top and bottoms didn't match so he'd mistaken it for an outfit. Pajamas.

"Don't fool yourself, Doug. We can die. We're not as difficult to kill as the movies would have you believe. We heal quickly, true, and we don't strictly need a fair number of our organs anymore, but a close shotgun blast to the chest will put us down as decisively as a stake in the heart."

Stephin was suddenly lively, like this was a favorite topic. Like he'd been asked about his great-great-great-great-grandkids.

"Though not as quickly," he added. "A sharp piece of wood will end it more quickly, for reasons that have never been adequately explained to me. Also, we still need to breathe. We still prefer not to be on fire. And though we might heal from a bayonet in the ribs we can't regenerate a whole limb. How long," he said, edging forward, "how long has any of us got before the big accident comes? The loss of arms, or legs? How do we hunt, then, with no wings? How much blood could a bloodsucker suck if a bloodsuck—and now I see I'm scaring you."

"What?" said Doug with a start. "No."

"I am. I'm sorry. I'm no longer practiced at human interaction. I've talked to so few people during the last fifteen or twenty years. I spent the whole of 1996 and part of '97 speaking nothing but a language of my own invention called Stephinese, just to see if it would make life more diverting."

"And?"

"And what?" Stephin drawled.

"Did it? Make life more diverting," Doug reminded him.

Stephin didn't answer. Doug glanced around at the small room, at the books and newspapers and dry furniture. There was a bell jar with a pocket watch inside. There was a small tin globe of the moon next to a cast-iron bank shaped like a slave holding a slice of watermelon. There was a picture frame on the floor, leaning against the wall. Behind the glass was something like a bouquet of dried flowers but fashioned from loops and braids of a fine brown thread.

"It's made from human hair," said Stephin. Doug frowned and leaned closer, and Stephin added, "It seemed like a good idea in the nineteenth century. So. You've told a friend about your affliction. Jay, was it?"

Doug flinched. His stomach lurched. Had he mentioned Jay? He had. What happened now? Did they fight? Did Doug have to fight to protect his friend?

"I frankly consider such complications unavoidable," said Stephin. "Of course you've told someone— How can one bear this half life alone? For your sake I hope you've chosen well. Would you like to try some peyote?"

:

"The rest of the hour went a lot like that," Doug reported to Jay afterward. The two boys sat heavily on Jay's backyard swing set, not swinging. "Less like school than like a school dream— you know: hazy, difficult to follow, full of weird surprises and wardrobe choices." When Doug had finally emerged, blinking, into the West Philadelphia afternoon, it had been like waking, and the memories of Stephin David faded in the sun. They'd

**160**

agreed to meet again on Monday.

"Did you ask any of our questions?" said Jay. "Did you ask how to turn into a bat?"

"Sort of. He said if I really wanted all that kind of stuff to happen, it would probably just happen. It would happen when I needed it to."

"Like, by instinct," Jay offered.

"Yeah. He said I'd change whether I wanted to or not."

Doug squinted up at the deck, where Jay's sister, Pamela, had just emerged from the kitchen door holding a watering can. She squinted down at the swings.

"Shouldn't one of you be pushing the other?" she called out. "That's how it always is with you young lovers, isn't it?"

On their best days Pam approached Doug as if he were a kind of hereditary illness—just something unpleasant she had to deal with because of family, like eczema. On their worst days, they had a sort of troll-hobbit relationship.

"I can come push you off the deck if you like," Doug answered.

Jay sighed. "Can you guys maybe not fight?"

Pamela was six feet tall and curly haired and now, in light of Friday night's movie, looked a little like Dr. Frank-N-Furter. Doug tried not to imagine her in fishnets, but you can't really try *not* to imagine somebody in fishnets. And now Doug's imagination was a slideshow of pornographic images starring himself and Pamela. The harder he tried to swap her out with a swimsuit model or something, the more his sweaty boy mind insisted on Pamela. Is this what being a teenager meant, that his fantasy life wasn't even his own? Pamela did have one thing

**161**

going for her—a big rack. Maybe that was two things. Okay, three—he supposed she was smart.

A year or two ago Doug and his friend Stuart got into a debate over whether Pamela was hot. Stuart said she was because of her tits, and Doug said that's sexist, you can't think a girl's hot just because of bra size if she's otherwise ugly, and then Jay overheard and shouted, *"HOW IS IT NOT SEXIST TO CALL HER UGLY AND, BESIDES, SHE'S NOT UGLY,"* and then he started crying. It had been a really fantastic afternoon.

The secret key to their relationship was that Pamela had once kissed Doug while their mothers played tennis. When he was six and she seven. Neither of them ever referred to it directly, though when cornered, she still occasionally blamed him for giving her lice.

Now she stepped down into the yard with her watering can, the potted plants apparently forgotten, and silently studied Doug like his face was a chessboard. "You need more sun, you know," she said.

*As if,* thought Doug.

"You're never going to grow any taller, hiding under that poncho all the time. Here, I'll water you."

She tipped the can over his ponchoed head. His ears filled with the spatter of water on plastic. It didn't get him very wet, but in his haste to escape he fell backward over the rubber swing.

"Gah—dammit!"

Pamela howled. Beside them, Jay said quietly, "Pam, Doug is my guest."

"Yeah!" said Doug once he was back on his feet. His eyes burned. He hoped Pam could feel the intensity of his stare, the conviction behind his hatred. "Jay's guest! So why don't you show a little hospitality, huh?"

Pamela wore an odd look.

"Just . . . fuckin' . . . fix me a lemonade and leave us alone," he told her.

She held his gaze for a moment, then walked off without a word.

"Well . . . good. Whatever," said Doug as he watched Pam climb back onto the deck. The swing set creaked as he settled again in the seat next to Jay.

Jay said, "Sorry."

"Forget about it," Doug answered. "So what are you doing for the rest of today?"

"I dunno. I thought Cat might call about changing her operating system."

"Yeah. Like *that's* really gonna happen."

The kitchen door opened again. Pamela stepped through it, crossed the deck, came down the stairs, and handed Doug a glass of lemonade. She looked pained. Then she walked off again and reentered the house.

Doug frowned at his lemonade. Jay frowned at Doug.

"Did you just hypnotize my sister?"

# 20

## SOUND BITES, REDUX

"**HELLO?**"

"Hi, is this . . . Mike Storch?"

"Speaking."

"Oh, hi. My name's Chris Spears, I'm a marketing assistant with Warner Brothers. I work with DC Comics, mostly, and I—"

"Oh! Great, thank you for calling me. Did you . . ."

"Yeah, I had a look at that police sketch of the kid you faxed to our offices. Someone put it up in the break room."

"I should stop you right there, Chris, and say that it's not actually a police sketch. It was done by a police sketch artist, but I am not with any law enforcement organization."

"Oh. Well, is this kid in trouble or something?"

"No, probably not. Some people are looking for him, is all. Did you see him at the San Diego Con?"

"Yeah, I'm certain of it. I moderated this DC editors panel, and we gave away a couple prizes before the show. The kid tried to win the prizes, made a real ass of himself, if you ask me."

"Okay. That's something. You're sure it was him?"

"Pretty sure. He looked like the sketch, and the height and clothes are right, and . . . you say something here about strange behavior? Aversion to sunlight?"

"Yeah."

"Well, this kid had a pretty bad sunburn."

"I don't suppose you talked to him much."

"Well, that's the thing—our prizes went to the people who'd traveled the farthest to be there. And this kid said he'd come from Philadelphia.

". . . Hello? You still there, Mike?"

"I'm here. This is outstanding news. You're sure it was Philadelphia?"

"I'm sure. He shouted it twice, and then he tried to convince everyone that it was farther away than Maine, and . . . I don't think I'd remember all this normally, but, like I said, he was a pain in the ass."

"A pain in the neck, if we're lucky."

"What's that?"

"Nothing, Chris. Thanks for your help."

# 21

# CROSS

**C**AT DID HOLD JAY to his promise to reformat her laptop. Doug barely found out about it in time.

He and Jay were IM'ing while Doug web crawled his way through Labor Day afternoon. He didn't care for chatting or texting much, but he liked talking on the phone even less.

Doug: Still there?
Jay: sorry had to answer the phone.
Doug: I think we should play this new MMORPG called Darkness. It's about vampires.
Jay: don't u get enough of that irl?

Doug: You chat like a 12-year-old girl.
Jay: lol! irl = in real life

Doug responded that he knew what it meant, though he had in fact been searching for the abbreviation in an online glossary.

Doug: Anyway, Darkness—you can play a vampire or a vampire hunter. Or a werewolf or demon or a lot of other things I don't care about.
Jay: i know, i've heard of it.
Doug: But get this: one of the goals you can work toward as a vampire is hunting down the vampire that made you. If you kill it, you become a superpowered human.

Doug watched the minutes tick by on his computer. He might get distracted from time to time while Jay was waiting for a response, but Jay was usually pretty attentive. He killed time watching clips on YouTube, but nothing moved him. Where he'd once considered it his duty to tell people who posted stupid videos that their videos were stupid, it felt less important now in the grand scheme of things.

Doug: Am I boring you?
Jay: sorry, getting some stuff together. i gotta go soon.
Doug: Where are you going?

Another long pause. Doug thought, *screw this* and flopped down on his bed with a comic book. The computer pinged.

Jay: ok i might as well tell u i'm going 2 Cat's 2 help her
w/ her os. i wasn't going 2 tell u cause remember when u
said Adam's nicer 2 us when no one's around? sometimes u
make fun of me more when there r people around. well not
more i guess but it bugs me more. but i feel weird going
over there alone so u can come if you want. ☹

Doug felt a twist in his stomach then, a vinegary taste in his mouth. He couldn't be the bad guy here. In a world of ass-holes, how could Jay think this of him?

Doug: I don't make fun of you. I just joke around. That's
what friends do. If it bothered you so much, you should
have told me.
Jay: my fault then.
Doug: That's not what I'm saying. I'm sorry. I'll try to be
more careful. I'm sorry.
Jay: it's nothing. so ur coming?

A quick bike ride and poncho refolding later, and Doug was at Jay's front door. He thought he'd better make it a front door sort of day. He rang the bell and listened as Chewbacca came barking, listened to his tiny terrier nails claw for traction on the hardwood floors, listened as he threw himself again and again against the inside of the door. Usually someone was right on his heels shouting, "Chewbacca! Shut up! Sit! *Sit!* Stay," and then the door would open. Chewbacca continued to bark and scratch at the door, but even his actions began to sound confused, a little lost, like a man in a bar fight who's expected his friends to hold him back before he embarrassed himself.

Doug was considering ringing the bell again when the door opened to Pamela's wary face.

"You can get your own drinks today," she said.

Chewbacca leaped toward Doug, licking and jumping and just hoping to catch a little bare flesh or get a good sniff of groin. After becoming a vampire Doug had braced himself for a lot of growling and biting from previously friendly pets, but if anything dogs seemed to find him mind-blowingly awesome now.

"Jesus," said Pam. Chewbacca had stopped leaping but was teetering like a trick dog on his hind legs, nose aquiver at Doug's crotch. "You hiding a hot dog in there?"

"Wouldn't you like to know."

"Probably one of those little cocktail wieners."

He wasn't going to let her get to him today. Today he would stay cool, cool as a tall glass of lemonade.

"What are you wearing?" she asked him.

It was the same shirt he'd worn at that party in San Diego. Long sleeved, lots of tiny pockets. It was a little snug, but the salesgirl had said it was supposed to fit snug.

"Oh, and you're qualified to give me fashion advice," he said, "because your swim team T-shirt is so incredibly awesome. Look! It has autographs all over it! Autographs of the

**169**

other members of the swim team! Are you gonna let me in?"

Pamela took a languid half-step to the right. "Jay gave me three dollars to get the door for him. You two have a spat?"

"How much would he have had to pay you not to tell me he paid you?"

"I don't know. Seven? But he probably didn't think he had to. He's so morally upright."

Doug followed her into the house, feeling carbonated and shivery. He would see Sejal soon. He and Jay would go to her house, Cat's house, and they would sit and stay awhile. Gentlemen callers.

"Where do you think you're going?" Pamela said suddenly. Doug had absentmindedly followed her all the way to the door of her bedroom.

"Uh, sorry. I just spaced out."

"Were you looking at my ass?"

"No," said Doug, who at the mere mention of the word "ass" had almost looked at her ass again. "I wouldn't look at your ass if it had a *Playboy* stapled to it."

"Nice."

Doug spun around and walked, pink cheeked, back to Jay's room.

"Okay," he said as he crossed the threshold. "I'm ready to go." Chewbacca stretched up Doug's leg, paws on his knee.

Jay didn't look up from his computer. "Cat's bringing her laptop over here now. Cat and Sejal. She said something like, 'No way with my mom on the rag' and said she didn't want anyone at her house."

Doug could tell he was trying to be standoffish, but Jay

still couldn't keep a straight face while saying "on the rag."
"They're coming here? Shouldn't you clean up a little?"

Jay looked around his room, which was spotless as always.

"Clean up what?"

"I dunno. At least take down the Darth Maul poster, right?"

Jay shook his head. "You're just like Adam."

"Okay," said Doug, "I'm sorry you're upset. I thought, you know, we've been friends a long time, and friends kid each other. I didn't know I'd been hurting your feelings."

It sounded reasonable to Doug as he said it, as if it could even be the truth. There was a flimsy nobility to it, like a paper crown. Just then the doorbell rang.

Doug nearly collided with Pamela in the hallway. Chewbacca rushed past to bark at the door.

"No!" Doug said. "This time we *want* to answer it."

Pamela held out her hand. "Three bucks," she said.

Doug stared at her, hard. "You will let me answer the door," he told her.

"Yeah. For three bucks. Stop looking at me like that."

"I thought," Doug said, fishing his Velcro wallet from his back pocket, "that trolls . . . were supposed to ask you a riddle"—the wallet was free now, and he paid Pamela—"not demand cash."

"You're thinking of sphinxes."

Doug ran to the entryway, then skidded to a halt and took a couple of leisurely steps to the door.

The door wouldn't open, so he turned the deadbolt, found

that he'd just locked it rather than unlocked it, turned the small handle lock instead, and soon he was looking out onto the stoop, and yard, and Sejal.

Jay's house faced the south, and that dazzling midday light made the neighborhood incandescent and traced a hot red edge around Sejal's small body. Cat was there, too.

"Cat, Sejal, come in," he told the girls. Chewbacca seized with happiness at having so many visitors.

Cat had her computer under one arm and a backpack over her shoulder. Sejal was wearing a long-sleeved red shirt that you could see through to a black tank top beneath.

"Hey, Meatball."

"Hi, Doug," said Sejal.

Doug led them down the hall and said, "Jay mentioned you might be coming by, but I thought I'd have to miss you. I have an appointment later."

"He paid me three dollars to let him open the door!" Pamela shouted from her room. "Which one of you does he have the crush on?"

"Sejal!" Cat shouted back, and entered Jay's room.

Doug winced at Sejal. "You look nice," he said.

She looked beautiful. Each time he saw her now, she was more lovely. It hurt a little to look at her, hurt in a part of Doug's body that he couldn't immediately define.

"Thank you, Doug. I didn't know you were going to be here," she said, as though explaining something, though Doug couldn't imagine what. "This dog is very taken with your pants."

"Yeah . . . well," Doug said. There didn't seem to be a

great way to spin a comment like that.

In the bedroom, Cat and Jay were talking like they were friends.

"Well, I hope you don't mind that I brought a bunch of music over," Cat was saying as she dumped a pile of CDs onto the floor. "I don't know what you're into. Where are your CDs?"

"I don't really buy them anymore," said Jay. "I have everything on a networked hard drive. I like They Might Be Giants, Jonathan Coulton, MC Frontalot . . ."

"Awesome! Nerdcore!"

"What?"

"That last guy was nerdcore. Are you nerdcore? I think that stuff's hilarious. Oh, my effing God! Is that a theremin?"

Cat jumped up from the floor and over to a long black box on a microphone stand in the corner. Dials and knobs studded one side of the box, and fat antennas trimmed the ends.

"He's really good at it," said Doug. "He can play anything. Play something, Jay."

"Maybe later," said Jay, his ears blushing as red as brake lights.

"Oh, you *have* to! That is so rad," said Cat. "A theremin's this electronic instrument you play without touching, Sejal. You just wave your hands around. You should totally start your own nerdcore band, Jay!"

"So what kind of music is all this?" asked Doug as he sifted through the CDs on the floor. "Goth?"

Cat made a face. "That word doesn't even mean anything anymore. There's a bunch of different styles in there:

darkwave, batcave, deathrock, death metal, queercore, slow-core, nocore, shoegaze, postindustrial—"

"Jesus. How many different kinds of music are there?"

"I don't know. Four hundred and twenty-seven. Lots."

"At Booktopia there's only, like, five," said Doug.

"Booktopia doesn't know dick," said Cat, and she turned to Jay. "So what do we do to get me using Linux?"

"Well," said Jay, "do you have all your files backed up?"

"Hell, no."

"We should back them up first."

"I don't know anything about computers," offered Sejal to no one in particular. Doug nonetheless treated it as an opening.

"I don't know anything about music, apparently," he said to her. "It's like . . . it's like how many different kinds of musi-cal labels do you need? There's almost as many as there are bands. Like in the future we'll reach some singularity and the ratio will be exactly one to one. 'Hey, you like the Rolling Stones?' 'What kind of music do they play?' 'Oh, you know—mid to late Rolling Stones.'"

Sejal smiled. Barely. If there had been a smile-o-meter on her face, the needle would have stopped at "Polite." Doug retreated and sat next to Cat on the bed.

"You're in good hands—Jay really knows computers," he said. Jay gave him kind of a weird look but he pressed on. "Way more than I do. He grew up learning a lot of stuff we didn't 'cause he was homeschooled."

"No way," said Cat.

"Up until sixth grade," Jay admitted.

His father had sent away for curricula and textbooks and *Cricket* magazine and acted as Jay's one and only teacher until he was ten. He had play dates with other homeschooled kids, and of course with Doug. Then Jay's mother came home one day with a child development study that concluded that homeschooled kids did worse in college interviews than their traditionally schooled peers. His parents panicked and rushed him into Doug's junior high. It didn't matter that another study refuted the first one just six months later—the damage was done.

It was as if he'd been raised in captivity, at Sea World maybe, and was used to popping his head above water every hour and showing off what he knew. But now out of a misguided concern for his welfare, he was being released into the worst kind of ocean. Middle school was shark-infested water, and even the other dolphins couldn't understand why Jay was so eager to jump through hoops.

This had been an uncomfortable time for Doug. Jay had never met School Doug before, and School Doug didn't want to be thought of as the sort of person who'd be friends with a boy like Jay. He hadn't been so complimentary then.

"Seriously. Jay's, like, a computer genius."

Jay glanced at Doug and connected a hard drive to Cat's laptop.

"What's that for?" asked Cat.

"I'm going to drag all your files over here," Jay answered. "I won't keep them or anything. I'll delete them after we're done."

"You better. I got tons of lesbian porn on there."

Jay flinched. Cat laughed.

"Kidding."

"So. Speaking of lesbians," said Doug.

It was a spectacular segue. It exploded and then lay there like a pile of dead clowns.

"Wow," said Cat.

"I mean . . . I just . . . I was thinking about what you said about Ophelia."

"I only said it because you asked," Cat insisted. "I probably shouldn't have. Don't spread it around, okay? She should get to decide who knows and who doesn't. If she even *is* gay."

"I think she is brave," said Sejal. "If she *is* a homosexual. It is not always easy, no? Even in America?"

"Are there gay people in India?" asked Doug.

Sejal shrugged. "There are a billion people there, so . . ."

So maybe Sejal hadn't been offended the other night after all. Or if she had been, she'd gotten over it pretty quick. Doug, for his part, didn't think he really had much of an opinion about gay people. He didn't know any. Except maybe Ophelia, now. If anything, he was possibly a little sick of them. They were always popping up in shows and movies and in the books he read. They used to be comic relief, but at some point it was like you weren't allowed to laugh anymore, and the gay characters were Very Serious. Their whole character would be about them being gay, and how serious and unfunny and also completely normal it was. In each new book, especially, there seemed to be one or two. Like the author wanted to prove what an open-minded, big-tent guy he was.

And, because he was thinking about books, and because the room had been filling with a cold silence and *someone* had to jump in, he said, "What do you guys like to read?"

"Kelly Link kicks ass," said Cat. "I read a lot of comics."

"Mmm . . ." said Sejal. "I am trying to think of someone I've read of whom you would have heard. Do you know Feluda? No? Jhumpa Lahiri?" she ventured, to dead stares. "Zadie Smith? Nick Hornby?"

"That last one sounds familiar," said Doug. "I think I've heard of Feluda, but I can't remember what she writes."

"She is a he. And he's a fictional character, not the author."

"What kind of comics do you read?" Jay asked Cat.

"Um . . . I like *Meat Cake* and this one graphic novel called *Ghost World*. And a lot of Vertigo stuff. Especially *Sandman,* but of course that's not a series anymore."

"Yeah, I liked *Sandman*," said Jay. "I have a few collections of it. Now that guy writes movies and books and things."

"Cat is having me read it right now," said Sejal. "I like it okay so far."

"It gets better, I swear," said Cat.

"It's gets better for a while, but . . ." said Doug, "Neil Gaiman doesn't know how to end things, you know? He builds everything up to this huge battle in Dreamland and then, poof, it doesn't happen."

"Um, spoiler alert," said Jay.

"It doesn't happen because a big battle would have been *juvenile*," said Cat. "It— Sejal, cover your ears and hum for a bit unless you want the ending ruined."

Sejal covered her ears and sang something Indian with lots of syllables.

"Okay," said Cat, but she couldn't continue without laughing. Sejal laughed back but didn't stop singing. "Okay. The Sandman doesn't fight because he's ready to die. The mess he gets himself into is actually this huge plan he's been setting up for centuries without even realizing it."

"I know," said Doug. "I know. Because he's depressed, and he doesn't want to be the Dream King anymore, but he doesn't have the guts to just off himself."

"He feels too responsible for his kingdom," said Cat, her voice getting sharp. "So he has this . . . secret plan to remove himself and be replaced with someone better, but the only way he can do it is to . . . not even let himself know he's doing it and . . . I'm not explaining it well."

"Because it's dumb," said Doug.

"It's about him realizing he's not a good person," Jay mumbled. "He knows deep down he should change, but he's too proud to admit he was ever wrong."

"Yeah," said Cat, and she smiled at Jay.

After a moment she threw a pillow at Sejal, and Sejal stopped singing.

"What was that?"

"*Jana Gana Mana*," said Sejal. "It's the Indian National Anthem."

"You guys are probably right," said Doug. He got down on the floor with Sejal. "Jay's always right about this kind of thing."

Cat put some music on. "I promised pizza," she said. "Is Agostino's okay?"

"You don't have to do that," said Jay.

"Whatever, I'm doing it." She checked her phone. "I'll be right back, I'm not getting any bars in here. Sejal, come with me."

Sejal and Cat walked back down the hall, followed by the dog. After the front door opened and shut, Jay rounded on Doug.

"Don't you think you're . . . I appreciate it and all, but don't you think you're laying it on a bit thick?"

"What are you talking about?"

"All your flattery. It sounds fake."

"God, there's no pleasing you," said Doug. He'd actually been enjoying it, being so complimentary. He'd noticed there was a way you could do it that made you look even better than the person you were complimenting. But it kind of ruined things if the subject of your praise was going to be all ungrateful about it.

"Just act normal," said Jay. "Except don't make fun of me as much. That's all."

"Well . . . *you* act normal. Except not so retarded. Then there won't be anything to make fun of. And you're acting totally weird, too."

Jay frowned. "No, I'm not."

"You are. You're all, 'I like *Sandman*, *too*, Cat. We have so much in common. Watch me code on your computer with my dick.' "

"Shut up."

"Screw this," said Doug, and he shuffled out to the front door. Cat and Sejal were coming back in as he reached for the knob.

"Oh! Hey," said Cat. "They're really backed up because of Labor Day. So the pizza won't be here for an hour."

Doug looked at his watch. "I have to leave in an hour. To see this . . . mentor guy by Clark Park I've been seeing."

"Mentor?" said Sejal.

"Uh, yeah, he's like a career counselor. You know. Helping me figure out what to do with my future."

Cat announced that she was going to see how her computer was coming along, and left the two of them alone in the hall. Now the stale house air seemed to crackle and bloom. He wanted to seize Sejal and hold her close. He wanted to shrink her down and carry her around in his tiny pockets.

"Maybe I should blow off my appointment," he said. He couldn't remember how to stand. What did he usually do with his hands? "The company is better here."

Sejal was looking at a potpourri arrangement on the side table. "Your future is important," she said.

# 22

# ORIGIN STORIES

*YOUR FUTURE is important,* Doug thought as he biked the last few blocks to Stephin's house. *What did that mean? Important because she wants to be a part of it?* He wondered if it was possible he was going to marry Sejal. He pictured the ceremony: huge families, lots of pink and red and orange, flowers everywhere, molting flakes of gold. Sejal with painted hands, in some complicated outfit, wrapped up like a present. Doug with a big mustache for some reason.

They get married and then they live together in some cramped little New York apartment. The trains rattle their knickknacks every fifteen minutes, but that's okay, they have each other, taking long walks by the river and breakfasts in the park.

They don't move to New York, they sail the world instead; and at each port of call the local constabulary calls upon them to solve mysteries in their own playfully pugnacious fashion.

So far away was Doug that he almost missed Stephin motioning to him from a bench in the park across from his house.

He had on a wide-brimmed hat that Doug thought looked effeminate. Like something his mother would wear to garden. But then he remembered his new, complimentary outlook.

"I like your hat," he told Stephin.

"I like your hooded poncho. I believe we share a bad habit of not feeding enough? I am a bit sensitive to the sun."

"Why did you meet me out here, then?"

"Because I believe, regardless, that I need to get out of the house. Can we walk and talk?"

"Sure. Um . . . is it okay if we don't meet too long today? I have a lot of homework to do."

They walked deeper into the park, away from the house, past groups of kids playing with foam swords. It looked to Doug like the sort of game he and Jay and Stuart used to play. He had to resist an urge to shout at the kids, "Run! Vampires!"

"I don't doubt you have homework," said Stephin, "but that's not really why you're impatient to leave, I think."

"How do you know that?"

"I've been watching people a long time. I'm good at reading them. And you're a teenage boy, which makes you about as challenging as *Dick and Jane*."

Doug huffed. "Fine. It's a about a girl—big surprise, right?"

"What's her name?"

"Sejal."

"Hm. A little padma from the subcontinent, eh?"

"Mmmm, sure. Yeah."

"Does this Sejal also know about your condition?"

"About being a vampire?" asked Doug. "No. No, definitely not. I wouldn't tell her. It would be dangerous."

"And yet how very dangerous not to. Can you afford not to tell her? If you truly care? The Vampire's Dilemma—you must have these kinds of human connections to retain your humanity. And yet they're impossible. And without them you'll become nothing but a hunter and a hermit."

*And a fucking downer*, thought Doug. *And a completely depressing pain in the ass.*

They circled the park, twining in and out of its concrete paths. At all times Stephin seemed to be distantly watching his leprous house.

"So," said Doug after a long silence, "did you ever have . . . someone? Were you ever married?"

"I never married. But, yes, there was someone."

"What happened?"

Stephin cracked a rare smile. "What a question. He died."

"Oh. Sorry." *He? You've gotta be kidding me.*

"We've been away long enough," Stephin said, then turned abruptly toward the house.

:

Inside, seated again in the small study, Stephin seemed more animated.

"So it occurred to me after your first visit that we'd spent

**183**

the better part of the hour not talking about anything. I blame myself. This time I've made a list."

Doug straightened.

"First, Miss Polidori has been most insistent that I glean certain information from you. Her ghoul Asa has been at my door twice in three days. Someone should do that man the favor of killing him, and I mean that in the friendliest sense. So. Perhaps you'll tell me about the hazing that got you into our little fraternity."

"Um. You mean . . . you want to know how I became a vampire? Like my origin story?"

"If you don't mind telling me."

"I guess I don't."

"Spare no detail, please."

Doug looked at his fingernails and told Stephin about the cabin in the Poconos, near Hickory Run, and the vampire that had come at him through the trees. The vampire was naked and wounded; the vampire held him down and fed. Then there was a bat where the vampire had been, and Doug told Stephin of the coyotes and what came after. When he finished, Doug had been speaking uninterrupted for seven minutes, and even now Stephin said nothing. Doug looked up.

"I am quiet," Stephin said, "because I'm trying to remember if you've always had such trouble with pronouns or if you're merely trying not to divulge that your corruptor was another boy?"

Doug sighed. "Yeah. Another guy."

"Is this so terrible?"

"It wasn't a gay thing or anything. He'd just been made

a vampire himself and he was out of his mind."

"In the Poconos. Near Hickory Run."

"Yeah. He's an okay guy. We're sort of friends. I hope you don't have to tell anybody I told you. I don't want him to get in trouble."

"He attacked you," said Stephin. "Killed you."

"Yeah . . . but he didn't do it to be mean or anything. He's not a big dumb monster like some of the guys at my school."

Stephin smiled—a joyless sort of half smile, like a smudge on an otherwise unused sheet of paper. He rose and faced a dusty sideboard topped with glasses, plus an old clock that never changed and a small telescope. "All teenagers are monsters. Misunderstood, hated, blamed for the evils of the world. Also, reckless, selfish. With huge appetites as they slowly change from innocent things into something new. Did you know there's a part of the brain, the part that makes plans, considers consequences? It's sort of the part that makes us responsible and less destructive. Teenagers don't have that part of the brain."

The eyepiece came off the telescope and, aha, there was liquid inside. Stephin poured himself a very full tumbler of something brown.

"That is, they do, of course, but it hasn't finished growing yet. It hasn't developed. It's not entirely human. Would you like a drink?"

Doug nearly answered that he wasn't allowed to drink alcohol, but stammered out a "sure" instead. He wasn't allowed to drink blood, either, but here he was.

"Mescal," said Stephin, and handed Doug a glass of it.

**185**

Doug sipped cautiously and was immediately glad he did. It was like drinking a campfire.

"So, teenagers," said Stephin, "they careen through life, self-centered, driving too fast, cursing those who care for them, gorging themselves on the world . . . how is it not monstrous, how they live?"

Doug nodded. He knew kids like that.

Stephin settled again in his warm, leathery chair with his warm, leathery drink.

"Second," he said, consulting his list, "is for me to discover if you're aware of a basic . . . cable . . . television vampire hunting show that's been airing a sort of docudrama about you."

Doug stiffened. "Oh. You know about that?"

"Not a bit of it. That's just what it says in Miss Polidori's note. I don't own a television. 'Basic cable television vampire hunting show?' That's at least three words I didn't realize you could use together in a sentence."

"It's a pretty good show," said Doug. "You should watch it."

"Is it a hunting show for vampires or a show about *hunting* vampires?"

"The second thing."

"Hmm."

"It's on tonight," said Doug. "I'm going to watch it, of course. Find out what they know. But . . . they picked up my trail in San Diego, and all the commercials for this week's episode make it look like they're still out there."

"I've admitted this is not my area," said Stephin, "but it's my understanding that most television programs are filmed in advance. Could they not be here right now? Could they not be right outside my door?" Doug didn't answer, and Stephin continued. "I believe I'll do a little research into this show of yours. In the meantime, take care, lie low, caution, and so forth. If these hunters come for you, you can expect no help whatsoever from the rest of the Delaware Valley Society Vampires."

Doug nodded.

"And," Stephin said while frowning at his list, "and for number three I seem to have drawn a picture of a tiny goat with a party hat. Give me a moment while I try to remember if this was significant."

Doug fidgeted. He wondered if he needed blood again, so soon. This drink was really going to his head.

"No. I believe it's just a goat," said Stephin.

"There isn't just, like, a manual I can read, is there?" asked Doug, enunciating hard to keep from slurring. "It's been really confusing. Getting changed, I mean. Like, after the shock and everything wore off, I noticed I wasn't branded by Fun-Time anymore."

Stephin sipped his drink. "'Branded by *Fun-Time*'."

"Yeah. Sorry—like, I worked at this movie theater all last year and part of the summer. And they have the most crappily designed Fun-Time popcorn maker, like it was from before we invented safety. I think Ford's Theatre made Lincoln some popcorn with this thing."

Stephin cracked a faint smile.

"It has a big metal kettle where you put the corn and oil," Doug continued, "and when the corn's done popping, you pull a handle and the whole thing swings violently out at you and dumps the popcorn below. Every person the theater's ever employed has caught that kettle on the same spot on their left arms, and they all have a burn there that reads 'Fun-Tim' backward. Except me. My burn went away. Becoming a vampire did that for me, at least. But what being a vampire apparently *doesn't* do is fix your eyes. I would have expected some Spider-Man moment where I discover I don't need glasses anymore, but I still do."

"Bats are not renowned for their eyesight," said Stephin to his drink.

"I just . . . want to know how it all works. I thought there would be rules. Some *Official Handbook of the Vampire Universe*."

"There are rules," said Stephin, "and I would swear that they change all the time. I haven't told you my 'origin story.' Are you interested? You may find it useful, and I am just now drunk enough to tell it."

"Sure."

Stephin rose slightly and resettled in his chair, then spoke. "I was in the Union Army. During the Civil War. Or do you call it the War Between the States? What have your schools taught you?"

"Civil War."

Stephin nodded. "There was a man in my brigade, Tom North, who was like the Virgil to my Dante. He attended me in that hell and became very dear to me. You'll think that he has very little to do with my turning, but this story always begins with Tom North."

Doug nodded, because it seemed like the thing to do. Stephin wasn't looking at him anyway.

"Tom had his belly opened for him by cannon fire. It could have hit me, but he was standing in front. Do you know what I thought?"

Doug shook his head. When Stephin didn't continue, Doug said, "You probably . . . wanted revenge. On the Southern soldiers?"

Stephin said, "I thought, Thank the Lord it wasn't me. Think about that."

He emptied the glass.

"Anyway, it was moot. I fell not two minutes later.

"The United States Army didn't know quite what to do with all the dead bodies back then. They thought I'd died. Or perhaps they didn't, but they knew I wasn't long for this world and wished to cover me like an old sofa should company come. I don't know. I was dragged to the center of camp with some of the dead men and covered as the sun set. My head fell to one side. Unable to lift it, I stared around a fold of canvas at the blue body of Tom North beside me, his face open to the sky, frozen as if sickened by what he saw there. Or didn't see. The length of him was painted with a bright orange stripe of sharp sunlight, and then that color did rise, and fade, until nothing but the tip of his nose still glowed with warm life. And as that little flame went out and night came on I imagined I'd watched Tom give up the ghost that very moment. A minute later they covered him, too.

"Soon the sounds of the camp dimmed and died away. I was forgotten, perhaps, but I could still see Tom's stiff shroud in the moonlight, could still smell campfire and copper, and I knew I still lived. Then there came into my sideways world a horrible figure. He appeared at the edge of my sight, very tall, I think, unsteady at the knees as though they'd been savaged and dislocated. But what struck me most was his wide, bloated torso, which I believe was quite red, covered here and there with tatters. Atop this, his head seemed tiny and keen, and with his long, thin limbs he looked like a monstrous tick just emerged from the woods."

At this Stephin focused on Doug's face for perhaps the first time that day, and asked if he might fix Stephin another drink. Doug rose, thinking that the story sounded just a little rehearsed. Like a monologue. He filled the glass again, expecting as he did so that Stephin would continue, but he didn't. In fact he didn't speak again until Doug had retaken his seat and the glass was half empty.

"He hobbled like a grotesque marionette toward me. But not directly toward me, no—he paused, bobbing for a moment, at what must have been a body some feet away. Then he lingered longer over Tom, leaning close, maybe taking his scent. His eyes were dry slits, his black lips were drawn back over long teeth like a Jabberwock. He . . . worried the air over Tom's shroud with long, white nails. Then he swiftly fell upon me."

Stephin finished his drink.

"He must have been looking for soldiers like me, dead but not yet departed. The war must have given him fields of fallen apples."

He looked for a while at the empty glass, then balanced it

on the top story of a book stack like a water tower.

"This is not a story I enjoy telling. Do you understand why I thought you might find it instructive?"

Doug didn't, but he wasn't in the habit of admitting that sort of thing.

"Sure," he said. "But . . . there's something I'm wondering about. I've done a lot of reading on vampires. Not just *Dracula*—lots of things. And there are a bunch of stories of vampires looking like the one who turned you: plump, and reddish or purplish. Long teeth and nails."

"Yes," said Stephin.

"But the books I've read just dis . . . dismissed those stories as a misunderstanding of how bodies decompose. When a dead person starts rotting, he often gets all bloated with gases like that. So it makes him look well fed, but it's just gas. And the skin around the teeth and nails shrivels up, and that's what makes them look longer. Stuff like that. If someone was dug back up when they looked like this, they could get mistaken for a vampire. But since I know a bunch of vampires now, and they just look like normal people . . ."

"You think I'm lying," concluded Stephin.

"No! No, just . . . Why would your vampire look like that, if the rest of us don't?"

"Exactly my point. You wanted to know the rules. I believe, sometimes, that the rules can change. That the rules are not rules at all. Why did 'my' vampire look like that?" said Stephin, sitting low and deep in his chair. "I have no idea. Maybe because he thought he should? Maybe because that was what the world believed of vampires in his day? I only know that I didn't become just like him. I was no treat in my early days, let me assure you, but I was never as loathsome as he. Then the years passed, and a notion of a different kind of vampire captured the popular imagination, and I sloughed off my dead skin, bit by bit. That's a metaphor, you understand. Do they still teach metaphor?"

"Of course."

"I'm glad to hear it. I thought perhaps school was all music videos and telephone messages. They teach books? I see from your face they do. So, shortly after our Mr. Stoker published *his* stuffy little book, I finally emerged, a fucking butterfly."

Doug assumed this was sarcasm. Stephin was clearly a moth, circling a dim light in a dusty closet, chewing holes in the world. *Metaphor!* Doug wanted to leave.

"So you see?" said Stephin. "I changed. The conception of what a vampire is, what he looks like and how he behaves, changed. It can change again. No rules."

Doug frowned, then realized he was frowning, and stopped. The whole idea seemed too unlikely. Too metaphysical.

"I wonder if we don't all have this kind of influence over each other," said Stephin. "Do you know that everything in the universe has its own gravity? It's not just planets that exert this force—it's anything with mass. You have your own gravity. So does a feather."

"I already knew that," said Doug. "We learn it in school. From books. But you have to be as massive as a planet or a moon or something in order to have enough of a gravitational pull that anyone'd notice."

"Yes. Precisely. But there are other laws of attraction—are

there not? The sort you don't learn about in school? How often do we find ourselves pulled to other people, becoming a different kind of person whilst inside their aura? How often do we remake ourselves to suit the expectations of society?"

Doug shook his head, which felt suddenly numb and elastic. He was possibly drunk. "I'm sorry. This sounds like touchy-feely crystal bullshit."

He was met with silence, and Doug imagined he'd probably said something he shouldn't have. He avoided the other man's face until it was too obviously deliberate, then was treated to a look that could sour milk. Stephin made a little cage of his fingers.

"I was a devil. I mingled with worms and dank earth. I slept as if dead by day and wandered by night, and by night I was diverted only by pretty screams and blood. A devil.

"And then came our friend Dracula, and the world changed its mind. The memory of my life came back to me. The memory of my death, and what I'd lost. Tom North came back to me. There are so many more of them than us, Doug. They have a planetary influence. And the vampire was only ever what they needed it to be."

Doug breathed and forced his head to clear for a moment. "Can you stop being a vampire if you kill the one who made you?" he said quickly, before his mind went soft again.

Stephin raised his eyes. "Ready to leave the belfry, so soon?"

"I've seen movies and read stories where you kill your vampire sire, or kill the one who started that vampire lin . . . lineage, and you change back to normal. Does it work? If so many people think it works, then maybe it works. Tell me."

Stephin stared for a long time, face blank as an old hat, while Doug fidgeted. Stephin could probably figure things out about Victor. He'd tell Signora Polidori or Borisov. Doug had been stupid to ask.

"I've never heard of such a thing firsthand," Stephin said finally, "but I've come across such stories myself. I can tell you that I know with great certainty that Miss Polidori's sire has gone to his final death, but she remains, up in her gilded bird-cage."

"But did she kill him herself?" said Doug, determined to see this line of questioning through now, screw the consequences. "Maybe you have to be the one who does it."

"Maybe. Maybe you'd even have to kill an 'okay guy.' One who was out of his mind when he made you," said Stephin. Then he was quiet again, and appeared to be thinking. Doug let him think, and felt his body sag and marinate. But then the sun set outside and the night filled him up like his whole body had a hard-on. Stephin must have felt it, too, because he breathed suddenly and spoke.

"I think you would find it useful to do a little genealogy. Find out more about your vampire family tree. I will consider this question of yours and do my own study. But offhand, I'd say do nothing to the boy who made you. I think you want the head of the family, so to speak."

"I guess—I guess the real question," said Doug, "is why would any vampire make another?"

"Why?" Stephin repeated. "Loneliness, of course."

"But I mean . . . why would a vampire create a younger

vampire if there was a possibility the young one might end up destroying the old one?"

Stephin stared. "If you can explain to me how this is different from parenting in general I might know how to answer that."

# 23
:

## GREAT WHITE HUNTER

**HE HAD BEEN** right, he thought, on the long bike trip home: getting low on blood *was* like being drunk. Drunk and hungry. *Being drunk and dry at the same time must feel terrible*, he thought. Drunk but sanguine—that felt a little better. He let his bike drift from side to side, giving in to the weightlessness, softening his eyes until everything was smoke and blurred edges. Then he was nearly clipped by a car.

"Dumbass!" shouted a boy riding shotgun.

"Nice poncho!" shouted a kid in the back.

*Screw you,* thought Doug. *This poncho is for safety. You're supposed to* wear *white when you bike at night. I shouldn't even have to explain this to you, but I do because you're all a bunch of fuck-wit future short-order cooks. You're a bunch of burger flippers. You're a bunch of batter-dipped fry guys,* he thought. Besides, it was easier to just wear the poncho than try to fit it in his pocket.

He ramped up onto the sidewalk and gazed into the park, through the hedges and tall trees, the statuary, the . . . deer.

There was a deer in the park. A West Philadelphia park, empty at night but for a man asleep on a bench and, over there, a deer. Doug stopped his bike. The deer, which may have been watching him pass, turned and stepped unhurriedly toward the far road. Doug trundled his bike around and pedaled back to a gap in the hedge, then into the park. The deer answered by bounding across the street to the south park, its hooves drawing a crisp, thrilling percussion out of the cracked pavement. Doug stood up on his pedals, shifted gears, and chased.

The night made him strong. He could feel it seep into his legs, an eldritch power, his prize and his curse, gained in a dark bargain with shadowy forces that he may better exact his vengeance on . . . this deer. Maybe he could pretend the deer was a mugger.

It dashed through the children's playground, and in that spray of sand and Tinkertoy architecture he lost it. At the far edge of the park he slowed and looked around.

There was a bewildered-looking guy on the sidewalk, and Doug asked, "Did you just see—"

"Yeah, man!" he answered, and pointed down a side street. "It went that way!" Doug thanked him and pushed off again.

Where had this deer come from? The closest real woodland was a few miles away, and even that was just a thin, fresh strip between two scabrous counties. Like Mother Nature had left her watch on while getting tattooed. It was too unlikely, seeing a deer here. Doug inflated the unlikelihood of it in his soggy mind until it was like mythology, until it seemed to him that the deer could be nothing short of a spiritual messenger or a gift. To catch it would signify something. In the fantasy sorts of stories Doug read the deer would have something important to tell him. Or he would trade its life for a wish. Or maybe it would actually be a beautiful woman, bound to him forever. If this last possibility strikes you as odd, then you have probably never been a teenage boy. There are an uncatalogable number of things that can remind a teenage boy of beautiful women.

The side street ended at a T, and Doug could see nothing in either direction. The deer was somewhere close, he thought. Hiding. He drew a deep breath through his nostrils and not so much smelled as sensed something wild in the air.

Near the T in the road was a gravel path between two houses, too narrow for a car, not quite a driveway. Doug left his bike by the street and crept up the path, conscious that he was approaching a strange house, ducking past a strange window, but the smell was overwhelming. The smell and a rhythmic, chuffing sound like a locomotive. He reached the end of the path. Crouching low, he craned his head around the corner, and the deer was there.

Large. Larger than he expected. It was looking slightly downward at him, fenced in by a postage-stamp backyard, no more than three feet away. Its mouth was white with dry spit. Its belly kept time like a huge, fiercely beating heart.

It was difficult holding it down, but Doug was strong tonight. And after a minute the animal grew calm. Its breathing slowed. Its blood was so much better than cow's blood, though not as satisfying as human. Still, there was an electricity to this feed that made even those bags of human blood seem a little like dead batteries.

He took more than he usually did. He took as much as he could.

He got a little of it on his poncho, but it wiped clean. That was the nice thing about vinyl.

The deer would never have found its way back home. The deer would have been shot by animal control, or got hit by a car. The deer might have hurt someone.

He was back on track now, tearing through the streets on his bicycle, his body warm and mighty. Was it the blood (or maybe the alcohol?) that made him feel both larger and smaller than himself? Like he was wearing a costume. Like he was looking at the world through eyeholes, narrowly. He really wished he could run into those guys in that car again. Those guys, or some just like them. Any guys, really.

There was a long way home and a very long way home, and Doug took the latter tonight, through streets that began to split and crumble beneath his tires, past the stumps of trees that had been cut down and made into posters for beer and cigarettes. He was looking for a little trouble, but it was only seven o'clock and barely dark, and a short white kid on a bike didn't attract the sort of negative attention he thought it would. So he'd already crossed the street that formed the abrupt and almost mystical barrier between the have-nots and the haves, and was nearing his own neighborhood, when he accepted that he just couldn't hold it any longer and pulled up to a MoPo convenience store to pee.

He couldn't remember the last time he'd urinated. It just wasn't something he needed to do much anymore. Was it because of the liquor? Alcohol made you pee, right? Or maybe because he'd taken too much blood from the deer.

Man, the deer. That whole episode already seemed so dreamlike, so long ago. He could almost wonder if it even really happened. But he could still smell the animal on his clothes and the blood on his poncho. And he was strong.

He locked his bike to the rack and pushed through the door of the empty MoPo, into the skim milk light, the smell of pretzels and freezer burn.

"Bathroom?" he asked the checkout girl.

"By the dairy case," she answered without looking up from her acrylic nails.

Doug minced through the faintly spinning store and found the bathroom. If he really did need to pee because he'd taken too much from the deer, did that mean he was about to piss blood? His stomach lurched at the idea, but when he finally unclenched the fist he'd made of his crotch, the only thing that splashed against the urinal was urine. He pumped his free hand victoriously in the air.

He washed up and glanced at his reflection in the mirror. Then he took a long look. Here was a nice-looking guy staring back at him. Doug couldn't quite place the face.

He retraced his steps through a swinging plastic door between the dairy case and the bottled water and found the MoPo a lot busier. There were two men near the checkout island and a third standing by the entrance with his hand over the lock. One of the men was pointing a toy gun at the cashier.

*No, a real gun,* Doug thought as he struggled to decode the situation.

*These guys are robbing the MoPo. Oh, hell yeah!*

This was important, the culmination of his origin story. This would be momentous. *Don't think,* he thought. *Don't think.*

He unbuttoned his poncho and pulled the hood over his head as he strode toward the men, arms akimbo. The cashier was fumbling underneath the register drawer. "All of it! All of it!" the armed man shouted. An unarmed man between Doug and the gunman saw him approach.

"Roy," he said, with a big-eyed frown.

"Hey!" said Roy. "No names! And, besides, uh, that's not my—" He flinched and turned the gun on Doug. "Who the fuck is this?! Chad, out of the way!"

"Now he said *your* name, Chad," said the man by the door.

"You've picked the wrong convenience store tonight, gentlemen," Doug announced in what he thought was an intimidatingly low rumble, like distant thunder. Too distant, possibly.

"What? Man, back off!" said Chad. With outstretched arms he threw all his weight into Doug. Doug sprawled backward, clutching at the counter, anything, to steady himself, to no avail. He was dumped backward onto the floor along with a clattering hot-dog cooker. Time slowed. The situation presented itself with intricate clarity.

"Just stay down!" the cashier shouted. "Let these men go!"

Doug said, "HOT DOGS!" and whipped a handful of the sweaty wieners at Chad's face. Afterward, he wasn't sure why he'd shouted it.

"Aah! Hey!" Chad screeched through upraised hands.

"Man, move!" Roy shouted as he pushed Chad aside, but when he raised his gun, Doug hurled the steel hot-dog warmer at his head. Roy fired at the stained dropped ceiling and went down.

The noise of the gun was deafening. Doug had never been so close to one before, and his ears went tinny. But it roused him off the floor and toward a snack display.

"POP-TARTS! POP-TARTS! POP-TARTS!" he shouted, throwing twin packs of them like shurikens at the heads and throats of all three men. *Again with the shouting,* he thought. He was reading too many Silver Age comic books.

Chad came close and threw a punch, but Doug found it surprisingly easy to dodge. Then he returned the punch, and Chad folded backward over the snack foods and didn't get back up. "Ha!" said Doug, then ducked when he realized he was being shot at.

"Roy, let's just go!" said the man at the door.

"MAGAZINE RACK ATTACK!" yelled Doug, deciding to just go with it. He swung the rack over his head and onto Roy's, and the man collapsed in a heap. All around them celebrity magazines and sudoku booklets flapped heavily like chickens and then slumped dead to the floor. The cashier was just finishing up a scream. Doug looked over at the doorman, the doorman looked back at Doug. Then he unlocked the door and ran out into the night.

"He won't get far!" Doug promised, and followed. His poncho billowed out behind him like a great white sail, a sail borne on the winds of justice. That would be a good name for him, he thought, as he narrowed in on his prey: *White Justice*. No, it sounded a little neo-Nazi. He might as well call himself Nordic Lightning. You can have black superheroes with "Black" at the beginning of their names, but you can't really do it with white superheroes. "Jewish Justice" just sounds like a law firm, he thought, before noticing he was about to get hit by a trolley.

# 24

## OPEN THE DOOR
## FOR YOUR MYSTERY DATE

**"I CAN'T BELIEVE** you guys watch it, too," said Cat as she squirted another slug of purple goop into Jay's hair. "I wonder if Doug'll get back in time."

"He has been gone longer than he said," Sejal observed. She considered how awful it would be if Doug had had an accident after she suggested he keep his appointment, and was feeling a little nervy. And this after having a mild panic attack on Friday, at the show. She was taking a full Niravam a day now, and wondered at how bad she'd feel without it. "Isn't it dangerous to cycle at night?"

"I think he's okay," said Jay. "Really. He's safer than most people." He turned on his television and began flipping up the channels to the Crypt, on which *Vampire Hunters* would be starting in a few minutes. "How is it looking?" he added, staring upward at the mysterious process that was playing out on his head. Cat had talked her way into coloring Jay's hair black with a half bottle of leftover dye.

"It doesn't look like anything yet. It looks wet. Don't worry, it's gonna be totally hot. Do you have any hair gel? I like that your hair's messy, but there's messy and then there's *messy*—you know?"

Sejal pulled her knees up to her chest and rested her chin. She saw a panicky thrill in Jay's eyes that told her that he *didn't* know but wanted to.

"My hair used to be a lot more messy," he said. "And blond. I used to have uncombable hair syndrome."

Cat laughed. "You had what? Is that real? It sounds like one of those bullshit drug commercials, like for restless leg syndrome."

"They're both real," said Jay. "I think. If you Google 'uncombable hair syndrome' you can find a picture of me from when I was four."

"Oh my god. When I get this shit off my hands, I am totally doing that. Forget Crystal Math, when we start our band we're calling it Uncombable Hair Syndrome."

Sejal was content to let the two of them flirt as she fortified her position on Doug. She had a decision to make, and she was beginning to notice the return of a cowardly, impetuous approach to problem solving that was not characteristic of the girl she wanted to become. Fear and guilt boiled holes in her stomach. She was not being honest with Doug, but that would come to an end tonight. Unless he'd had an accident.

"Wait, what was that?" said Jay. He flipped backward two stations and stopped at a newscast that was live and in West Philadelphia. Police lights strobed on the screen. The sound came up by degrees.

                    REPORTER (V.O.)
          . . . dria Franklin, an employee at
          the MoPo, describes what happened
          next.

                    MOPO CASHIER
          After he . . . after he knocked out
          those two he chases after the third
          guy, an'—an' they run out into the
          street, an' just as he was about to
          catch the guy there's this screech
          and the trolley comes and POOF!

                    REPORTER
          Poof?

                    MOPO CASHIER
          Yeah, poof! The hero guy disappears!
          An' the trolley rolls right by! And
          there ain't nothing left but his
          clothes!

                    REPORTER
I just want to be clear about this.
The vigilante vanished and left his
clothes behind?


                    MOPO CASHIER
Yeah. The cops took them.


                    REPORTER
What was he wearing?


                    MOPO CASHIER
A white cape and a hood. Like in a
comic book.


"Oh my god. Like in a stupid comic book," said Cat. Jay
didn't answer, only stared with hard features at the screen.


EXT. A WEST PHILADELPHIA DELI CALLED
SAMMY'S II


                    REPORTER
The story may continue at this
nearby deli, where a startled
shopkeeper says he had a close
encounter with the hero shortly
after the foiled robbery. A
close encounter of the . . .
thirst kind.

CUT TO THE SHOPKEEPER, WHO DOES NOT
APPEAR SO MUCH STARTLED AS VACANT.

                REPORTER (off camera)
          What makes you think it was the
          hero who came into your deli?

                SHOPKEEPER
          Well, it was, like, right after
          I heard what happened at the
          MoPo, you know? And . . . then
          there was suddenly this guy at
          the counter, right? And I thought,
          that's weird, I didn't even see
          him come in. He was just there,
          all of a sudden.

                REPORTER
          Was he naked? Or wearing a white
          cape?

                SHOPKEEPER
          Um, no. But he was really tall and
          musclely. Like a superhero.

                REPORTER
          And did this mystery man identify
          himself to be the MoPo hero?

                    SHOPKEEPER
Not exactly. Not exactly, but he
acted like he was in a real hurry,
right? And he bought some beer and
some BullShake Energy Drink, right?
*Energy drink.*


                    REPORTER
I see.


                    SHOPKEEPER
Plus, his driver's license looked
totally fake. Like it could be a
secret identity.

PAUSE.


                    REPORTER
Should you have sold him the beer if
his license looked fake?

SHOPKEEPER LOOKS CONFUSED, STARES
NERVOUSLY AT CAMERA.


Just then something smacked hard against Jay's bedroom
window, and all three kids jumped.
"Holy shit," said Cat. "Is that a bat?"
It was without question a bat, twitching, pasted flat

against the glass like a Halloween decoration. It shook itself and flapped away.

"It must have been attracted to the light," said Sejal.

"I . . . don't think it was a bat," said Jay.

"It was definitely a bat."

"IT WAS A MOTH," he answered in a voice that was suddenly like a car alarm. "A big moth. I have to go to the bathroom." And with that he hopped to his feet and strode out of the room without moving his arms.

Cat smiled after him. "Weird guy."

"He likes you," said Sejal.

"Yeah. Probably just because his best friend likes you."

"I don't think this is true."

Cat changed the channel until "Last week on *Vampire Hunters*" could be heard.

"You're really not into Doug, are you?" asked Cat. "You're just naturally nicer to him than everyone else."

Sejal nodded. Her stomach seethed.

"If he asks you out again, you have to tell him no. Guys like him who haven't hooked up much . . . they get clingy real fast."

"I know this. You could say the same of Jay."

"I'm handling Jay. But with Doug . . . trust me, it's better you say something sooner than later. Just say dating's not allowed in your country or your religion or—"

"I know, I know. I will tell him. Don't eat my head."

"Sorry, *yaar*," said Cat.

Silence followed, and Cat turned up the sound.

EXT. FLOODLIT, TREE-LINED FIELD AT
NIGHT

VAMPIRE HUNTER CREW STANDS IN A LOOSE
LINE, REDEEMERS IN HAND. THEY FACE A
SECOND LINE OF DRESSMAKER'S DUMMIES.
ALAN FRIENDLY IN FRONT. MUSICAL STING
#24 (REDEEMER THEME)

                ALAN FRIENDLY
      There! The San Diego vampires are
      before us! Present Redeemers!

CREW MEMBERS RAISE THEIR WEAPONS

                ALAN FRIENDLY
      Send those mothersuckers back to
      hell, boys! Fire at will!

CREW FIRES WEAPONS. QUICK CUTS OF
DUMMIES STRUCK IN THE HEART WITH
STAKES, DUMMIES STUCK IN THE HEART
IN SLOW MOTION, DUMMIES STRUCK IN THE
HEART IN BLACK-AND-WHITE WITH DRIPPING
BLOOD EFFECT #3 (BLOODY VENETIAN
BLINDS)

ALAN FRIENDLY

Equipped and confident, we set back
out on the trail. Last week we
learned that two individuals, quite
possibly a vampire and his ghoul,
robbed a bloodmobile outside the
San Diego Convention Center. A
convention center that was playing
host to the largest pop-culture
gathering in the world, Comic-Con
International.

MONTAGE OF SCENES FROM PAST CONS,
COURTESY OF COMIC-CON INTERNATIONAL

ALAN FRIENDLY (V.O.)
Comic-Con: four days of sights,
frights, and delights in the heart
of San Diego—

"They're stalling," said Cat. "They must not have anything good this week."

"No," said Sejal.

"I really didn't mean to . . . eat your head?"

"Do you not say that here?"

"I don't know, but I'm saying it every chance I get now."

"I did not mean to snap. I've been testy. I thought I should
try to like Doug. But I think I understand now that he is not

my sort for a number of reasons. Jay is nicer."

Cat nodded. "And kind of more fun when Doug isn't around. Hey, you're not gonna like Jay now, are you? Not that it wouldn't be okay, but . . ."

"No. It would not be good for me to date a boy with an Intel Quad Core with E-Line connectivity."

"Right. Hey, stormtroopers."

EXT. THE BEACH—A REGIMENT OF
STORMTROOPERS RUN DRILLS

            ALAN FRIENDLY (V.O.)
On Mission Beach we caught up with
two Imperial Stormtroopers of the
501st Legion, who were attendees at
the convention. Do you remember any
people who could have conceivably
been vampires?

            STORMTROOPER #1
Dude, tons. (to Stormtrooper #2) You
remember that vampiress with Arcade
Comics? She was all kinds of hot.

            STORMTROOPER #2
Totally. Her <bleep> were all
(motions with hands) . . . can I say
<bleep>?

                    ALAN FRIENDLY
Not on basic cable.


                    STORMTROOPER #1
Remember those slave Leias that
posed for that big group photo with
Jabba?


                    STORMTROOPER #2
(laughing) They weren't vampires.


                    STORMTROOPER #1
Oh, right. Vampires. Well, there was
that old lady dressed as Elvira.


                    STORMTROOPER #2
That *was* Elvira.


                    STORMTROOPER #1
And there was that guy dressed like
that guy from Dark Shadows.


                    STORMTROOPER #2
And that girl dressed like that girl
from that video game.


                    ALAN FRIENDLY
These are not the vampires we're
looking for.

"Heeey," said Jay from the doorway, and he had Doug with him. "Look who I found." Doug said hello and the girls answered.

Sejal supposed it was the sun allergy that made Doug always look better at night. He wasn't wearing the same clothes he'd left in, and these new clothes were less than flattering—the T-shirt, in particular, looked like the sort of thing you'd get free for opening a checking account. Still, there was something very ripe and alive about Doug now.

"His clothes got all sweaty from the bike ride. So he stopped at his house on the way back. That's what took him so long," said Jay. Doug said and did nothing to confirm or deny any of it. He stood calmly in the doorway as though waiting to be invited in.

"What did we miss?" asked Jay finally as he went and sat down beside Cat.

"Whole lotta nothin'. They're just fartin' around San Diego."

"Good."

"Good?"

"Yeah, I mean . . . I didn't want to miss it if they caught him."

Doug had taken a seat behind the rest of them, but Sejal could feel his eyes on her. She stole a glance and regretted it—he was gazing at her, all right. *That's the word for it,* she thought. *He is gazing.* The light of desperation, that faltering candle, was gone from his eyes. Now they were steady, warm, and even, and Sejal couldn't explain the chill that seized in her chest.

"Excuse me," she said, and left the room.

The hall bathroom did not lock. She didn't really have to go, but she hiked down her pants and underwear nonetheless, going through the motions as though the dance itself might bring rain. She sat on the toilet and tried to work out why a girl from a house where people did not lock doors might now have groped every inch of a bald doorknob for something to turn or press. What was wrong with her? This was only Doug.

After what seemed the right amount of time she rose, dressed, washed her hands, and opened the door to where Doug stood in the hallway. She had to make an effort not to laugh or scream.

"I need to talk to you outside a minute," said Doug.

Sejal stood silently for a moment, then sighed and followed him through the kitchen and out the back door. Across the deck, down stairs into the yard, he stopped by a weathered swing set. Sejal sat on one of the swings and curled her arms around the chains, because who could come so close to a swing set without sitting on a swing? But Doug stood before her.

"That's perfect," he said. "You on that swing set." He didn't elaborate on what was perfect about it. "I just wanted to tell you that things are going to be different now. I'm a different person than I was when you met me."

"That is . . . remarkable," said Sejal. "I met you only a week ago, no?"

The moonlight touched off a single cold spark in each of his eyes, and it was only now that Sejal realized Doug was not wearing his glasses. Sejal had had a good look at those lenses before, at the Coke-bottle curves of the glass, so now she relaxed, no longer clothed in the scratchy self-awareness that comes from being on display. There was no way Doug could see anything but smears of color. His familiarity with Jay's house had been a good cover, but he was blind as a bat.

"A lot can happen in a week. A lot has happened to me just tonight—I'll tell you all the details someday, but it can wait for now. I just want you to understand that we can take things slowly if you want, I have all the time in the world."

*Dating is not allowed in my country,* Sejal repeated in her thoughts. *It's against my religion. I'm arranged to marry a cricketer. In fact, I'm already married now!* A dozen dodges and excuses formed in her mind, but she stayed silent. If she could, she would have remained silent forever, but there was Doug above her like a *vetala*, a folktale spirit, demanding answers. Say the wrong thing and she'd never be rid of him. Speak properly and she could set him free.

"Doug, I'm not interested in you as a suit—as a boyfriend. I think perhaps we should not hang around anymore."

Doug smiled. "You don't mean that."

Sejal blinked and skimmed back through her last statement for typos. Everything checked out.

"I do mean that. Actually."

"There's a lot you don't understand," Doug answered, "but you will. I'll take care of you."

Sejal laughed now, half from nerves. But then she laughed harder as a sort of slap in the face, the best she could do to soothe a bright animal whisper in her to flee, to put doors and distance between her and this boy—or else to attack, to push her sharp thumbs into his soft eyes. Gods, was it just a panic attack? Why did it feel like Doug was to blame? Her laughter, anyway, had the effect she wanted—Doug flinched, and a little of that old uncertainty flickered across his face.

"You'll . . ." Sejal sputtered. "You do not need to take care of me, Doug. I will manage on my own, thank you. Why do you Americans think we are all orphaned children? For only pennies a day you can buy me a donkey! Excellent! Thank you. I'll put it with the rest."

"Hey. Hey! Why're you . . . where do you get off saying shit like that to me?" said Doug. "No one says stuff like that to me. Anymore."

"I'm sorry," said Sejal, looking away.

"Do you have any idea what you're doing, saying stuff like that?"

Sejal sighed. "I am doing what needs to be done. I'm sorry if I . . . got mean about it."

"You've been giving me signals. Don't pretend you haven't. You've been going out of your way to lead me on."

"I am like that only," Sejal insisted. "I've been trying to be friendly. I did not know you would . . . not see it like this."

"So what's wrong with me, then?"

*"Doug—"*

"No. Really. I'd like to know. I'm too short? Too fat? I can tell you without bullshit that I am maybe the second-strongest guy in school. Do you want to know how?"

"You are not kind!" Sejal said, braced forward, knuckles white around the swing set chains. "You are no better than you have to be. Why are you no better? Because people treat you poorly? You treat others poorly. You treat Jay poorly."

"I've been nothing but nice to Jay today—"

"Yes. Today. It is like you've been running for office."

They fell silent and the old nag of a swing set creaked and groaned. The leafy tangles at the property's edge shuddered in the night air.

"You don't know what you're doing," Doug said. "It's not my fault, if you say these things."

Sejal stood, feeling suddenly foolish, and put the black curved seat between her and Doug. It shimmied and bumped against her hips. "I know what I'm doing. I have been trying to find something in you . . . I have been looking for your heart. There should be something divine in all our hearts." She swallowed hard and her eyes rimmed with tears.

"Hey," said Doug. "Hey, hey, hey, it's all right." He tried to take hold of her, but Sejal backed away and in between the swing and struts.

"There's something wrong with me, too, Doug," she said. "Something missing. That is how I can see it. But I'm trying to be better. You're only trying to be admired."

"Oh, and—and I suppose *Adam's* a good person."

"Adam? This has nothing to do with Adam."

"He likes you."

"He likes Sophie," said Sejal.

She was cold and her feet were damp and she wanted to go inside and then to leave with Cat. After a moment Doug said something. Sejal couldn't make it out as he barely moved his lips, so tight were they over his teeth. He looked as though he might be biting the inside of his mouth.

"I can't hear you," said Sejal. But Doug didn't repeat

himself, so after a moment she added, "I'm going in." She walked back up the deck stairs and into the house *(don't turn around,* she thought, *don't look),* and left Doug alone below in the dark.

"How dramatic," she whispered to herself sourly. "I should try out for the school play."

# 25

## BLOOD BROTHERS

**I**T HAD RAINED in the early morning. By lunch the world was as fresh and clean as a green apple. The air was spiced with the smell of new possibilities and taquitos. While most of the usual lunch group was occupied with a loud and stuttering debate over whether Andrea did or did not sleep with Blaine on *Lexington Avenue* (it was like watching toddlers play soccer, this debate—each new idea was swarmed and kicked simultaneously from all directions), Ophelia asked Sejal about the rest of her weekend.

"Saturday we went shopping on South Street," she answered. "Is that right? South Street?"

"Was it all body jewelry and sex shops?"

"There was also a comic book store."

Ophelia nodded. "South Street."

South Street had felt a little more like home than the Main Line suburbs. There was bright, messy life on the streets. Colors. And here the colors had not been washed and scrubbed until they faded into taupe and eggshell.

Not that there weren't still differences, big differences. There was an almost stultifying array of choices—kinds of people, kinds of foods. Here, amid the produce wallahs of the Italian Market, she'd counted six fruits she'd never even seen before and gasped at a line of ripe mangoes—their blushing skins looking suitably embarrassed to be spotted so far from home and in September. They practically shivered in the autumn air.

"What'd you do on Sunday?" asked Ophelia.

"Ah—I ruined Cat's Sunday by asking to accompany the family to church."

Cat overheard this and disengaged from the TV show argument, which had just devolved into personal attacks and name calling anyway. "I didn't say you ruined my Sunday, *yaar*. I'm just disappointed. I thought you were going to be my Get Out of Church Free card for the whole year."

"I am here to try new things." Sejal smiled. "Tough shit for you!"

"Ho, *ho*!" Cat shouted.

"New things, huh?" Ophelia purred as she leaned in. "What kind of new things do you want to try?"

Cat puckered her lips in a silent whistle and turned back

to the others. That left Sejal alone with Ophelia, so to speak, in this tangle of thorns that had suddenly grown up around them.

"I don't know," she said, looking at Cat. "Things." She considered what to tell Ophelia about her visit with Doug and Jay when a shadow fell across her lap.

Doug's head was blotting out the sun. Jay stood behind, looking vaguely apologetic.

Sejal hadn't expected him to show up for lunch. He had rather pointedly ignored her in math class that morning. "Doug," she said.

"Hey, Meatball, Jay," said Sophie.

"I prefer 'Doug,'" answered Doug, and he sat down at the base of the tree where the roots were packed in tight, intestinal coils.

"Okay," said Sophie. "Doug. You look different. You got contacts! But there's something else."

Conversation wilted. Faces turned and became transfixed by this something else, this question of how exactly Doug had changed. Doug seemed unfazed by the attention, almost bored with it. Where he would have previously only had eyes for Sejal, he now examined Abby with all the careless detachment of the mean judge on a reality talent show.

"But, hey," Cat broke the silence. "What about Jay? Isn't his hair rad?"

Jay flinched as the group came back to themselves and stared at his head. He smiled sheepishly and bobbed it back and forth.

"That looks so good on you, Jay," said Ophelia.

"Although—and you know I'm only saying this because I like you—your new hair doesn't really go with your Simpsons T-shirt."

"Or your cargo shorts," Sophie added.

"It's like your head's on the wrong action figure," said Adam, and everyone laughed.

"Fuck you," Doug said suddenly like a whip crack. "You don't have to take that from him, Jay."

"It was funny," Jay mumbled. "He wasn't being mean."

"I really wasn't," said Adam. "I'm just, like, Jay's too cool for his clothes now. That's all."

Doug gave a princely nod. Everyone seemed to avoid his gaze. Everyone except Abby.

"Jay and I are going to start a band," Cat said. "Me on bass, him on theremin and MIDI. We're inventing a new genre— early goth plus nerdcore. We're gonna call it nerdcave."

"What's a theremin?" asked Sophie. "What's a middy?"

And so they talked about electronic music, and they talked about nerdcave, and they talked about Cat and Jay's theoretical band (which was now called Primordial Soup for the Teenage Soul) until Victor approached.

Even Sejal knew his name. He had been impossible to miss on campus. And though Cat had once referred to him as a "meathead asswipe," even she stared now with unabashed longing.

"Hey, Victor," said Adam.

"Can I talk to you a minute, Doug?" said Victor. "I have a homework question. About the chiroptera family."

Doug made a face. Then he got up, and the two boys walked

away. The drama group watched them depart in silence.

"I never noticed before," Cat said finally, "but . . . don't those two look kind of alike? In a really weird way?"

Sophie nodded. For a few moments the rest didn't nod or say anything, but even their lack of reaction to such a patently absurd claim was in itself a kind of endorsement.

"It's like they're a 'before' and 'after' picture," Adam said. But nobody laughed.

**:**

"You look better," said Victor as they walked around to the far side of the gym. "Not as douchey. You get some neck?"

"Maybe," said Doug. *Get some neck?*

"Maybe?"

"All right, no. But I did try some deer. It's better than cow."

"Huh," said Victor while scratching his cheek. A cheek that had a blue grit of stubble, Doug noted—unlike his own face, which had never produced more than a thin cotton-candy fuzz on the sides of his jaw. And never would, he supposed. "You hunted a deer?" Victor continued. "Well, that's . . . it's not actually cool, but it's closer to cool than before. Like, now maybe you can at least see 'cool' if you stand on something."

"Thank you. Your brotherly encouragement is the fucking wind beneath my wings."

Victor laughed. "Not a bad crowd," he said, pointing his chin in the direction of the drama kids. "A couple of those girls are definitely fuckable."

Doug looked lazily over his shoulder as if the thought hadn't occurred to him. "That was real subtle—'chiroptera

**225**

family'? Are you *trying* to give us away?"

"Relax. Nobody knows that 'chiroptera' means bat."

"*I* knew. Jay might know."

Victor looked back at the tree. "You think he could figure out what I meant?"

"No," said Doug, too quickly. He pretended to consider the possibility for a moment, and shook his head. "No. No way. Jay's really rational. Like, scientific. I happen to know for a fact that he doesn't believe in us."

"Seriously? I know you two have been best friends since preschool or whatever. You used to talk about him all the time at the cabins in the summer. Made him sound a lot cooler than he actually is, too, but . . . admit it—you've told him, right?"

"I have not told him. Seriously. You think I want to get him killed?"

"Good," said Victor, "'cause the other vamps really have their panties in a twist lately. Where were you guys yesterday?"

Doug frowned. He didn't know what Victor was talking about, and he was conditioned to be distrustful of situations where he didn't know what some taller and more popular boy was talking about. They always reeked of a setup. At worst they were a kind of entrapment. At best they were like a friendly hand to be yanked away at the most humiliating moment. But these sorts of stunts required an audience, and the boys were alone.

"Me and Jay?" Doug asked.

"You and Stephin David," Victor explained. "We were all supposed to meet and talk about this *Vampire Hunters* thing, didn't he tell you? Everyone's freaked. The signora sent Asa. Borisov sent me. But you and David weren't at his house at five-thirty."

*That's true,* thought Doug. *We were walking around the park.*

"Stephin didn't say anything to me about it. I mean, he mentioned there was concern about the TV show, but he didn't say anything about any meeting. Maybe he forgot."

"Well, he owes me," said Victor. "I want the half hour back that I spent alone with that ghoul Asa. That guy's depressing as boiled steak. And now Borisov's got me watching that lame show for homework so I can report back to him."

"I missed it," Doug admitted, "but they still think I live in San Diego, right?"

"Right. Those fucktards couldn't find a vampire in a phone booth."

Doug nodded. Then he said, "You use a lot of colorful expressions."

"Well, you know . . . we're from Tennessee."

*Look at the two of us,* thought Doug. *Talking like we're old friends.* He sort of wished more people could look at the two of them, but on this side of the gym they were visible only to the crows and a band teacher in a golf cart.

"So what do you and David talk about?" asked Victor.

*Last night we talked about whether I should kill you.*

"Nothing much. He rambles. Tells me about the Civil War. I'm thinking of asking the signora if I can meet with someone else."

"You should definitely go see her. She'll want to talk to

**227**

you about the show. She'll want to talk to you about that other little stunt of yours last night."

Doug started. Victor grinned his corn-fed grin.

"I knew it was you! Superhero powers, white cape and hood? Okay, that's officially cool. You stopped an armed robbery! Up here, Batman!"

Victor held up his hand, and Doug slapped it awkwardly. It was a bit of a miss—too much fingers, not enough palm.

"Lost all your clothes, didn't you? I figured that was why you didn't have your poncho today."

"Well," Doug said, and he gave a glance back at what would plainly have been the drama tree had there not been a gym in the way. "I don't think I'm going to be needing it anymore."

Then Jay emerged from that same direction and approached them—stiffly and with that ridiculous new hairstyle and a look both of apprehension and concentration on his face. Like he was walking toward a bomb while trying to remember a telephone number.

Before Doug's cat had died the previous winter, he'd become all too familiar with a particular smell, a kind of tangy feline musk she'd produced at the vet's, during car rides, or whenever you tried to give her her ear medicine. A fear smell. He was getting a whiff of something like this now. And no wonder, he supposed—Jay looked terrified. Then Victor cleared his throat, and Doug turned his head.

It was altogether possible that Victor was making the smell. Doug inhaled deeply, tried to narrow in on it, but now it was gone. Gone, or else his nose, like a gracious host, was already pretending it hadn't happened at all.

"Sorry to— Are you guys still talking?" Jay asked. "I need to talk to Doug, alone."

Victor glanced from Jay to Doug. His face was inscrutable.

"We're done," he said, and walked off toward the parking lot.

Jay watched him go.

"You haven't told me everything about Victor Bradley," Jay said after a moment. "Have you?"

"There's nothing to tell. What's this about?"

"What's *this* about? What was last night about? What's everything about?"

Doug rolled his eyes. "I'm not really in the mood to discuss the meaning of life right now. I could probably find you some pamphlets in the counselor's office—"

"You know what I'm talking about. You're walking around suddenly like you got a stake up your butt."

Doug glared at Jay's serious face. But then the corner of Jay's mouth twitched and a laugh came coughing out his nose. Doug lost it, too.

"A stake up my— How long have you been waiting to use that?"

"Just since last night."

The boys stared at each other, smiles fading.

"You look better," said Jay. "Did you . . . get some blood last night, or—"

"I think it would be better if I didn't share every little detail of my life now," Doug answered.

"Oh. Well."

The truth, as Doug considered it, was that he had not become a vampire in the Poconos so many weeks ago. Last night had been like a ritual, and he told Jay so. *Now* he was a vampire.

"Huh," said Jay. "Like a dark Bar Mitzvah. Like a . . . well, I was going to say *Bat* Mitzvah, but that's for girls, right?"

"Okay, see? This is what I can't have anymore. I'm different, now. I'm getting a do over on my life. I can't get my do over if you're always around being all . . ."

Jay frowned. "What?"

The bell rang, signaling the end of round one and of lunch in general.

"We'll talk after school," Jay insisted. "Well . . . not right after school, 'cause I'm going over to Cat's and I guess you wouldn't want to . . . but later, maybe? After dark?"

"I have something I have to do after dark," said Doug.

# 26

## FADE TO BLACK

"**THERE,**" Mike said, tilting his head toward the passenger seat where Alan Friendly sat but never taking his eyes off the MoPo across the street. "What about that guy?"

"Maybe," said Alan. He'd seemed distracted all day. Mike wasn't used to being the enthusiastic one.

They were sitting in the front of a windowless white crew van. They'd had to cover the large, red *Vampire Hunters* logo on its side with butcher paper and duct tape. It had been Mike's idea to monitor all the local news stations after they'd relocated to the Philadelphia area, and they'd seen the story about the thwarted holdup. And it had been Mike's idea again to stake out the convenience store.

"Stake out," Alan had repeated, and laughed. "Get it? *Stake* out?"

Mike ignored this. "Look. So we're pretty sure our guy is a kid, right? He's short, he looks young as far as we've been able to tell, he went to a party full of teenagers."

"He may only *look* like a kid," said Alan. "He may be thousands of years old."

Mike sighed. He didn't know what to think anymore. There was something off about this kid, but it would take more than that to get Mike to say the V word. According to the MoPo clerk, the hooded vigilante from the previous night had shown some remarkable strength. According to her he had vanished into thin air. "Turned into mist," Alan had suggested. "Or a bat or rat." If only they could have seen the MoPo's security tapes, but the police had taken them as evidence and they weren't sharing.

"Whatever," said Mike. "Somehow he vanished from the scene, and when he vanishes he leaves his clothes behind. So he must have gotten *to* the MoPo the old-fashioned way: in a car or on a bike or on foot. Otherwise he would have *arrived* naked, too."

Alan nodded. "So . . ."

"So if we're lucky he left a bike or a car behind. Probably a bike, if he's as young as we think. Maybe it's still there and he'll come back for it."

It made sense. Enough sense that the two of them parked themselves in sight of the store on the morning after the robbery. But by now one or both of them had been sitting there for twelve hours and Mike was beginning to feel a little foolish.

Still, there *was* a bike there, locked out front. Customers had come and gone, the MoPo employees had even changed shifts, and the bike remained.

The short man they were watching now had arrived on foot, but he left that way, too. "Okay, that wasn't our guy," said Mike. "But the sun's going down. We wouldn't really expect our guy to come for his bike during the day if—if, you know."

"Right," said Alan.

"Man, what's with you?" said Mike. "I've seen you more excited about traffic school. I've seen you more excited about that Best Lighting award you got for *CatCops*. We're actually close to . . . something here. We're not just harassing Eurotrash like we usually do."

Alan was quiet for a moment. "You can't tell the rest of the crew," he said. "Not yet."

Mike listened to the silence a moment, then exhaled and stared back out at the road. "Shit," he said. "We're canceled."

Alan nodded. "Almost certainly. I have a conference call tomorrow, but . . . yes, we're canceled."

The sky had darkened to the color of a bruise. Across the street, the MoPo's exterior lights flickered on.

"We're under contract for two more shows," Alan added. "So. I'll be pitching something new tomorrow, I'm calling it *America's Top Psychics*. If they go for it, I might be able to bring the whole crew over without much downtime."

A trolley pulled up to the corner just past the MoPo, as

trolleys had done every ten to twenty minutes throughout the day. Someone got off, as someone often had.

"There," Alan whispered. "There."

Mike followed Alan's eyes and was surprised to find the bass suddenly turned up in his chest, his heart pumping out a beat he could feel in his ears. Something had stepped off the trolley, something he'd only seen in grainy black-and-white video.

"There's our Bigfoot," he said.

The boy walked directly to the bike and unlocked it.

"This is bloody amazing," said Alan, switching a handheld camera on and training it on the boy. "What is he, five four? Five five? The Littlest Vampire."

"The littlest . . . person of interest," Mike answered, and started the engine.

"Easy."

The boy wheeled his bike around and started off quickly, glancing back only for a moment at the bright lights of the MoPo. Then he turned onto the road, settled into the bike lane, and pedaled west. Mike pulled out behind him.

"Not too close," said Alan. "Give him room—"

"I've seen the same cop shows you have, Alan. I know what to do."

In fact, following a bicycle in a van turned out to be far more difficult than Mike expected. Their quarry was by no means riding slowly, but he wasn't traveling at thirty-five miles per hour, either. They would pass him, then have to casually crawl below the speed limit to give him a chance to catch up. But then their van would get caught behind traffic or stuck at a light, and the boy would weave through the red and have a two-block head start again.

"I can't see him anymore," said Alan. "You're losing him."

"I'm not losing him."

"Maybe we could just offer him a ride. Lure him with candy. That's how you get kids into vans, isn't it?"

Mike glanced at the camera. "I think we're going to have to edit that last part out."

"Oh, what are they going to do—cancel us?"

Mike closed the gap just in time to see the bicycle turn off the main road and onto smaller, quieter streets. There were no traffic lights here and few cars, but every corner was pinned with a stop sign.

"Won't lose him now," said Alan.

"But this is worse. I have to roll through every stop just to keep up. He's going pretty fast. And it's only a matter of time before he—"

The boy looked over his shoulder, looked right at the van.

"Shit!" said Mike.

"Turn off the lights."

"Then we'll lose him. Look, he's turning east again. Why is he—?"

"Don't do it."

"I have to do it."

Mike turned right and followed, and the rider was already far down the block, just a shining mote in their headlights. He'd picked up speed.

"He's turning again," said Alan.

"He's taking us around the block. Making us prove we're following him. Dammit! Look how fast he's going!"

Now they were hurtling through intersections, bucking over cracked pavement and divots in the road. Alan held the camera in his left hand, braced himself against the dashboard with his right.

"You should really put on your seat belt," said Mike.

"Uh-huh," said Alan, gazing cross-eyed at the camera's bright LCD.

"This is . . . really fast. I couldn't ride a bike this fast."

"Uh-huh. Uh-huh."

"Should we stop?" said Mike with a glance toward Alan. "This is really dangerous. And it's not like he's gonna lead us home at this point."

"It's fantastic footage. Like nothing we've ever had. Something like this could save the show."

"Yeah. Yeah, get a shot of the speedometer." Alan leaned over and focused on the backlit dial. Forty-five . . . forty-seven miles per hour through residential streets. "Good," Mike added, and laughed. "They can use this as evidence at our trial."

The rider swerved past another stop sign and narrowly missed an SUV. Mike slammed on the brakes and the horn at the same time. The SUV honked back, the driver shouting through his tinted glass as he crept through the intersection.

"Aah! Shit! Move!" said Mike.

The SUV finally cleared a path, and Mike urged the grumbling van forward into . . . fog.

"What the hell?" he said. The headlights barely cut into the thick white cloud ahead of them. He switched on the high beams, but that was worse.

"My god," said Alan. "My god. Go, go! We're going to lose him!"

Mike accelerated cautiously. They passed another stop sign. It emerged from the bright mist suddenly, like a magic trick.

"There's no fog down the side streets," Mike muttered. "Did you see? It's only ahead of us."

"That's how we know we're still on his trail. Go faster."

Mike went faster. "Alan?" he said. "Alan, what are we gonna do if we catch him?"

Then a white face came out of the smoke, a bright, hideous face. Mike looked into the eyes. He saw the teeth. The bike and its rider came at them and swerved to their left; and Mike swerved to the right and saw briefly the shapes of houses and an electrical pole and then red.

His head hung forward, tingling, and then it was all dark, like he'd been pulled by his hair into sleep. In a moment the sleep faded and he thought of Alan.

"You okay?" he groaned, and turned his head slowly.

The vampire's face was in the window. Between Mike and the vampire was Alan, slumped like a dead man against the dash. All around was the fog, which was fading and mingling with a turbid black smoke that rose out of the van. The passenger door opened. The night air came in, smelling of tires, and the dome light flickered on, flickered off. In the flickering light he could see the vampire, see *(thank god)* Alan's chest rise and fall. He could see, through a space between the dashboard and the rise and fall of Alan's chest, the vampire reach in and take the camera.

"This is your fault," it said, and was gone.

# 27

## ROLES

**IN THE COMING WEEKS** the school buzzed with speculation about the superhero of Philadelphia. He had stopped a robbery at a MoPo. A few days later, he saved a woman from rape, or worse, at the hands of a group of young men in West Philly. A week after that, another group of men were found badly beaten in Upper Darby. No one knew what they'd done, but they said they'd been assaulted by a short man in a white mask and cape and so were assumed to be up to no good.

Several names were put forth for the character, by the newsreaders and by the populace he presumably served, but the Ghost was the name that stuck. There were no more stories of the hero vanishing, leaving his wardrobe behind like the mark of a clothing-optional Zorro. Stranger stories spread to fill the vacuum, however: the Ghost could fly. The Ghost had a snow-white wolf companion. The Ghost rode an invisible motorcycle.

Then a new piece of information, separate at first, was braided tentatively into the thread: Alan Friendly, host of the Crypt's *Vampire Hunters*, had been in a car accident in West Philadelphia, only blocks from that legendary MoPo, on the night after the robbery. He'd almost died. No one was sure if he'd even walk again. And his organization wouldn't confirm that he'd been in the area hunting vampires, but why else would he be there?

Opinion on the Ghost grew mixed and vague. The woman he'd saved in West Philly changed her story: she'd been in no danger—the boys had been loud and crude and were bothering her, but they'd done nothing to deserve . . . what he did. Now that she thought about it, there had been something weird about the Ghost. His mouth had looked like an animal's.

Fanboys and goths and readers of black-clad paperbacks found their stars suddenly rising. They were the keepers of all the abruptly popular atavistic knowledge that You Needed to Know: the myths and folktales, the talismans and apotropaic spice racks that could keep you safe. *If* he was a vampire. *If* he wasn't a hero. Adam, who was suddenly an admitted scholar of speculative fiction, thought he might even be both, like Blade from the comic books. Jay said he didn't believe in vampires. Doug said little that was not mocking, when he said anything at all.

:

Sejal actually did try out for the school play. Cat was going to anyway—if she didn't land a part she planned to volunteer for crew—and so Sejal imagined quiet, airless evenings alone with Uncle and Auntie Brown while Cat remained at school for rehearsals. Acting would be therapeutic, she thought. Besides, she had seen *West Side Story* before. She already knew the music.

And because she had a nice singing voice, and because the Ardwynne High School drama teacher, on a subconscious level, felt that a girl from India was somehow specially qualified to play a Puerto Rican, Sejal won the role of Maria. The lead role.

"Rock out!" Ophelia said to Sejal as they crowded around the freshly posted cast list. "Look at you!"

"And you got the part of Anita," Sejal replied.

"That means we'll have a lot of scenes together."

"Sorry, Cat," Sophie said. Sophie and Abby had won parts, Cat had not.

"Whatever," Cat answered. "I never get anything. But I talked to Ms. Todd and she wants me to be assistant director."

"That's cool."

"It beats carrying furniture."

"I bet you're happy for Jay," said Sejal. Jay would be playing the shopkeeper.

"Are you guys dating or what?" asked Sophie.

"Yeah," said Ophelia. "You two eating a big bowl of Humpees cereal?"

"God! Shut up!"

"Are you drinking the milk?"

"Fuck you! Shut up! We're in a band together! You can't date your bandmates! Have you learned nothing from VH1?"

Sophie looked worried. "*I* haven't."

The real surprise was Doug. He had never won a part before, either, but now he'd be playing one of the Jets. "Look at that," said Ophelia, pointing to his name.

"Doesn't surprise me," said Cat. "He's been so much more confident lately."

"Not as funny as he used to be," said Ophelia. "But he's been looking a lot better."

"He always looked good," said Abby quietly. It was the first thing she'd said in an hour.

No one spoke. Doug had asked Abby out two days after Labor Day, and they'd been dating for a few weeks. And during those weeks he'd only seemed to grow more charismatic, stronger. Almost good-looking in a weird sort of way. But Abby looked terrible. She'd lost weight; her hair was like burned straw. She always looked like she was getting over the flu. She'd won only a nonspeaking role in *West Side Story*, despite her record with the department.

"Well," said Ophelia with a dip at the knees. "Shall we?"

They gathered their bags and turned back through a cluster of other students who'd come to check the cast list with craned necks and achingly hopeful faces. Like pallbearers the girls carried a slow and heavy silence between them until Sophie turned at the lobby door and, having held it for Ophelia and Sejal, let it fall suddenly against Abby. Abby flinched and caught the push bar against her knuckles.

"Bwah-bwah," Sophie sang with a smile.

Abby kept her head down. "Thanks a lot," she said.

"Jeez. Where's your sense of humor?"

At the parking lot Sophie and Abby walked together to Abby's Volvo, and Ophelia, Cat, and Sejal approached Ophelia's old Mustang convertible. It was just the car for her, flashy in its spotless orange and chrome; but like bangs or a Blondie T-shirt it gave a nod to the graduated classes of beautiful young things that had come before her.

Sejal was flattered by Ophelia's attentions. It was hard not to be. Wasn't the whole world in love with her? Who could help it? But Ophelia was also not her type—she suspected that no one was, right now—and Sejal was determined to be straight with her.

*Be straight with her,* she thought. *I made a joke.*

"Shotgun!" said Sejal.

"I never should have taught you that," said Cat. She climbed into the back as Ophelia put the top down. "What? No! It's gonna be cold."

"It's a convertible," said Ophelia. "You gotta put the top down. Plus, how much longer are we going to be able to do this? Plus it looks better."

"Convertible. The halter top of car parts. You'll shiver all night, but *woo*! *Halter top!*"

The car crawled and stopped, a hiccupping ride down the busy avenue. Cat fiddled with her iPod while Sejal and Ophelia sang songs from the musical:

*"Ev'rything free in America*
*For a small fee in America!"*

They turned off the main drag and into neighborhood streets made precious with coppery leaves and late-day sun.

"You're going to have to kiss a boy," Ophelia taunted. "Tony Petucco's playing Tony." She frowned petulantly. "You gotta wonder if that's how he got the part. I think Ms. Todd's kind of suggestible."

Sejal smiled. "You are going to have to kiss a boy. Adam. He's playing Bernardo."

"Yuck," said Ophelia, pointing her tongue.

Sejal laughed. "Yuck."

*"Boys."*

"Boys."

They dropped into silence. Sejal replayed the previous exchange in her head and cringed.

"I'm going to imagine Adam's someone else," said Ophelia.

"Do you think that will help?"

"I think it'll help a lot. A *lot*. Are you going to imagine Tony's someone else?"

Sejal hummed. "I will . . . think of a boy I liked back home."

"Yeah," said Ophelia, her voice now squeezed into a different shape. An indifferent shape. "That works."

At the Browns' house Cat and Sejal disembarked and said good-bye. They started up the thick grass to the front door.

"Are you mad about the shotgun?" Sejal asked.

"What? 'Course not. Shotgun is sacred. You don't hold that against a person."

"You didn't speak in the car. You only listened to your music."

Cat shrugged. "Just giving you two some privacy."

"I could have done with a little less privacy," said Sejal.

"Sorry. I couldn't tell. If you want her to back off, you might have to ask her to marry you. Drama isn't just an extra-curricular activity for Ophelia, you know? And nothing makes her lose interest faster than when a person likes her more than she likes him. Or her. Whatever."

"Can homosexuals do that here? Marry?"

Cat fiddled with her keys. "Not in this state." They went inside. "You've been a popular girl."

"Yes. I have my theories about that."

She'd been thinking about it more and more. She was possibly being too friendly, for a start. Overdoing it. And she was alone and far from home and from a country that, to Americans, was mostly known for its spicy food and its quiet, not-so-spicy people. And wasn't there a weakness in her? A space that needed filling? So to some people here she was a crippled bird. There are people who pointedly ignore a crippled bird and there are people who want to put it in a shoe box and keep it under a strong lamp in their room, and she was attracting a lot of the latter.

Cat said, "Such as?"

"Oh, nothing. Is Jay coming over tonight to practice the band?"

"Yeah. We might even get some real practicing done now

245

on Mondays, with *Vampire Hunters* off the air."

An idea occurred to Sejal then, a strange idea about vampires and Monday nights with Jay. And Doug, and Doug with Abby. A ridiculous idea.

A completely strange and ridiculous idea.

# 28

# LADIES AND GENTLEMEN

**DOUG PULLED UP** to the gates of Signora Polidori's estate in his father's Prius. It was his birthday, or the anniversary of his birthday. That afternoon he'd taken and passed his driver's test. Victor had driven him.

"This is nice of you and all," Doug told him as they drove to the DMV, "but my dad would have taken me this weekend. You're just going to have to sit in a boring waiting room while I take the test in *your* car."

"It's nothing," said Victor, his eyes on the snaking road. "I wanted a chance to talk away from school."

"Official club business?"

"Heh." Victor laughed, but it sounded to Doug like no more than a polite social noise. Victor was in a serious mood.

"So how are things going with you? I've seen you around with Abby Dawes."

"We're dating."

"Dating . . ." Victor intoned, as if it wasn't the word he'd have used.

"What?"

"Nothing. And she's doing good? What does she think about it? I mean, how much do you think she understands—"

"She thinks we've been messing around. That's all. Boy, you think I've been blabbing to everyone, don't you?"

"No—"

"Abby knows nothing, Jay knows nothing. Everyone's safe."

"I know. Forget it," Victor said, waving his hand in the air. "That wasn't what I was getting at. I just wanted to know how things were going."

"They're going good."

Victor nodded, and then they were silent until the next red light. "You haven't been having any problems dealing with people?"

"You mean recently?" Problems Dealing with People had actually been sort of a major theme of Doug's life from the fourth through the tenth grades, but lately there had been nothing but improvement. Except with Sejal, he supposed. And Jay. "No. Have you?"

Victor frowned. "Everyone's saying I'm acting different. I think *they're* acting different. They're all being stupid. Fucker!" he shouted at a sedan that had merged a little too close. He tapped the brakes and the three lemon-yellow pine trees hanging from the rearview mirror tangled their lines. "God, I hate being in cars now. Maybe while you're getting your license I can turn mine in."

They parked in the DMV lot and walked up to that squat, joyless building.

"It's like . . . you know how people look at you when they know they've got more money than you?" asked Victor. Doug didn't, really, but he kept that to himself. "I catch myself looking at normal people like that, now. Like I know they're gonna be forgotten, and I'm not. We're gonna live forever—do you realize that?"

"Are you just figuring this out?" said Doug. "We're always going to be as we are, right now."

Victor stared at his feet. "I guess I've *always* felt that way. But now it's true."

Doug left him reading magazines in a room where all the stiff plastic chairs had been bolted in rows into the floor. He took his driving test, screwed up the parallel parking section a little, but the administrator let him retry it. He took his paperwork to the license photographer and felt a moment of panic. What if the license came back and he wasn't there? But a half hour later he left the DMV with a little rectangle of plastic with his picture on it, and it felt like he'd gotten away with something. He wasn't really a year older.

Nor a year wiser, maybe. Now, outside the gates of the Polidori estate, he thought about what Victor had been trying to tell him. Doug recently had two different people suggest he wasn't as nice a guy as he could be. You had to consider each source, of course. Jay was like a little kid—he didn't understand how the world worked. It didn't do him any good to be so thin-skinned. And Sejal . . . Sejal hadn't been in America long. She'd learn.

He was just being funny. On television people insulted each other all the time. For laughs. Humor made the world a better place. Clever insults were the basis of all humor.

No, he realized with sudden clarity. Not insults. *Control.* Control was the basis of all humor. Even at its most innocent, what was a joke or a clever comment if not a way to take control? To become King of the Moment.

People like him—the unbeautiful, the less popular—were almost inhuman in some people's eyes. They were a kind of pitiful monster, an aberration, a hunchback. You made eye contact only by accident and then you turned quickly away. The word "geek" had once only referred to a circus freak, hadn't it? A carny who performed revolting acts for a paying audience. Was it so different now? See! him bite the head off a live chicken. Behold! as he plays Dungeons & Dragons at a sleepover.

Wasn't this how they always tried to compensate? To overcome a girl's disgust or another boy's contempt and make them laugh despite themselves was to take some small measure of control. No wonder the popular, good-looking kids were so seldom funny. They didn't have to be. Why else would people find it so hilarious to see some short kid's textbook stolen, held high above his head, out of reach? It wasn't funny—it was pure control. Insult comedy minus the comedy.

*So humor is a kind of weakness,* Doug thought as he approached the house. He couldn't understand why he'd never seen it before. Enough jokes, then. He was going to become the least funny person he knew.

The scent of cloves mixed with an oddly nostalgic smell of wet leaves. Absinthe was sitting on the front steps of the Polidori house, smoking a cigarette. She knit her brow at him as he approached.

"Hey," said Doug.

"Oh," said Absinthe. "It's you. Douglas."

"Yeah."

"You look different."

"So I've been told."

They studied each other for a second.

"It's fortunate I ran into you," said Doug. "I was going to leave your clothes with Cassiopeia." He held out the neat little pile.

"That *is* fortunate," Absinthe agreed. "Mama Cass probably would have had Asa burn them in the backyard."

Doug couldn't tell if he was supposed to laugh. He pushed a noncommittal little puff of air through his nose and sat down on the step. "Are you having . . . problems with the signora?"

"Problems?" said Absinthe. "No. No, we don't have any problems. I'm learning so much, thank god I can command rats now—that's going right on my college applications."

"You can command rats?"

"Yeah. All I ever want to do is command them the hell away from me."

Doug nodded, and looked out of the corner of his eyes at her breasts. Deep in his mind there was a space like a basement where he kept ideas he'd used once or twice but had mostly forgotten. Self-improving ideas, like exercise equipment, gathering dust. One of these was the realization that sexy people were not always, themselves, hypersexual, that just because Doug could only think of sex—sexy, hot nude intercourse sex—when he looked at Absinthe didn't mean that it was on her mind at all. There was probably no clever conversational password that could get her making out with him at this moment. Probably.

"I can make fog," he said.

"Hey, look, so can I," said Absinthe. She took a drag and blew a plume through her plum lips. It smelled like Christmas.

Doug laughed. "That's not what I meant. I—"

"Do you like your tutor guy? Mr. David whatever?"

"Not really."

"I can't stand this anymore," said Absinthe. "I hate her! It's like, I get to hang out with this totally hot two hundred-year-old vamp and she's just like my mom. Worse, even—at least my mom will die someday."

Doug managed to say, "What's wrong with—" before she started up again.

"I mean, what's the point of being a vampire if everything is 'don't do this' and 'I forbid you to do that'? She's even got the nerve to insult my clothes, like her *Masterpiece Theatre* wardrobe hasn't been out of fashion for, like, *ever*. I'm all, like, 'You should talk. Nice empire waist. I bet you were the belle of the Industrial Revolution, bitch.'"

Absinthe sighed.

"I totally should have said that."

"I like your clothes," said Doug.

"Jesus. Of course you do. You're just another horndog boy. But Madam Polidori says I look like a hooker, and I say, no, I look like a vampire, so she says I look like a vampire hooker. Then she shows me a photo of this vampire hooker she knows in New Orleans and we're wearing the same top."

*Vampire hooker*, thought Doug.

"And all the time she—she wants me to . . ." Absinthe quailed, but recovered quickly. "Did you know that Asa really isn't a vampire? He's a . . . thrall. It's so fucked up."

"She introduced him to me that way. As her thrall."

"Yeah, but do you know what it means? It means she almost made him a vampire, but she didn't give him enough blood. She just gives him a tiny bit at a time, so he's addicted. It means he's her slave. He can never leave—he has to do whatever she says. What kind of person does that to someone?" Her face pruned. "Shit! I'm in such shit," she said, and she folded up against her knees.

Doug put his arm around her as he'd seen people do on television, but she only seemed to stiffen and lean away. Like the way an unhappy baby could almost pitch herself backward out of your awkward clutches. He let her go as she got to her feet. She turned and hugged her arms, though Doug knew she could not possibly be cold.

"I told my boyfriend. Almost right away I told him. He was cool with it. Well, not so cool with the whole getting-ravished-by-a-vampire thing, but . . . I made it sound like I hadn't been into it. Like it was more of a . . . rape or whatever."

"Uh-huh," said Doug. *Where was this going?*

"I guess he . . . I guess he really never was okay with it. He started making all these little comments, not much at first, but then all the time, and . . . I finally got tired of it and dumped him."

She dropped her cigarette butt and ground it out with her toe.

"But then people started asking me these questions, everyone's looking at me different, and I know he's been talking about me . . ." She raised her face and pinched her eyes shut. "God, Travis! Don't you know I have to kill you? Don't you know you're making me?"

"Elizabeth?" said a voice behind Doug, and he turned to see Cassiopeia Polidori stepping onto the porch.

"Oh, perfect," Absinthe said, her eyes shining. "Perfect timing."

"Hello, Douglas," said the signora. "You are welcome inside. Elizabeth, why don't you come back in—"

"Don't look at me," said Absinthe, and then her whole body exhaled and was only mist, a lewd column that shed its clothes and lost its shape and rose into the sky.

Doug looked at the pile of clothes, next to the other pile of clothes.

"You can't keep transmogrifying away from your problems, young lady," Cassiopeia called to the vapor as it drifted over the trees. She watched, for several beats after it had vanished from sight, then turned as if suddenly remembering that Doug was also there. "Douglas. This is a surprise. Leave the clothes. Asa will see to them." Doug followed her inside.

They walked through the parched, candlelit hall. "You're

looking well," said Cassiopeia. "I can't confess to agree with your recent flair for vigilantism, but I daresay it agrees with you."

"You shouldn't believe everything you've been hearing about me," said Doug.

"Hm. So I suppose you *don't* have an invisible motorcycle? What a disappointment—I was rather looking forward to not seeing it."

They settled in the drawing room near the harpsichord, Doug on an uncomfortable chair and Signora Polidori on what Doug assumed was an uncomfortable sofa. He thought they should be drinking tea and remarking on the latest society gossip and news from London and whenever would Mr. Fucklesby settle down and marry? A moment later Asa arrived with the tea.

He glanced briefly at Doug with eyes that, while not exactly approving, no longer carried the hint that Doug was something to be scraped from his heel. So that was something. Doug thought about what Absinthe had said. If true, it was Doug who was the superior being—Asa probably wished he were him.

"Mr. David tells me that you did not attend your last appointment with him," said Cassiopeia after Asa withdrew. "And that he's heard naught from you since. Milk?"

"Uh, no," said Doug, looking down at the tea.

"Sugar?"

"No. Thanks. So . . . I didn't feel I was learning with him. And I didn't like his attitude, to be honest."

"Mr. David, despite his many fine qualities, could have a more winning disposition," Cassiopeia admitted.

"Right. Well, I heard from Victor that there was supposed

to be some big meeting a few weeks ago. Stephin forgot about it, or just blew it off. I dunno."

"And I have not pursued the matter because I believe the issue at heart has been . . . settled? The television show?"

Doug allowed a beat to pass before speaking. "Let's just say I took care of it," he said. It was something else that happened on TV a lot, these kinds of enigmatic statements. *They were probably a kind of story shorthand,* thought Doug. It was all that needed to be said, because the viewer already knew the details, or wasn't meant to yet. *It wasn't going to work in real life,* he reasoned. *Nobody just let you say a thing like that without explaining yourself.* But here, now, was Cassiopeia's curt nod, and then silence. *Don't you want to know what I did?* thought Doug. *Don't you want to know how I did it?* He had a sense that he was moments from being dismissed. That the signora would stand, and Doug would have to stand, and then Asa would come from wherever Asa came from to guide Doug through such uncharted territory as the stair hall and the foyer.

He didn't want to leave. He was kin to women like this. Why had he ever thought vampires smelled bad to one another? Here he was in a vampire's chambers, and he couldn't smell a thing. The world outside smelled like a farm.

"Have you found out anything about the mystery vampire?" asked Doug quickly. "The one that made . . . all us guys."

Cassiopeia shifted in her seat. "We are investigating. It's no fox hunt. It can be a long and delicate process, finding a fellow cousin."

"Oh, right," said Doug. "Obviously. I didn't expect you would have found her yet, it's just Stephin thought I ought to try to learn more—"

"I don't suppose you have any further details about your benefactor you may have neglected to mention . . . ?"

"No. Like I said before, it was dark. I didn't get that good a look at her."

Cassiopeia pursed her lips. "It would seem no one did. Douglas, may I be frank? When one considers young Victor and Evan and Danny, the inescapable conclusion one reaches is that our mysterious stranger has a . . . type. One positively leaps to this conclusion. Do you take my meaning?"

"I'm not sure. You're being awfully subtle."

"Yes. Very good. Most of our kind develop 'types,' Douglas. The older we get, the more distasteful we find the notion of supping on anything but our ideal. Like . . . a restaurant 'regular' who always orders 'the usual'. Yes?"

Doug didn't like where this was heading. He needed a change of subject.

"Perhaps we search out subjects that remind us of first loves. Or past enemies, punishing some former rival again and again," Cassiopeia continued, though she made it clear by her tone that she found this latter habit offensive. "Others simply have a physical preference. I have known a hundred kinsmen, and we are all the same in this regard. All but our Mr. David, who has always claimed a more egalitarian lack of preference. But our Mr. David is given to invention."

"You mean he's a liar?"

"A dreadful liar." Cassiopeia smiled sweetly. "Quite

unapologetic about it. To hear him tell it, he has been in the night tide reborn so many different ways. Bitten by a despondent New York banker in October 1929. Or in Reconstruction South. During five distinct wars . . . at the culmination of the Boston Tea Party . . . whilst a cast member in the original touring production of *Faust*."

Doug frowned at his hands. "He told me he'd been made in the Civil War." He remembered Stephin's narrative and felt like a chump. *Tom North? Oh, and let me guess—he was shot by Dick South?*

"It is a favorite of his. Mayhap it's even true! Something has to be. But to return to my earlier point, Douglas: it would be passing strange that our cousin should have ennobled the three boys and also you. And so soon after Victor!" She laughed airily. "Is this woman trying to assemble a baseball team?"

"We could play night games," Doug said, because he was nervous. *I could be batboy.*

"Is there anything you'd like to tell me about your benefactor, Douglas? Is there anything you'd like to tell me about Victor?"

"I don't know what you're talking about. Part of the reason . . . part of the reason I'm here is because Victor and I have been talking about the vampire who made us." Doug saw Cassiopeia flinch at the word "vampire," but he pressed on, seeing an opening. "I told Victor that I was going to try to find out more about her, and he wanted me to tell him everything I learned. He wants to find her." This wasn't the least bit true. Doug and Victor had been talking more and more at school, even nodding to each other in the halls, but in fact the hot mystery vampire never came up. "He keeps bugging me about it. Like . . . he knows I'm smarter, so he figures I'll have better luck figuring out who she is. It's like I'm doing his homework for him." He forced himself to take a sip of his tea. *Wait for it,* thought Doug. *Don't be too obvious.*

"Hm. I suppose we all want to discover her."

"I guess. I mean, I'm curious, but it's all he talks about."

"And has he indicated why he's so keen to make contact?"

It was just what Doug hoped she'd ask, and he nearly pounced out of his skin. "You know . . . I didn't think so, but . . . a while ago, like weeks ago, he mentioned this movie he'd seen where a vampire—an ennobled person, I mean—turned normal after killing his . . . ennobler."

Cassiopeia put her teacup very firmly down on the table. Not on its saucer. Not on a coaster, even.

"I'm sure it's nothing," Doug added. "I wouldn't want to get him in trouble or anything. It probably doesn't even work, right? Killing your maker? I told him you'd probably have to kill the head of the family or something—and, besides, don't do it. I said."

Cassiopeia stood. So that was it. "I must beg your forgiveness, Douglas. There is a matter that needs attending." Doug stood as she passed him, and he turned to see Asa suddenly at his shoulder like Droopy Dawg, like you'd only just wrapped him up in chains and nailed him inside a crate and shipped him to Albuquerque but, surprise! there was Asa.

"Does it work, though?" Doug asked Cassiopeia. "If it does, I won't tell Victor 'cause, hell, who wants to encourage him, right? But if it doesn't, I can get the whole stupid idea out of his—"

"Of course it does not work. I bid you good night and good hunting." With that Signora Polidori swept out of the room.

Doug looked at Asa. Asa looked back, not so much at Doug as at the empty Doug-shaped space he'd soon be leaving in their drawing room.

"If young master would—"

"Yeah, yeah."

They walked the familiar path back to the front door, Doug all the while staring out of the corner of his eye at Asa's face, smelling his strange smell. He remembered, suddenly, the back lot of a café near Jay's house. It was one of those unwanted places, free from adult supervision, where you were permitted the pleasure of doing nothing. He and Jay and Stuart had spent a lot of time there in middle school. Asa smelled like the Dumpster in that back lot, the surprisingly sweet smell of pastries slowly melting into flies' nests and poison. It didn't seem like the sort of thing you told a person, but it made Doug feel kindly toward him.

"You know, um . . . Absinthe told me about your and Cassiopeia's . . . relationship," Doug said, and Asa paused at the door. "I think it's really . . . Well. I wouldn't do that to a person, personally."

Asa's long, bell face was absolutely still and silent.

"I just wanted you to know that I understand . . . It must be really hard, your . . . situation. And I just wanted to . . . say that." Asa opened the great door and stood to one side. *Fine,* thought Doug. He stepped out onto the front stairs and into the night air.

"Young master," said Asa behind him.

Doug turned. Asa was still standing in the doorframe, blue-skinned against the warm embers of the hall behind him. Silhouetted like this, Doug could just barely make out a jagged smile in the corner of Asa's lips, like a crack in his bell.

"My mistress misspoke. It works," he said, and closed the door.

# 29

## THE UNDYED

**OPHELIA HOSTED** a hair-dyeing party for all the girls playing Puerto Ricans. It was something of a magnanimous gesture, after fighting tooth and nail for the right to keep her brown-sugar hair and pink bangs. Her family had Puerto Rican friends in New York, she argued—real Puerto Rican New Yorkers—and they didn't all have black hair. But Samantha Todd, the theater director, was adamant—now that she'd cast Sejal in the leading role she wanted the other girls to match.

Mostly they watched the Natalie Wood *West Side Story* and ate. Ophelia, Sophie, Jenny Underwood, Emily Purvis, and Jordan Belledin needed to dye their hair, but of course Sejal didn't.

And Abby was playing a white girl, essentially an extra. And Cat was just there to assistant direct the whole thing.

"I can deal with the hair," said Jordan as Cat picked across her scalp, "but are we really going to wear dark makeup? Isn't that supposed to be offensive or something?"

"Offensive?" said Sejal.

"I don't mean offensive to have dark skin," Jordan assured her, though it hadn't occurred to Sejal to consider this until she was assured not to. "I mean, it's blackface, right? I think people get really upset if you wear blackface."

"This'll be brown face," said Sophie. "And brown neck."

"And arms," said Emily.

"You're so lucky," Jordan told Sejal. "You don't have to change anything."

"Good thing we're not doing *Grease*." Ophelia laughed.

The girls fell silent. Sejal supposed they were thinking the same thing she was: If they were doing *Grease*, she wouldn't be playing the lead.

"Crap, that's my phone," said Cat. "I have goopy gloves."

Ophelia fished the phone from Cat's boxy velvet purse and sang, "It's Ja-ay."

"Put it up to my ear. Hey, Jay! No, I'm at Ophelia's. A bunch of us girls are here, trimming each other's bushes."

A couple of girls gave scandalized shrieks, and everyone laughed except Emily, whom Sejal had come to think took everything a little too seriously. "Aah! Tell him we're not really, Cat!" Emily said. "He'll spread it around school."

"Shave a lightning bolt in mine!" shouted Ophelia.

"He knows when Cat's joking," Sejal told Emily. "He'll not spread it around."

"He'll tell Doug, maybe," Emily whimpered.

"So what if he does?" said Abby. "Doug doesn't care about your business."

Silence, again, apart from Cat's brassy laugh—Jay must have said something funny. She looked abruptly startled, chastened, as if she'd just remembered she was in church and surrounded by sober, serious people. "It just got really quiet here," she said into the phone.

*What did the other girls think when they heard his name?* wondered Sejal. Surely they couldn't be having the same thoughts as she. It really was a ridiculous idea. The way Doug had been acting, and Abby's decline, and the stories from that store robbery and the bat that night—you didn't just put all those pieces together any way you pleased. They had their own order, or lack of order. And although these pieces were all cut from Western cloth, she knew how it would sound to American ears if she, the Indian girl, started talking about vampires. That was the gaudy image she was embroidering from all these loose threads, wasn't it? That Doug was a vampire? It was the Niravam, certainly. She had to stop taking it—it only made her worse. Poor Indian girl—her head is full of superstitious hoodoo. It's a culture of confusion—too many gods, all those arms—what do you expect?

"Can I talk to you a minute, Abby?" asked Emily. *"In private,"* she added in the least private tone possible. It was discreet like a kazoo was discreet. The two girls rose and went off in search of some quiet corner.

"I don't know. Some drama," Cat told Jay. "We're a dramatic people."

"Okay, so what's the deal with Doug Lee?" said Ophelia. Sejal imagined that a less brazen version of this question might at that very moment been posed to Abby in another part of the house, but Ophelia's seemed to be directed primarily at Sejal.

"I know, right?" said Jordan as Cat tucked the last of her slick hair under a plastic grocery bag. "So creepy. My uncle pulled this really weird Jekyll and Hyde thing a few years ago, and that turned out to be a stroke."

"Why are you looking at me?" Sejal asked Ophelia. "You have known him longer."

"Yeah, but I've only been paying attention to him as long as you have. And he has a huge crush on you, so maybe you got to know him. For a while some people thought you might like *him*, too."

*So we're not just talking about Doug*, thought Sejal. "Maybe you should shout your questions louder," she said, "so Jay can hear. So Abby can hear."

"Ophelia wants to know what's up with Doug," Cat said to Jay. Ophelia winced. Cat leaned away from the phone. "Jay says nothing's wrong with Doug, but he's saying it in this weird way he gets whenever he's lying. Like he's talking in all caps. What? No, I'm just telling them what you said."

"This is gonna sound all weird," said Sophie, "and if you tell anyone I said so I'll kick your ass, but . . . like, I know you said you thought he was looking better, 'Felia, but does anyone think he actually looks . . . good? Like not *good* good, but . . . like you see some eggplant and you actually feel like trying it even though eggplant makes you throw up."

"I know what you're saying," said Jordan. "I'll admit it. It's like he got some kind of Guido body spray and it actually works like the commercials say it does."

"Do you think they've . . . you know," asked Carrie. "Do you think he took her virginity?"

"Ha!" said Ophelia. "He's not a time traveler."

Cat had by then hung up. "Jay says he and Doug haven't hung out much lately, but . . . he thinks it all has to do with Doug wanting to go with Sejal and her saying no. Doug thinks she led him on—sorry, Sejal, I don't think you did. Maybe he's just bitter or depressed or something."

"I need a glass of water," said Sejal. "Does anyone want a glass of water?" No one did. "Excuse me."

She didn't know this house well, and at the bottom of the staircase she veered away from the sibilant whispers of Abby and Emily ("Jodi thinks so, too," Emily was saying. "She called him evil . . .") and down one hall, past a loo, and into a laundry room.

"Damn," she whispered. She turned and found Ophelia blocking the hall.

"Hi," said Ophelia. "Here." Then she leaned forward, her still-sugary-brown locks breezing fragrantly past Sejal's nose, and switched on the dryer. The empty tumble made the small, slightly chilly room inexplicably more inviting. Dapples of warm light like goldfish appeared on the blue moonlit wall behind the dryer. Ophelia half closed the door. No one would hear them speak.

"I didn't lead Doug on," Sejal said. "I thought I might grow to like him, isn't it? When I realized my mistake, I stopped it."

"I'm sorry."

"What I did was proper. I do not mean to lead *anyone* on."

"I believe you. I'm sorry."

They paused. Sejal listened to the warm, snoring dryer.

"I'm trying to learn to be a better person," Sejal said. "A stronger person."

"You're good. You're strong."

"I'm not," Sejal insisted. "I have the Google. Did you know that?"

"Oh," said Ophelia, stepping back. "That internet disease?"

"It's not contagious."

"Sorry."

"It makes you forget what's important. I lost track of myself for a while. I forgot who I was. You can do terrible things when you don't know who you are, *na*?"

Ophelia shifted from one foot to the other. She shrugged slightly.

"I became a ghost, and I only cared about other ghosts. I was not available to people at school, on the street . . . I wasn't there. But move your mouse like on a Ouija board and you could speak with me. You could conjure me up. I lost every one of my real friends, but I had a box full of trolls and demons, like Pandora."

"You don't have to tell me all this if you don't want to," Ophelia whispered.

"No, I don't," Sejal said. "That's true. Will you let me?"

Now that she'd started, she was impatient to get it off her chest, finally. The story of it all stuck to her like wet clothes.

A second passed, then Ophelia nodded.

"There was this girl," Sejal continued. "A girl from my neighborhood, one of the only ones to follow me onto the web. One of the only kids I still talked to who knew me in real life. Maybe that was part of it . . . She had a blog. She posted videos, bad poetry. And we *haunted* this poor girl. Me and the other ghosts. They were awful to her, and I was awful. We posted terrible comments, things I would never say in real life. Because I only cared for the people online and for what they thought of me—and when I was mean, I was funny, and when I was funny, I could make them laugh out loud."

Ophelia was shaking her head. "Lots of people are meaner on the internet."

"And those people will have to deal with what they've been. Or they won't, I don't know. But listen: This girl, Chitra, she posted a video, singing and playing the ukulele. Because pretty girls playing the ukulele was a thing then. And this girl . . . this poor stupid girl always left the comments on."

"What did you say to her?"

"I wrote that she had made me pukelele with her bad singing. I—I and the other commenters suggested maybe she wasn't really pretty enough for the pretty girls-with-ukuleles meme."

"God."

"Yes." Sejal nodded. "She singled me out—I was the only one who actually knew her. 'Why was I being so mean?' I had my own blog pages full of posts and videos and hundreds of comments, good and bad. Some terribly bad. In the outside world I felt numb and half dead, but then I could look at my hit counter and read the comments, and every little vicious word was like a paper cut that got my heart beating again. And this fat ukulele player wanted to know why I was being so mean?"

"Um . . ."

"I became something awful. I made personal attacks. I revealed all her crushes and told all her embarrassing secrets. And because I never knew her all *that* well, I ran out of secrets fast and began pinning her name to some of my own. Even the trolls started telling me to back off, in their way. They claimed the thread had gotten stale and I was getting boring and, besides, Chitra hadn't said a word in days. She hadn't posted in days because she'd tried to kill herself."

"W-what?" said Ophelia. She covered her mouth with her hands.

"When I found out I just . . . I broke it off with the real world. Entirely. It could not touch me. When my mother came home that night, she found me sitting in front of my own video blog, watching myself watching myself. Like I was trying to fold right up into one single electron. My parents got me help. When Chitra's parents found out my part in the whole thing, they tried to bring me up on charges, but I hadn't done anything against the law. But I got help. I got better. That was the best I could do for them, for Chitra. I'm lucky in that way—I had this horrid event to tell me I was not the sort of girl I thought I was, and now I have made the decision to be good. I don't believe most people think to make this decision, you know?"

"Uh-huh."

Silence.

"I thought I saw something familiar in Doug, but . . . I'm trying to be good, and I don't need any more friends who are not also trying."

"Yeah."

Silence.

"Also I think Doug is a vampire."

"Um." Ophelia frowned. "You mean, like, a metaphorical vampire?"

"No, the regular kind."

Silence.

"So, watch out for that," said Sejal. "I'm going to go," she added, and waited for Ophelia to let her out of the laundry room.

:

Cat tried to talk her into staying, or at least accepting a ride home, but Sejal told her she'd prefer to walk. It wasn't even a kilometer, and the streets were sort of familiar. Jay lived nearby.

She supposed Ophelia would tell everyone that she had the Google. And maybe that she thought Doug was a vampire. *Well, good,* she thought as she pulled her coat closer and started down the hill. *Fine. What better way to kick-start this new, improved Sejal—this strong girl who's good and who knows her own mind and doesn't care what other people think?* She shuddered and pulled her coat closer still.

These neighborhoods looked fake at night. In the dim lamplight one could see only a scant spill of stars, and the colors and details of the lawns and houses flattened out and gave the impression of huge miniatures. And now there was a thickening fog at the bottom of the hill. It reminded Sejal of the fogging of distant objects in some video games. There was not enough processing power to render the bottom of the hill. The bottom of the hill would not exist until she got there.

There was a rustling behind her, and then a rustling to one side as she turned to look, and then it was down the hill and gone. Sejal considered suddenly the wisdom of declaring someone a vampire and then taking a walk, alone, at night. Had she never seen a movie? Did she not understand how these things worked? She comforted herself, however, with the insight that the movie would not kill off the well-meaning foreign exchange student with the comical internet addiction. Sejal wouldn't be the main character, the hero—not in an American movie—but she might be the best friend or the comic relief or the one you think is dead but turns out to be all right in the end. She wondered who the main character in her life was.

When she finally saw the person standing at the bottom of the hill, she was almost on top of him. Given more warning she might have nonchalantly crossed the street, but now she could do nothing but pass him by. Or else stop, turn, walk or run, risk embarrassment and offense against what was probably just a man walking his dog. A short man, about Doug's height. No dog. A man staring right at her.

Not Doug. This man was a little leaner and older. Just a man. Who seemed to be trying to hoist his careworn features into an unpracticed smile.

"Hello," said the man.

"Hello." Sejal smiled briefly, then dipped her head as she passed.

"A quiet night," the man replied, and kept pace with her, though whether he was now following her or merely continuing on his way, she couldn't tell.

"Mmm."

"You know, when I was your age, one didn't often see a girl walking alone at night. You would be tempted to draw conclusions about such a girl. You would say she was no better than she should be."

This seemed like an insult, something that begged for an answer, though maybe it was just harmless chitchat. *Times have changed—what a world*. She stole a glance at the little man out of the corner of her eye: a dark, long-sleeved shirt over a white tee. Gray wool pants. That was all, despite the chill. Sejal suddenly wondered if this man was in need. Perhaps he only meant to ask for spare change.

"I do not think they have the sort of girls you're talking about in a neighborhood such as this," she said. "Is your . . . house nearby?"

"No. I have two homes, but one is in the country, and one is in the city."

"Like the mice," said Sejal, "in the fable." It was a puerile thing to say, but she always felt more at ease when she pretended to be at ease.

"Yes," said the man. "Very good. I hadn't thought of that in ages. I'm like a mouse that flies from city to country, country to city. But I have no houses in the rarified half life that is the suburb. I've only been spending some time here, observing. We're both far from home, I think."

"No, my home is close. Very close," she added, though it was still many blocks away.

"Then you'll permit me to escort a young lady just a little bit farther. To her home, or to the place that serves as home for now. Am I right?" His sleeve brushed her coat, and she sensed if not felt it through three layers of clothes—a cold sting. "I think we have this in common: we'd both like to go home but we have now only houses. I have a house in the Poconos, but it's not my home. I have a house in West Philadelphia, next to Clark Park—do you know it?—but it is not my home either."

Sejal was surprised to find that Clark Park did spark some glimmer of recognition in her. A name like that, once heard, could never be entirely forgotten. Had Cat mentioned it?

They turned a corner. The Browns' house grew closer, but was still achingly far away.

"I think I've heard of the Clark Park," Sejal said. "I cannot remember why. Is it nice?"

"It's perfectly nice. You should visit. I expect you will."

"Well, this is me," said Sejal, stopping in front of a well-lit flagstone house with THE HOLSTEINS painted on the mailbox.

The man stopped a few feet off and watched her. Could body language be mistranslated? What was expressed on his face as a smile clearly meant something different where he came from.

"You have nothing to fear from me, young lady. Not directly. You're not my type."

Sejal tried to tell him that she just really needed to get inside and was dimly surprised to find she slurred her speech.

**273**

She was so tired, in a moment, and the fog was thicker than ever.

"Do you know something?" said the man, and it was like the hum of a voice that you hear a moment before waking. "I'm going to tell you everything. I'm going to explain it all. And you won't remember a bit of it until it's much too late."

# 30

## CURTAINS

**THIS WAS HOW** Doug's dates with Abby went: they'd rent a movie or go see one. Doug had half watched the first fifteen minutes of a number of movies from the back rows of theaters or from the tweed cushions of his great accomplice, the Lee basement sofa. He'd initiate some kissing, and Abby would respond willingly at first, but eventually return to the movie, as if anyone could possibly care what Matthew McConaughey was doing. He'd have to keep restarting things, keeping both of them on track. Then he'd feel a breast, and she'd guide his hand away, and he'd wait what seemed like the requisite amount of time before he could do it again. She'd let his hands be on the second try, sometimes the third, but get squeamish when he went under her shirt, so he'd go back to just kissing, as if they both didn't know what was going to happen. Once he was under her shirt he'd hike it up a bit, maybe feel her ass, and if the movie wasn't too short he'd finally get to the business of biting her neck and sucking out a half pint of blood before the closing credits.

At her front door, or his, they'd have a kind of coded conversation about how Doug always rushed every evening to sex. He didn't know how to tell her they'd hardly had any. If he was leaving Abby's house she might wonder aloud why she always gave him what he wanted, they should be more careful, she couldn't vouch for his safety if her parents ever caught them. Doug wondered how her parents would react if they ever caught him doing what he was *really* doing to her. In monster movies there were usually torches.

She was a little overweight. He reminded himself constantly that extra weight meant extra blood, that this was a good thing. Swimsuit girls would be like light snacks. They'd be small Diet Cokes. He'd hear himself noisily sucking air after the third date.

It was confusing to see Abby at school, or after school rehearsing the fall musical. Her proper context was now in basements and back rows and humid media rooms. What was she doing here, so fully inflated and out in the world? Why did she sit in the theater seat next to his in this school auditorium, so far from the back row and so near these prying eyes? What was she doing talking to that other guy?

:

Onstage, Sejal sang with Tony Petucco. Cat stopped them and reminded Tony of a crucial bit of blocking he'd missed, and they began again from "Somewhere, We'll find a new way of living, We'll find a way of forgiving." Tony Petucco had certainly not been cast because he could sing or act or dance in any fashion that did not give the impression he was plagued by invisible insects. He more than once even failed to respond when another actor called him by his character's name. Which was also Tony. He *did* look good in a T-shirt. It was much discussed.

In scenes like this, when facing the audience, Sejal's eyes sought out Cat. Cat was her anchor. When Maria closed her eyes, it was Cat's face in bright negative on the insides of Sejal's eyelids.

There had been no fallout from her conversation with Ophelia that night. Ophelia was being discreet or hadn't found the details worth sharing or she was holding them in reserve, waiting until they could be used to greatest purpose.

Now Sejal and Ophelia were onstage together, rehearsing their big scene, their big song. Cat rose from her seat at the behest of the director and left the room on some errand. Most of the rest of the cast was scattered around the theater, in the aisles, lobby, or backstage. Talking quietly to each other, flirting, consoling one another at the end of a long school day with electrically charged rounds of truth or dare and surprisingly smutty neck rubs. Sejal sought out a new face, an anchor in the audience, and she stammered through a line as her eyes fell on the only person who was at that moment staring straight back at her.

:

She had a beautiful voice, Sejal. Doug remembered Abby having a good voice, too, but lately it was scratchy. Hoarse. She

**277**

wasn't taking good enough care of herself. If you didn't take care of yourself, who would?

He was still mad at Sejal for leading him on, then rejecting him, but he sort of admired her for it as well. You couldn't just give it away like Abby did. Not if you had any morals. Not if you had any self-respect.

"God, take a picture," said Abby as she slid back into the seat next to Doug's. "It'll last longer."

"Take a picture of what?"

"You know what."

"No, I really don't—that's why I asked. You see how that works?"

"If you had a picture, you could spank off to her later. That's the best you'll ever do, you know—her picture and your right hand. She's not interested."

"If you're talking about Sejal," said Doug, "I think you'll find you don't know her any better than I do."

"I know what she really thinks about you."

Doug struggled to get a grip on himself. It wouldn't do to let her think he cared.

"Look, I don't know what we're even fighting about. I was looking at the stage. There are people on it. Singing. I don't know where I picked this up, but I was under the impression that you were supposed to look at people when they sing on a stage. It's good manners. You don't see me picking fights over you talking to that guy over there for ten minutes."

"Who, Kevin? We've been friends since kindergarten. I can't talk to Kevin?"

"You can. That's my point. I didn't throw a hissy over you

talking to that guy, but I can't watch a girl—*two girls*—on a stage singing? Without you going insane?"

They sat in silence for a while before Abby apologized. "But if you're still thinking of trying to get with her," she added, "I wouldn't. You don't know what I know—that's all I'm saying."

**:**

This had been a semi-dress rehearsal. There were new costumes to try on, and makeup tests. All the Puerto Rican girls apart from Sejal had already dyed their hair black, or tried to. Sophie's fine blond hair was giving her trouble. It was more the color of mold.

Because it was a semi-dress rehearsal it was also the semi-official start of the Cleanest Dressing Room Contest. Each night Ms. Todd and Cat inspected the boys' room and the girls' room, and tallied the nightly winners. The losing gender would have to clean the better half's dressing room on closing night, plus their own, before being released to attend the cast party. It was all a bald-faced ploy to get them to clean up after themselves, and it worked. It more than worked—you could only get a room in a fifty-year-old auditorium so clean, and this invariably sparked an escalating arms race of baked-good bribes, flowers, throw rugs . . . even the utter transformation of linoleum floored, white cinder-block spaces into gaudy nightclubs or the Garden of Eden.

Doug left the other boys behind to sweep and wipe mirrors. He didn't care about the contest, and the ammonia smell was burning his nostril hairs. Outside, the sun was setting—he could feel it. He could feel his blood rising.

There were whispering voices, the furtive *pssts* and shushes of secrets leaking into the air. He could follow the wispy trails of their echoes, down the hall, through the woodshop, to the black-painted floors and red flowing curtains of the stage's right wing.

Sejal and Ophelia were here. Doug lurked behind a curtain. Sejal was upset about something, and Ophelia was trying to smooth it over. He only picked up bits and pieces. To him the whispers were loud, rough, buzzing his eardrums like they were broken speakers, but they didn't resolve themselves into useful shapes. *Yet another part of being a vampire that's not all it's cracked up to be,* thought Doug.

The thought surprised him. Wasn't everything getting better? Wasn't this new life so much better than the one before? There was a girlfriend and respect. Strength. But throughout, a glimmer of something inside him like a warning light on his dashboard.

Ophelia pressed herself against Sejal. Footsteps approached from behind.

"Why aren't you helping the other boys?" asked Ms. Todd.

"Too many of us," Doug replied as he turned and walked back through the shop toward her. "We were getting in each other's way. I promised to bring some sponges and stuff tomorrow." Not a bit of it was true.

Ms. Todd studied him. "You better tell Jay not to miss another rehearsal or he's out."

She had actually been pretty clear about this when she'd called roll at the beginning of the evening. When Jay hadn't responded, she'd made an announcement to all cast and crew that anyone missing rehearsals without an excuse would be cut, she didn't care who they were, no exceptions. She'd made the announcement while staring straight at Doug, like Jay was his responsibility.

"Either Jay or his sister has to go let their dog out after class," Doug breathed. "They both have after-school things. If he didn't come back, he must have had a good reason." This was true—Jay would have a good reason. With a dull pain Doug realized he hadn't wasted a moment wondering what it was.

:

Later he walked with Abby to her car. She was talking to him or something. Doug was too occupied in contemplating what he'd seen of Sejal and Ophelia and what it meant. Only when Abby suddenly lowered her voice did he give her his attention, and then only to hear her say, "There's a guy by my car."

He scanned the dark parking lot and fixed upon the small figure of Stephin David, standing just in front of the passenger door, arms heavy at his sides. Face flushed, probably from drink.

"I know him," Doug told Abby. "You go ahead home."

"With . . . without you?"

"Yes."

"I was hoping you'd drive. I feel dizzy."

"What? No, I'll find my own way home. Don't worry about me. Good night." He walked off toward the edge of the soccer field, leaving Abby to sway unsteadily under a yellow, moth-battered lamppost. Stephin gave her a clipped nod and came to meet Doug on the grass.

"What are you doing here?" Doug asked, looking around him. Cast and crew spilled slowly out of the auditorium. There were other students, too, here and there, coming from the quad or the track.

"I was in the neighborhood," said Stephin. "You've been so elusive, I had to find some way to grab your attention."

"Well, okay, you've got it. And good move, too: single guy, single *gay* guy, hanging out at the high school? You look like a child molester."

Doug knew he wasn't supposed to throw Stephin's sexuality in his face like that, but the man was making him supremely uneasy. He did not belong here.

Stephin said, "We play the roles in which we are cast. Every play's a tragedy, if only you leave the curtain raised long enough—"

"God! Please, just . . . What do you want?"

Stephin took a moment before speaking. "I received an interesting message about your friend Victor. It seems Cassiopeia is under the impression he's hunting his maker. It seems that you gave her that impression."

"Shit," said Doug. "That was . . . I didn't mean to throw Victor under the bus like that, but I needed a diversion. It's no big deal."

"I doubt Victor will see it that way. But can we be clear? Victor does *not* aim to find and kill his maker, with the intention of undoing his curse or for any other reason?"

"No," said Doug. "No, and I'm not even sure I want out anymore either. I . . . have to think about it."

"You should. It's a big decision, an enormous responsibility. Consider all the people you may meet during your long existence. Souls you can't even imagine. People not yet born. Would you deprive all these people the pleasure of your company?"

Doug chewed his lip and watched Stephin for some hint that he was joking. But his dead face was as illegible as ever.

"Of course, you have also to consider all the lives that may curdle at your touch. You could be a curse to others, something worth breaking. Such responsibility."

"Well, I guess I'll just kill myself."

"Suicide is ungrateful."

In the parking lot engines cleared their throats, and red and white lights winked on. Doug was dimly aware that Abby had not yet pulled out of her space. She was just sitting in her car. Was she watching them?

"So, then . . . is it possible? Becoming normal again? You sound like you're saying it's possible."

"Hm. Well, I've been doing some research, purely with the intention of dissuading you from this course, you understand. But, I can't lie—I've uncovered evidence that such a thing may be possible, if certain conditions are met. But do leave Victor alone. It has to be the head of the family—the oldest active vampire in the lineage. I think a stake in the heart may be necessary. You won't do it, will you? Of course you won't—you don't even know who made Victor. And you with your newfound zest for life."

"Asa told me you only have to kill the next vampire in line," said Doug, though he wasn't really sure *what* Asa had meant.

Stephin was silent for a moment, during which a steady pulse of red taillights passed like heartbeats behind him.

"Did he, now."

Doug heard a distant squeal of tires. He looked over Stephin's shoulder just in time to watch Abby run her car into a fence.

# 31
## :

## PALE

**HE WASN'T** the nearest student to Abby's car, not by a long shot, but he was the first on the scene. Her face was lost in the white pillow of the airbag, tassels of curly hair splayed like creeper all around. She wasn't buckled in. He wrenched the door open and was already pulling her from her seat as Troy came running up yelling, "Don't move her! Don't move her!"

There was a right thing to do in a situation like this, and a wrong thing. The right thing was to call 911 and wait by Abby's side, maybe even initiate CPR until the paramedics arrived. The wrong thing was to load Abby into another car and move her yourself to the closest hospital. A distant third might have been to lift Abby into your arms and run thirteen blocks to St. Mary's Emergency in Pennwood, despite shouts of protest from the mob of kids that had gathered at the school gates.

*I just acted without thinking,* Doug explained to an imaginary jury of his peers after he'd been running for a mile and his mind had cleared. *In emergencies a person can sometimes demonstrate astounding feats of strength.*

He didn't notice the wood-paneled station wagon that followed him all the way to the hospital. He was in another world.

The hospital waiting room was filmy and crowded with people. One man had a piece of rebar in his foot, but apparently not enough of a piece of rebar in his foot to leave the waiting room. CNN silently played on a television bolted to the ceiling.

After handing Abby off to the ER nurses Doug had been unable to answer, for various reasons, the following questions about her:

What kind of insurance she had

Whether she had a middle name

How her last name was spelled

If she was allergic to any medications

How, exactly, she'd come to have only three liters of blood in her body

Abby's parents had been called. He'd have to face them soon. No one had actually asked him to stay, but leaving now would feel like fleeing a crime scene. He got up and sat down, got up again, walked to the hospital gift shop and stared at Mylar balloons and fist-sized teddy bears, then returned to the waiting room to find all the seats taken.

A lot of people had come to the ER in sweatpants. A thin, well-groomed woman in a tailored skirt and hose shivered in her seat while the sweatpants crowd seemed to look askance at her and wonder: *Did she change clothes before coming? Did she freshen up?* Doug wondered if his own clothes communicated the right amount of human concern and went to the restroom to check.

It wasn't getting any easier, looking in mirrors. Most days he could focus below the neck, examine his clothes, all but ignore his hair now that it never seemed to get mussed up anymore. Tonight was no different, except that it was completely different. Putting aside for a moment that he was actually trying to muss himself up a bit, he also sensed the insistent stare of a pair of eyes in the mirror.

*His eyes*, nominally. They were set in his face, or in a kind of counterfeit of his face. There was something wrong with the expression. Something wrong with the eyes.

They looked old, inevitable. Like they'd always been here in this hospital, waiting for Doug to arrive. He didn't like their air of blunt satisfaction. He wanted to give them something to look surprised about.

Exiting the bathroom he took this hospital scene in again and wondered, suddenly, if Abby was going to die. The white floors, white walls, cold white light that robbed everything of shadow and substance, the flimsy gowns and white coats and pajamas—were they trying to make it all look like some cheap heaven? Were they trying to prepare you for what came next?

"Doug?"

Jay's sister, Pamela, was down the hall, looking a little

fragile, unsteady. Doug tried to recall—Was she friends with Abby?

"Hey, Pamela."

"How did you find out?"

Doug didn't know how to answer this question, didn't understand it, really, but then Pamela was just hugging him so he hugged back.

"Have you seen my mom?" asked Pamela.

"No."

"Okay. I'll take you up. They moved him upstairs."

*Him? Jay?*

"God, what the fuck? Who would do this?" said Pamela, suddenly a fury, as she let Doug go and turned back to the elevators. "Do you have any idea who would do this to a person? A person like Jay? Anyone at school?"

"No. Look," said Doug, "I don't really know much. I just heard he was here because . . . because Abby my girlfriend is here, too. What happened to him?"

The elevator opened, and Pamela tucked herself into a cold corner of it. Another woman got in with them (a young and Indian-looking doctor, Doug noted), so Pamela whispered, "He's lost a lot of blood. He was unconscious. Someone or . . . something bit his neck. Actually bit his neck. And Chewbacca's dead."

Doug would have liked a chance to explain a few of those details to the doctor, but the opinions of strangers didn't seem like the right thing to be concerned about right now, and besides—the woman just exited on the third floor like she hadn't been listening.

All the fire had gone out of Pamela and she hugged her shoulders. "There was blood everywhere at home. You could smell . . . and now Dad's being all stupid and telling the police all about how Jay dyed his hair black and started dressing better," she said, and with a target for her anger she rallied a little. "He told them to talk to Cat. He thinks they're doing drugs. Jay and Cat, I mean. Not the police."

The elevator doors opened, and the hallway they stepped out into was indistinguishable from the one they'd left: white walls, white ceiling, polished white floor. The same odd sensation of floating.

Through the third door Jay lay asleep in a bed with his arm strapped to the side. A clear tube connected the inside of his elbow to a plastic bag on a metal stand, a plastic bag that looked like those Doug had once stolen from the Red Cross, though the liquid inside this one was colorless.

Jay's dad rose from his bedside chair and crossed the room to meet Doug. "There he is. There he is. How are you, Doug?" He seemed to consider and then quickly reconsider hugging Doug, and instead gave him a firm, vigorous handshake, like he was trying to sell Doug a shiny new optimism. "It's so good of you to come. Thank you." He looked over at Pamela. "You didn't find your mother?"

"I'll try her cell again."

Pamela left the room, and Doug and Mr. Rouse stood at the foot of the bed, watching Jay. He didn't look like he was sleeping. Doug could see the place on Jay's neck where the blood had been taken. Even through a patch of gauze he could see it was big, obvious, surrounded by a scribble of broken blood vessels just beneath the skin. It didn't look anything like the evidence Doug left (or didn't leave) on Abby. This was like graffiti. This was sending a message.

"How . . ." Mr. Rouse began, "how did you know to come, Doug? Did Pamela call you?"

"No, actually . . . I was already here for this girl I know. Abby. She . . . passed out while driving."

"Abby . . . Abby. I've met her, haven't I? She dresses just like that Cat!"

That wasn't really true. Cat dressed more punk, Abby more romantic, but they both wore a lot of black. Dark makeup. That was probably enough for Mr. Rouse. Doug knew it didn't take much for some parents to see Satanists and death worshippers. His mom had once described his cousin Kristi as "pretty goth" for wearing plum-colored lipstick. Which matched her plum-colored polo shirt and the embroidery on her cutoffs. Mrs. Lee insisted she only wore it for "shock value."

Doug looked at Jay. He looked at the boy who was ostensibly his best friend and willed himself to have a feeling. Any feeling, but it should be fierce, and raw. Nothing came. There was nothing in him anymore that was fierce or raw except his lust. And even as he thought this, he knew it wasn't true. Increasingly, his vampirism wasn't a lust, it was an itch. An itch that needed a lot of scratching, sure, but . . . just an itch. A constant irritation; a rash; a chicken pox on his soul.

"You kids are falling in with a dangerous group of people, Doug. You have to see that. Before it's too late. It was almost too late for my boy." His voice cracked, and he pressed a red fist against his mouth while Pamela reentered the room.

"There are some bad, bad kids at that school."

That was true. There were some very bad kids at that school. Monsters. Pamela had wanted to know if any one of them might have done this to Jay, and the answer was of course.

*Of course.*

# 32

# THE WOLF IN CREEP'S CLOTHING

**D**OUG COULD SCARCELY believe his luck. No sooner had he vowed to hunt Victor down and destroy him, than a pale wolf charged at him through the trees.

He'd left the Rouses abruptly, left the hospital before meeting Abby's parents, and it *did* feel like fleeing a crime scene. He walked swiftly through the first doors he could find marked EXIT, corkscrewed down the ramps of a parking garage, and emerged into the night air.

He had no car here. He'd have to walk home. Or fly home as a bat? No, he liked this shirt.

He was picking his way through the shared woods between the hospital and the seminary when the wolf appeared, upwind, and it smelled like Victor. It slowed and made a wide circle before him and bared its teeth, but stopped short of growling. Doug wondered how best to fight a wolf. He'd have to snap Victor's neck, he decided. Maybe sacrifice his own arm. He was walking through trees—why hadn't he picked up a stick?

But there was no attack. Wolf Victor reared back on his hind legs and in that instant Doug realized he was turning human again. Despite himself, Doug looked away. It seemed like a private moment. There came a squeak, the sound of a million discrete hairs pulling back into the skin.

Doug was seeing altogether too much of naked Victor.

He would try to get Victor circling again, he thought, try to get close enough to a tree to snap off a branch, then drive it into Victor's chest. There was a sternum in the middle of the chest, wasn't there? And ribs. He'd break the ribs.

"Who were you talking to at school?" Victor snarled, his chest heaving. "Who was that?"

It wasn't the question Doug was expecting. "Who was who? I talk to a lot of peo—"

"Today! In the parking lot, just as the sun went down."

Doug narrowed his eyes. "Are you spying on me or something?"

"I was coming off the field after practice. You were standing right there in the open with . . . some guy."

"It was just Stephin David. My so-called mentor? You know."

"*That's* Stephin David?"

"Sure. What?"

293

Victor just looked away, into the ether, and Doug side-stepped gingerly to a tree with a low-hanging branch. He could just make out Victor's mutterings, despite the wind: "That's Stephin David . . . I know where he lives."

"So you were at school, at practice," said Doug. "What'd you do before practice?"

Victor looked at Doug, but his mind might have been racing through the trees. "What?"

"Let me lay out your schedule today as I see it. You had school, lunch, school, a quick errand to kill my best friend, then back to school to spy on me. Did I leave anything out?"

"I killed your best friend?"

*Better to let him go on thinking he did*, thought Doug. *If he hears Jay survived, he'll just try to finish the job.* "You know what you did," he said, his hand closing over the branch. It was thick enough to be strong and already snapped by wind or lightning. If he could wrench it free from the trunk, it would be just over a foot long. Perfect. "Did Borisov tell you to do it? To protect everyone's precious secret identities?"

"Where are you getting this shit? Jay's dead? I didn't do anything to Jay. And I haven't been talking about him and I never told you anything about wanting to kill the vampire who made me, either. Yeah, I know you've been spreading that around. What the hell?"

"I didn't say that. The signora misunderstood me. But that's no reason to go try and kill Jay—"

"I told you, I didn't kill Jay. But you're gonna get *me* killed, you know that? I'm in a shitstorm of trouble now with the old vampires. I thought we were friends."

Doug caught his breath. He swallowed away some of the dry crust in his throat. "You . . . we were." In an instant Doug saw that what he'd assumed was a monster was actually a boy his age, a boy he used to play with on summer vacations. He lost his grip on the tree and his arm sank. Victor did not currently look like a killer. He looked sickly and naked.

"You're always asking about Jay," said Doug. "And that day behind the gym when he walked up to us . . . it almost seemed like you were afraid."

"I was afraid. I am afraid. For Jay, for us, about everything being different," Victor mumbled. "Aren't you afraid?"

"Why are you so pale?" asked Doug.

"Being a wolf . . . it makes you burn through blood kind of fast."

"Then why do it?"

"I just . . . feel like I'm in my right skin when I'm a wolf. I'm not real good at being people lately. I've been . . . scary, I guess. I scared my *mom*."

Maybe he felt exposed then. He stretched to cover his crotch, his arms stiff as a clock's. Six-thirty, Naked Standard Time.

"Does it work," he asked, "killing the vampire that made you? Does it make you human?"

"Oh, so now you want to do it?"

"I just want to know if it works."

Doug frowned as a new possibility occurred to him. "Asa says it does. So . . . do you remember everything you do when you're a wolf? Afterward?"

Victor bit at his thumbnail. "You can't really trust that Asa," he said. "Who knows what he's up to—you know?"

"Do you remember your time as a wolf?" Doug asked again. "Are you in control? Or do you just go on autopilot, like when you're driving?"

"I don't know. I gotta go."

Victor became a wolf again and disappeared into the darkness.

Doug couldn't follow. He wasn't that fast on foot, or as a bat, and he didn't know how to turn into a wolf. He considered trying, thinking wolfish thoughts, confident that getting stuck halfway this time wouldn't be as big a problem as it had been that night at the farm. Why, he might even turn into some sort of man-wolf. That didn't sound so bad.

Then, in a moment of honesty, he imagined what sort of animal might really fall halfway between a wolf and himself, and the image that came to mind was purebred American hairless terrier.

Chewbacca had been an American hairless. Small, spotty skinned, a face like a butcher-shop window. Doug allowed himself to think of Chewbacca then, pictured the dog's final moments: probably so happy to be meeting another vampire; confused to find he was, in a moment, small game in his own house.

Doug felt the chill suddenly. Something noxious rattled up in him, and he crumpled into a pile of leaves and sobbed. Thinking about a dog he'd never liked, he cried like he hadn't cried in years—retching, convulsive tears. A dog. A boy and his dog. Jay and Chewbacca, like Batman and Robin, like Han Solo and . . . Chewbacca. Jay, his friend, nearly dead in an indifferent room in a building behind him. He cried until his tears ran red and he had to staunch the flow with his palms.

*Okay,* he thought when he could stand again. *Okay,* and he snapped that tree limb free of its trunk and cleaned it of smaller branches. *Right,* and he ran toward the lights of the city.

Even if he hadn't had a pretty good idea where Victor lived, Doug could have followed him home. He was arguably the only vampire wolf who'd trespassed through the seminary grounds in a while, probably the only one who had crossed Lancaster Avenue that evening. Certainly the only one who'd threaded the Taco Exchange drive-thru so recently that the paper-hatted attendant was still pressing his clotted, dumb-struck face against the cashier's window.

Victor lived on a narrow street lined with the sort of smallish, vertical houses that were all stairs and U-turns. Doug stood panting at the bottom of Victor's driveway, the tree branch in his hand. He'd lost an opportunity, sure, and that was stupid of him. He'd let Victor talk his way out of a staking. It wouldn't happen again. Victor had obviously acted while in wolf form, and he couldn't remember the details any-more. Each time doubt reached in with its wet fingers, Doug banished it with thoughts of Jay. Jay in the hospital room. The largely theoretical tableau of Jay bloody and helpless in his own living room, kitchen, or backyard.

He crept up the driveway, tasting the air. The concrete

under his feet was cracked into puzzle pieces and stained with faded, continental shapes. Grass grew optimistically through the cracks.

He couldn't really expect to be able to sneak up on another vampire, Doug realized. He would just have to stay on guard. He ignored the front door—nobody ever entered through their own front door—and stepped up a small, steep flight of stairs to the side door. But, no—the trail cooled here. Where was Victor?

The driveway ended at an open carport. It was a good place to hide, a good place to wait for someone who was following you.

"I'm coming, Victor," he said in a soft voice that he trusted would be heard by wolf ears. "I don't care. Get the drop on me if you want, I know how low on blood you are."

The carport was crowded with the detritus of modern life—paint cans and mulch and cracked flowerpots formed a car-shaped bunker around a dull gray Accord. It sort of *wasn't* a good place for an ambush, after all. Doug could barely move. A bright white square on the windshield of the car caught his eye. He prized it free of the wiper blade and it unfolded in his hand.

MOM—
*I'm going to see a man tonight. I'm going to see*
*if he'll give something back to me.*
*I'm sorry for how I've been acting. I'm sorry for*
*sneaking out. I know I said I'm not on drugs, but I*
*kind of am, too. It's hard to explain.*

*If you're reading this, it means I didn't come back.*
*Send police to the ugliest house facing Clark Park*
*in West Philly. Send a lot of police. Tell them he*
*has a lot of guns, and he deals drugs to kids. And*
*that he's only there in the daytime.*
*I'm so sorry.*
*Victor*

Doug folded the note again and put it in his pocket and thought for a long time. *All right*, he sighed. *I'm going to Clark Park*. It seemed so far away, and he'd been running all evening. If he wanted to be prepared, he needed blood.

That was okay. He knew a couple places he could try on the way.

# 33

## VANT

**THEY SAT** in Cat's room, not doing their homework. Sejal was not doing her Pre-Cal and Cat was not writing an essay about the Louisiana Purchase.

"Honest, I don't think she's told anyone," Cat said. "I heard it from Abby. You were all downstairs at the same time—maybe she overheard you?"

"I did not exactly ask Ophelia to keep it secret anyway," Sejal said. "I was only nervous. I couldn't stop talking."

"So you really think Doug's a vampire? *Really* really?"

"I don't know. Tell everyone I was only joking, yes? Tell them . . . Lord, tell them it is just a saying in India, and that I was misunderstood."

"That's good," said Cat. "That'll work."

There was a lull. Cat made as if to read a page in her text-book, the same page she'd been reading and rereading all night. Sejal pushed some numbers around, and looked askance at a plastic shopping bag that was just visible inside her backpack.

"But do you see why I might think it?" asked Sejal.

"I don't know . . . *a vampire?*"

"I thought you believed in the vampires."

"I . . . kind of believe in them when they're on TV, but we're talking about Doug."

"Okay, fine."

"I mean, I know he's changed this year, but—"

"I was probably just hopped up on Niravam. Is that right? 'Hopped up'?"

"It's awesome, if you're trying to sound like my dad."

"I got rid of it. The Niravam. I flushed it. I'm sorry."

The doorbell rang, followed immediately by four crisp knocks. Cat pushed up to her feet and scrambled out of the room, down the stairs. In distant tones Sejal heard Mrs. Brown bluster, and Cat say, "I told you, never answer the door!"

Sejal returned to her math and kept her head down for half a minute before she heard a faint cry, from Cat she thought, as if some little terror had just been squeezed out of her. Sejal rose and ran to the top of the stairs. There were police officers by the front door. Just like from the American cop shows.

"*How?*" said Cat to the officers. She had her arms folded tight into her chest, her fists pressed up against her chin. "Is he going to be okay?" Mrs. Brown put her arm around Cat, and Cat leaned into it. Mr. Brown appeared now from the living room.

"They're telling them about Jay," said Doug, behind her. Sejal flinched, turned. He was there in the hallway. She opened her mouth to scream. "Don't scream," said Doug. "You already screamed, and they didn't come. They're too busy with their own stuff."

Sejal nodded. She had already screamed and they didn't come. Had she?

"Don't make any noise," said Doug. He was curling his arm around her, cutting her off from the staircase. Downstairs voices were rising. Cat was upset, Mr. Brown asked someone, "Just what are you implying? That my daughter is hopped up on drugs?" Sejal ducked Doug's arm and rushed back into the bedroom. She fumbled with her book bag, with the flimsy loops of the plastic shopping bag inside. Everything had the tarnished tunnel vision of old films and nightmares. Finally she produced a clove of garlic and a pocket Bible that someone had handed her on South Street. She had also been handed three nightclub flyers and an ad for carpet cleaning before she'd learned to keep her hands at her sides, but at least she'd gotten the Bible. The contents of her little bag had seemed embarrassingly crackpot only moments ago, but now she brandished them like they were the chakra of Vishnu.

Doug was in the doorway. When he came near, she got a foggy feeling, a feeling she was certain now that she'd had before.

"What are you holding those for?" asked Doug. "Here." He approached, and Sejal backed right up to the wall, pressing against it until the pushpins dug into her shoulder blades. Doug took the Bible, and she dropped the garlic.

"Come sit on the bed," he said.

"What did you do to Jay?"

Doug looked horrified. "How can . . . It's what Victor did to Jay. And now I have to settle things with Victor. Then I can be a better person, like you said. But first . . . I have to do one more bad thing." He took hold of her wrist.

"It does not work like that," Sejal shuddered, and she thought, *Victor, too?* "You have to be it all the time. You have to be it for yourself and no worries about the other fucking people."

Doug winced. "I don't like it when you swear."

"Fuck, fuck, fuck, fuck, fuck."

Doug reached for her other wrist.

Sejal threw her fist forward and punched him in the face. Not a slap—a real punch. The pain of it creased her knuckles and jolted up her arm. It didn't seem to make much of an impression on Doug, and in a moment he had both of her wrists pinned against the wall.

Now the fog really rolled in. She could feel her breathing grow shallow, and all sounds faded away. Doug was still talking to her. Doug, or someone who looked like Doug. Close. A little blurry. She could feel his breath, which seemed to her an impressive detail since she knew none of this was real. She nearly laughed because vampires were only real on television.

The person who looked like Doug was still talking. Trying to explain something. *And now look. He's crying. That's hard to watch. I'll close my eyes.*

The darkness was absolute. But then the hot breath faded away.

Cat was shaking her awake.

"You look like Cat," Sejal slurred, and tried to get up from the floor.

"What the hell?" said Cat. "Why were you sleeping like that? Didn't you hear us?"

Sejal stared at her, confused. Cat had been crying. It reminded her of Doug. Doug had been here.

Cat crossed behind her and closed the window. "Jay's been attacked, but they think he's going to be all right. They think me and Abby and Jay are all part of some goth cult or something because we all wear black and Abby's anorexic or whatever. Asswipes. You know who else wears black? Fuckin' asswipe cops—they wear black. Ooh, they're a danger to society, they—"

Cat burst into tears again and sat down on the bed. "I'm sorry," said Sejal, and she sat beside her. "I'm sorry."

As she held Cat she remembered Doug. And someone else . . . an older man . . . and Clark Park. She couldn't recall much of what either had said. One thing she was sure of— Doug had come here for something, and he hadn't taken it. He'd changed his mind.

Well, she still thought he was a vampire. There was a way she could check. She'd thought of it before.

By the time Cat finished crying, Sejal had something like a plan.

:

She silently cursed herself for taking Cat's key ring, especially when her friend was in such a state. But she remembered how Cat had looked at her earlier when the subject of vampires came up, and she knew this was just something she was going to have to prove to herself. She was tired of feeling fresh off the boat.

The nice thing about her new wardrobe, she thought, was that it was good for sneaking. In her black velvet dress, she was like a frilly ninja.

Before she could do whatever it was she expected to do tonight she would need to know where she was going. She thought again of her lost (no, *disowned*) suitcase and whispered a prayer that Ganesha, Lord of Beginnings and Remover of Obstacles, might keep the Browns' geriatric internet connection free and clear long enough for a web search and a set of directions. Despite her many faults. Despite her leaving him at the airport. And then, once the directions were secured and silently copied, she considered asking for a fresh obstacle—a browser crash, a frozen cursor, some prudent rockslide to cut her off from the World Wide Everything. But, no—she'd had enough favors lately.

If she ever saw her Ganesha figurine again, Sejal thought they might have a little talk. It could be that she was willing to manage her own obstacles for a while.

She did send one email. A much overdue one to her parents:

amma and bapa,
i am sorry i have not written for a few days.
i am sorry this will be so short. i promise to
write again soon and tell you everything. my
studies go well. rehearsals go well. cat is a

great friend, and i am trying to be a help to
auntie and uncle brown. i continue to enjoy
america, but could do without the vampires.
much love,
sejal
p.s. can you believe I'm writing on a
pentium II? did these people rob a museum?

Then she took a breath and turned the computer off.

Now she crept out of the dark house with Cat's key ring, and approached the older of the Brown family cars. She eased into the driver's seat and closed the door as quietly as she could. She barely knew how to drive. The steering wheel was on the wrong side of the car. This would be interesting.

She shifted into neutral and let the sedan slide down toward the street, and flinched against her seat belt when she felt the rear tires sink into soft grass. The Brown mailbox passed inches from the passenger side like a dark sentry and set her heart pounding.

Finally, safely in the street, she started the car and jerked forward into destiny.

# 34

## DONOR

**A GRIPPING** half hour later, Sejal pulled up to a MoPo convenience store and parked next to a champagne-colored SUV. She got out of the car and squinted into the bright store windows.

"Hey, how you doin' tonight?" said a voice.

There were two boys in the SUV. High-school age, maybe a little older. "I'm fine," Sejal said, and she made an effort to smile. Americans were always smiling.

"There's nobody in there," said the boy in the driver's seat as he jerked his chin toward the MoPo. "Door's open, though."

That seemed odd. Odder still was that the boys appeared to be opening fresh bags of crisps and sipping fountain drinks.

Perhaps they had left their money on the counter.

"Well, I suppose I will go in and wait," said Sejal.

"We got snacks. Why don't you come with us to this party."

"Thank you, no."

"I gots this book I think I seen you in. *The Kama Sutra of Love*."

Sejal flailed her hands. "Look here. Why do you eve-teasers keep saying that? Do you even know what the *Kama Sutra* is?"

A flutter of doubt crossed the boy's face. "Of course I know. It's Indian for 'sex book.'"

"I assure you it is not."

"I'm . . . pretty sure it is."

"Oh, pooh—I'm done with you now. Go."

She turned toward the store, and after a moment the SUV's engine started. "Bitch!" called one of the boys as she pushed through the jingling door.

"Yes, yes. Bitch. Very good," she said, scanning the store. There really didn't seem to be anyone in here. She weaved through the shelves and stepped over a spill of candy necklaces. There was a swinging plastic door the color of old tires in the back, and Sejal pushed it open a crack.

"Hello?"

Nothing.

Then, a small noise behind her, from the middle of the store. A clicking. She approached the checkout island, a stomach-high oval counter piled with impulse items and two cash registers. *But there's no one here,* she thought as she leaned into the counter.

"Oh! Hello."

A young woman sat on the floor in the center of the oval, tapping long nails like stick candy against the linoleum floor. She wore the green belted dress of a MoPo employee and the vacant look of a slightly-more-dazed-than-usual MoPo employee.

Sejal tried again. "Hello?"

The girl stirred and touched a hand to her hair. Then she looked up at Sejal, and down at herself.

"I'm on the floor."

"Yes," Sejal agreed. "Are you all right? Do you want me to call someone?"

"Nah . . . I'm all right," said the girl with a guilty smile.

"I'm sorry to bother you, but is this the MoPo where the Ghost stopped a robbery?"

The girl nodded, then nodded harder with an ever-widening smile. "He was just here! He came back. I think . . ." She seemed to notice her legs, which were stretched out in a V, and pulled her knees together. "I think we did it."

Sejal had her doubts. She tried to examine the girl's neck, but could only see the left side. She circled around the check-out island, pulled a yearbook from her bag, and opened it to the page she'd marked.

"Did he look like this?" Sejal asked with her finger by a photo of Douglas Lee. The girl squinted.

"Yyyyyeah, but . . ."

"But better. I know." There was a small spot on this side of the girl's neck. It could have been a bug bite. It could have been anything. "He didn't happen to mention where he was going?"

The girl stared for a moment, then shook her head.

*All right then*, said Sejal in her mind, as fragments of half-remembered conversations bubbled up to the surface. *That's fine*. Someone had once told her where this was all going to end anyway.

"Could you direct me to Clark Park?"

# 35

# VAMPIRE HUNTERS

**LOOKING UP** at the house of Stephin David, Doug couldn't imagine why Victor had come here. It was just a rusty birdcage, and an old crow, and two hundred years of crap. Still, there was no doubt he'd arrived. His smell was in the air, and the front door was just slightly ajar.

Doug stepped onto the porch, grimaced at the groaning boards, and slipped inside. The entry hall was more spartan than before—the stacks of books were gone, and the only remaining detail was that conspicuous portrait on the wall, no longer covered with drapery. Doug paused. It was a Civil War soldier, the same as when he'd stolen a glance during his first visit. Now that he had a chance to let his eyes linger, the soldier looked a bit like Victor. More so the longer he stared.

But a small brass plate on the frame said CORPORAL THOMAS NORTH.

He passed the tree branch to his left hand and wiped his clammy right hand across his shirt. Then came the strains of floorboards above. And, if he remained still and listened keenly, voices. A low voice first.

"It was easy. You were a Nancy. You're a Nancy now. Or what would you kids say? A bitch?"

"Shut up. You had no right."

"Nonsense. You know what we are. It gives me the right. I'll do it again."

Doug crept toward the stairs slowly, holding his weight only on the outside edges of his feet.

"You can't keep ruining lives! I should . . . stop you."

Doug started up the stairs.

"You? You cannot stop me. A pretty little thing like you?"

The stairs were noisy.

"Wait," said the voice that was almost certainly Victor's. "What was that?"

*Shit,* thought Doug.

"That," said Stephin, "is probably your friend Doug Lee. Why don't you invite him up?"

Doug held the branch behind his back. There was a cacophony of squeaks and groans, and Victor appeared at the top of the stairs. Clothed, for a change.

"What are you doing here, Doug?" Victor hissed.

"What are *you* doing here?" Doug said, and braced himself against the banister.

Victor studied him a moment. "Is that a wooden stake?"

No sense hiding it anymore, then. Doug brought the stake out in the open.

Victor nodded. "Do you want to stop being a vampire?" He'd been wondering just this for weeks, but when Doug spoke his answer still surprised him.

"Yes."

Victor waved him forward. "Then come on!"

It was the best invitation Doug was ever going to get, so he lunged up the steps and swung his weapon high toward Victor's chest. But standing on a lower step put him at a disadvantage. Victor deflected Doug's arm to the side, both boys lost their footing, and two entangled bodies came tumbling down the stairs.

On the ground floor Doug collected himself but couldn't account for the stake. He couldn't even remember dropping it.

Victor coughed, still on his back. "What are you doing? Not me! Stephin David!" He tried to get to his feet, but Doug pushed him off balance again. Victor's back hit the wall, the portrait of Tom North came down on his head. The glass shattered.

A creaking upstairs told Doug that Stephin was now on the move. And so was Victor. He scrambled backward to the front door. Doug went at him again, but this time Victor found his footing and hit him, hard. Everything went red. Doug felt and heard a door slam right between his ears. He staggered and took a few halting steps backward. Glass crunched under his heels.

"I've been punched by a vampire, an Indian girl, and a panda," he mumbled. "I should be a video game."

He took two deep breaths and charged again. A moment before Victor tossed him over backward and through Stephin's front door, Doug questioned the wisdom of rushing a varsity football player, and as he lay at the bottom of the porch steps he silently congratulated himself on his insight.

He was acupunctured all over with splinters. Victor came to the door, breathing hard. Doug was counting on this—*he* was full of convenience store blood, but Victor was running on empty.

"Stop it, Doug! I didn't kill Jay! Stephin David probably did it—he's a seriously bad guy!"

"Very bad." Stephin's sonorous voice tolled behind Victor. Victor scrambled forward and turned, and both boys could see the man was holding Doug's lost stake. "Did anyone drop this?"

Victor made as if to grab it, but Doug grabbed Victor and dragged him down the porch steps into the street. The boys traded punches and the fight lurched across the street and into the park.

Doug could feel an itching in his gums. Victor's fangs were bared, too. Victor got under him and threw Doug up against the thick branch of a tree. There came the cracking of wood, maybe ribs, and when Doug picked himself off the ground there was a sizable piece of tree next to him.

Victor was on his back, winded from the effort. Doug took the tree limb over his knee and snapped it in two. Then he went after Victor, swinging, but Victor clambered away, tottered at the edge of a hill, and went down.

Nearly half Clark Park was given over to a huge natural bowl, the length of a football field, which had once been a millpond. Victor tumbled into the basin and Doug came tumbling after.

"I'm sorry, Victor," Doug huffed, "but you've gone bad. And I need a do over for these past few months."

"I didn't hurt—" Victor began, but Doug clubbed him with the tree limb. Victor reeled and collapsed.

Doug breathed, light-headed, and tried to focus on the limb. It was thick for a stake, and it wasn't sharp, but hadn't Stephin told him all the old movie tropes weren't really that important? He stood over Victor with the branch like a great spear, and heard a faint voice calling his name.

"Doug! No! Don't do it!"

Looking up, Doug could see two people had joined them in the basin. Stephin, and Sejal.

"Sejal?"

She was running toward them from the other side of the bowl, dressed like the heroine of some dark story. *His* story, maybe.

:

"Don't do it, Doug!" Sejal shouted again. "I do not know what Victor has done, but he didn't hurt Jay."

Doug went to her, his head swimming.

"You've got to leave here. This is a very dangerous . . ." He struggled to finish, but dropped to the ground by her feet.

"Your back," said Sejal. "You're bleeding."

"Didn't know . . ."

**315**

"Well, this has been a super evening," said Stephin. "It's nice to see you again, young lady—I assume you've remembered our little chat."

She scowled at him. "You could have just killed yourself, you know."

"Suicide is ungrateful. And my life is not my own."

"And so you make vampires of boys like Victor. The sorts of boys who you think will want revenge."

"Hmm . . ." Stephin began, his hands folded in front of him, holding a spike of wood. "I'll volunteer that my selection of Victor was a little more complicated than that, but you're essentially correct."

Stephin stepped to the base of the hill. "It came to my attention several months ago that my behavior had become reckless, inadvisable. What seemed at first to simply be poor decisions began to look like a subconscious plan. I was scouting my own executioner. When I heard all these boys had concocted some fantasy of a mysterious female vampire, I thought the end was near. They obviously would not let it stand, being assaulted by someone like me. But now look at them," he said, his gaze falling on both Victor and Doug in turn. Victor wasn't moving at all.

Sejal was cold. "That night I met you, you said you were observing. Observing me, perhaps, but also Jay, isn't it? He lives nearby."

"Yes. Trying to get people motivated. Doug wanted to kill the head of his vampire family. He had only to realize who that was. How is Jay?"

"You don't care," said Doug, trying again to stand.

His breathing was labored, and his arms gave out from under him.

"I suppose neither of you would believe I do," Stephin told them.

"Victor left his mom a note . . ." Doug whispered. Sejal could barely hear. "I get it now . . . He wasn't here to kill you 'cause you're gay, just an asshole."

"I'm sorry," said Stephin to Sejal, "what was that last bit? Our Doug seems to be losing steam."

"He said you're full of shit," Sejal hissed. "These boys are better than you think."

"What a comfort. So. Your champions seem to be down for the count. Are you going to kill me yourself? Here."

He tossed Sejal the tree branch stake. It landed out of reach but rolled a few feet in the crackling leaves. Sejal watched it with a sick feeling.

"Is this why you brought me here? Am I your plan B?"

"Brought you here? My dear, I haven't made you do a thing. I only planted the merest suggestion in your mind. But, no, frankly, you were only meant to be here to assuage my ego. I'm just vain enough to want a witness."

Sejal looked from the stake to Doug. She couldn't tell if he was awake or asleep. Alive or dead. She satisfied herself that he was still breathing as Stephin continued.

"You have to strike very hard. I wonder if you have the strength. And the catch is, for all my dreams of oblivion, I don't believe I'll go without a fight. I may just let you do it. Or I may take your little stick and snap it along with your neck." He gave an embarrassed smirk. "I honestly don't know."

"Don't do it," groaned Doug from the ground. "I'll get him. I screwed this all up, but I'll make it right."

"Yes, there's an idea. Put all your faith in Doug Lee. What could possibly go wrong?"

There was a lot to occupy her mind, but in truth Sejal was most taken with another figure who had just appeared on the lip of the bowl, a thickset man in an army coat with something in his hands. He slid down the hill behind Stephin.

"Make up your mind, dear," Stephin said, walking toward her, "or I'll win. I'm a monster, a murderer, and I'll be worse— I can feel it."

The vampire was close—thirty feet away, maybe twenty.

"Will you run?" he asked, still closer. "You can't run. I'll CATCH YOU. PICK UP THE STAKE, SEJAL, I'M—"

His whole frame shuddered, and he halted, mouth slack. Eyes heavy. With his long fingers he touched at the sharp tip of a cone, a cone at the end of a shaft, a shaft of wood that had emerged from the center of his chest.

"Finally," croaked Stephin, and he dropped. Behind him stood the man in the army coat, holding a gun Sejal had seen on TV.

:

"If he's a murderer, it's justifiable," Mike breathed, and tried to make sense of these people in the park. These vampires.

"There's so many," he whispered with rising panic. "They're everywhere."

There was the one he'd killed, and then the vampire boy there, on the ground, and maybe another one a little way off.

And a fourth, on her feet—wearing a vampire dress. Saying something.

Mike couldn't hear anything over his own heartbeat, and the scratch of his hands against his coat as he fumbled for another whippit, and a new stake to reload. Then he raised his Redeemer and sighted the vampiress down the barrel.

:

Doug had been bracing to come between Stephin and Sejal. He was sure of it. But Stephin was gone, and now there was a man, a familiar man with a gun. He saw what was about to happen and forced himself to his feet as the gun hissed and fired.

In another story he might have slapped the stake away, plucked it out of the air and returned it to sender. Or the stake's coarse point could have found his shoulder, or his arm, but it didn't.

How could it?

What could it find but his heart?

# 36
## THE FALL

**THROUGHOUT** the frigid early morning Sejal sat at Doug's side. His eyes were closed, he lay on his back, there was a wooden stake in his chest. His breath came like smoke signals. Like empty word balloons.

The vampire hunter, trembling, had keeled over, thrown up on the hillside, and fled. As he ran to his wood-paneled coffin of a car, she thought he called back, "This is his fault," but she wasn't sure. Doug struggled up into consciousness, gasped for air, and went under again.

Next Victor woke, or, rather, a wolf awoke and stepped out of his clothes. It shook its head and coat and strode silently over to where Doug lay and where Sejal sat. She glared at it, her body balled up like a fist. But the wolf just nosed at Doug's arm and sniffed the air.

"I can't take him to a hospital, can I?" she asked the wolf. "Could they help? They will find him out." And then she wondered—should he be helped? Would it be better for everyone if he were gone? *No. No, no, no,* she thought. She would pluck this wish out by the roots, tear it to pieces.

Victor hung his sleek head and waggled it. It might have been an answer to her question. Then he loped up the hill, and with distance his twitching tail and white legs flickered and then slipped like a nightmare into the sleeping neighborhood. Sejal wondered if she'd see him again. She'd read too many fairy tales to expect a happy ending for the wolf.

The sky had brightened to a sort of tarnished silver before she rose and looked at the distant houses. She'd run to one, a friendly one—that one, trimmed with pink and yellow. She'd pound on the door and explain to whomever answered that her friend in the park had a stick in his heart. Then she heard Doug speak.

"Oh yeah," he whispered. "Forgot."

"You keep passing out," she said. "You wake up, look at the stake, pass out again. But shouldn't you be dead? I thought a stake through the heart was supposed to kill you."

"It seems like a good . . ." wheezed Doug, "guess to me."

What Doug didn't need right now was morals. What he didn't need was to be taught a lesson, to be put in his place. What he needed was less stick in his heart. Still, Sejal heard herself say "I think . . . I think sometimes you think you're the hero of the story, and sometimes you think you're the victim. But you're not either."

"That's . . . going to change," said Doug, and he tried to lift himself again. He failed. Sejal thought he might have fallen back into unconsciousness, but he rasped, "You know what I think? You know what I bet . . . Dracula thought . . . when they stuck that knife in his chest? . . . I'll bet he thought . . . *Why me?*"

"I have to go get help," said Sejal. "I'll come back with help."

"No . . . no, please stay. It's going to be fine . . . I'm going to be . . . fine. The head of the family is dead."

Sejal stayed where she was. She stared at the stake.

"It'll . . . just work itself out . . . like a splinter," Doug said. "I'll have to hide it . . . for a while . . . with—with—" He began to laugh, then to cough smoke like an old train. "Christmas lights. I'll tell people I'm a Christmas tree holder."

He laughed again, and Sejal smiled at him.

"Not a vampire anymore . . . I can be good now. I'll be so good," he said, and went to sleep.

**⁚**

Doug pulls the stake out, the wound heals, he goes about the rest of his natural life in Philadelphia as a graphic designer.

**⁚**

Doug pulls the stake out, he and Sejal marry, divorce, he rises to manager of a Kohl's department store and is shot and killed while trying to prevent a stickup.

**⁚**

The stake never comes out, Doug files it down to a nub and hides it under his clothes. He finds he can't readjust to life as a human—each new experience seems pale and flavorless. He never does anything of any importance and dies alone.

:

He rises, wrenches the stake from his chest, snaps it in two. He now has all the strengths of vampirism and none of the weaknesses. He becomes a celebrated crime fighter and occasional vampire hunter, and a founding member of the League of Champions.

:

In alternate histories we learn what the world would be like
    —if he had become a werewolf
    —if he'd been born a Russian
    —if he'd lived in Nazi-occupied Europe
    —if Jay had become the vampire instead
    —if he'd killed Victor
    —if he'd killed Stephin
    —if Sejal had loved him

:

He sleeps, in a state like death, for two thousand years while his body heals and his mind clears. He is accidentally unearthed and revived on the construction site of a future prison for poorly socialized clobots. Everyone in the future is either a vampire or a clobot, and his wild anecdotes from the twenty-first century make him a popular talk show guest.

:

He dies.

:

It took a long time to get home. There were people to talk to, calls to be made, a story to tell again and again and again. There were the Browns—Mr. Brown bleary-eyed, Mrs. Brown in a mismatched sweater set, stunned and bobbing through the gray police station like a rubber duck in a bathtub. Cat looking hurt. Sejal mouthed a "sorry," to her, sorry for rushing off on her own, sorry for going on a quest without her American guide. The hurt look lingered for an hour, but on the car ride home (during Mr. Brown's loud and impassioned speech about personal responsibility; hospitality; American values; and then, less clearly, outsourcing and the Marshall Plan), Cat's hand drifted across the backseat to take Sejal's own.

They pulled into the driveway as Mr. Brown reached the end of his sermon and started over from the beginning. "Something came for you this morning," Cat whispered at the door.

A half-dozen tags printed with colors and codes were tied to the handle of a bag, a scarlet-pink bag like a huge heart in the foyer.